Ask Me No Questions

JOAN KINGSLAND

Mater Ecclesiae College
60 Austin Avenue
Greenville, RI 02828

Editor: Trish Bailey de Arceo
Cover design: Lisa Small. All rights reserved.
Interior layout, design, and proofreading: Claudia Volkman, Creative Editorial Solutions. All rights reserved.

ISBN: 978-0-692-01410-3

Printed in the United States of America

5 4 3 2 1

ONE

The great wall toppled down while reveling Berliners on both sides took their turns at it. But the young woman in the waiting room seemed oblivious of this great historical event even though she was staring right at the television. Her breathing tight, her back cold with sweat, her mind transfixed on the possible outcomes, she earnestly tried to appear calm and sure of herself.

As soon as the nurse began to open the door to the inner office she was on her feet. There was nobody else waiting, so it had to be her. When the doctor came in, he presented a single sheet to the patient.

"Do you need any explanations?"

She gave him a withering look in response. He knew full well that she could understand just as well as he. A quick glance was enough to grasp what was there. It was handed back without a word or a change in her expressionless face.

"I recommend a month of rest and then we'll set a date for beginning the treatment again."

"I'd rather not. I'm more worn out than I expected to be by all this. I've had enough. I'm done."

The doctor looked displeased and took on a reasoning tone. "Are you sure? Don't you think it would be better to wait a while before deciding that? This probably isn't the best moment for—"

She cut him off.

"I'm very sure. I've had it. I'm exhausted, but no amount of rest is going to change my mind!"

There was nothing more to say. He looked at the nurse and shrugged. "Would you prepare her discharge papers then?" Once the nurse had turned her back, he gave the patient a reassuring smile. She tried to muster one in return but only succeeded in grimacing.

The room was quiet when the nurse returned a few moments later with the sparse data entry form, deliberately cryptic.

> *Patient: J*
> *Age: 18*
> *Update: Miscarriage*
> *Status: Discharged at patient's request*

All three signatures were required at the bottom: Dr. Henry Foster, Nurse Silvia McEnroe, Patient Elizabeth Smyth. The nurse didn't perceive the tension of the other two signers. They were both deliberately cool and said nothing, only permitting themselves one quick, meaningful look over her head while she signed. The nurse, for her part, was delighted that it was over so fast. That was the last patient slotted for the morning, and she would be left alone in the office with time to redo her nails and make a few personal phone calls.

Elizabeth had already packed her things and only needed to return to her room to collect them. She tried not to betray her intense relief as she submitted her precious discharge paper to the man at the door. She had tried to go out earlier; however, on other days the "doorkeeper" had politely but firmly referred her to the head doctor. Nobody had used the word "prisoner." She had come of her own free will; nevertheless, she hadn't been permitted to leave until now. This time, the man was already pushing the door release button.

She walked down the hallways and through the precincts of

McGill University as quickly as she could without drawing attention to herself. She opened her bag to check once more that her plane ticket for Buffalo was still there. When could she begin to relax? Not until she had left the country. And not even then. At least, not for a long time, if ever. From Buffalo, the goal was Texas, and from Texas to Mexico, where she knew she would remain for many years.

TWO

The whole team was a group of misfits. And that's precisely why David Johnston was devoted to them. His perfectly straight posture and trim condition were signs of the strong will and determination that had driven him far up the ladder of success in the Dallas business world. At such a young age he had reached apparent success. Yet here he was, approaching forty, in this backwater Texan town of Fort Davis, coaching kids who might not even be legal in the country. But success meant something different now, and he could help these kids. They trusted and admired him, knowing that his interest in them went beyond the soccer field.

One of the Mexican players turned to him and said, "Hey, Coach, you see that kid on the bike over there? He's new in town, a home-schooler in his junior year. I told him maybe he could play on our team. Do you think he could try out? He played with some of us on the weekend, and he's not bad."

David looked at the motley team on the field: just twelve of them. Some of the Spanish speakers had to work to help support their families, so they couldn't make all the practices. Jeff and Nick kept losing their sports eligibility because of low grades, never mind Josh and Roberto who had been caught drinking again… Besides that, the players didn't work as a team. No surprise they hadn't won a game all last season.

"Carlos, if he has legs he can play on our team. Do we look like we're selective?"

Carlos smiled back."I thought that would be your answer."

He waved to the boy. "Hey, Jimmie!"

During practice, David observed how easily Jimmie fit in with the rest: low-key, easygoing, and a real team player. But Carlos' estimation was about right. He was just okay. Nothing great. It was a relief to see that at least he was on par with the rest, though many of the others had a lot of undeveloped talent. When practice was over, David clapped him on the back companionably.

"Welcome to the team. We could use another player."

Jimmie smiled, and with a simple "Thanks, Coach," headed off.

Carlos was also going by bike so it seemed the most natural thing for them to go amiably down the road together into town, though his house was really in the opposite direction. Jimmie was careful to be the one to ask Carlos questions about the town, sports, school. With his frank, open manner, he was happy to fill the new kid in about everything. When Carlos lamented about how tough algebra was for him, Jimmie offered to go over to his house to help him out right away if he wanted. The other boy was glad to accept. He lived on the other side of town, on a street where all the houses were small and run-down.

Upon entering his home, Carlos greeted his mother warmly in Spanish and then started to introduce Jimmie in English, but Jimmie joined in with fluent Spanish. In response to their questions, he downplayed his expertise, stating that he'd spent the first eight years of his life in Mexico, where his parents did humanitarian, medical missionary-type work in little towns. He neglected to mention that he was also fluent in some other languages… in fact, he gently diverted the conversation away from himself.

It was already dusk when he emerged again into the open air. Jimmie cycled steadily through the small town and then pumped hard once he reached the back road he had come from earlier that day. The townsfolk only knew of a few sheep ranches out in that direction.

THREE

Two weeks later practice ended with an especially encouraging pep talk by Coach David, since their first game would be the next day. At least they were in good spirits as they went their way. Jimmie, as usual, biked to Carlos' house, but now with a few more players who also wanted tutoring. He was already popular among the players because of his amiable manner and quick, dry sense of humor.

"Nice kids. Just wish they could be more united on the field!" David muttered to himself as he picked up the bag of balls and headed for the school.

On the edge of the field stood a lady he didn't recognize, waiting for him. She wore a classic style black dress over her slight frame. Her hair was back in a tight bun, not a wisp escaping. The overall impression should have been severe except that her face threw everything off. It would have been hard for her to apply her makeup worse: dark red lipstick that seemed to have been smeared on without reference to the shape of her lips; thick mascara with eyelash prints under her eyes.

"Coach Johnston? I'm Jimmie's mother, and I need to talk to you about my son."

"How can I help you?" He hoped she wouldn't keep him long or create some kind of scene. He glanced furtively around but there was nobody about who might be able to help him somehow.

Her voice trembled as she spoke.

"It's about my son. Jimmie's a very special boy. He's so talented. But it wouldn't be good for him to attract any attention right now. My husband died just eight months ago, and it's been so hard. This would complicate matters, and I'm not sure I can bear anymore..." She choked up, struggling quietly to gain control of herself.

Overwrought females were not his specialty. "I'm sorry," he ventured. She aroused pity in his heart... besides a fair amount of disgust. At this weak attempt to show sympathy, tears immediately flowed, smearing her makeup all the more and giving her an even more comical look. He was at a loss, but then dug for a handkerchief and offered it to her. She blew her nose morosely and wiped her eyes, mussing up the makeup still more. He thought to himself, *Poor lady!* and wondered if she were fully with it.

"What we need right now, Coach Johnston, is peace." Her voice had begun to take on a shrill tone from her efforts to stifle her grief and tension. "We haven't even settled in yet to our new home and…" The next words were spoken in an accusing tone. "Jimmie wants to be on your team. He's a very special boy, you know."

David began to feel annoyance creeping over him. "Um, I'm afraid I don't quite understand your concern. Soccer's not considered by the general public to be a dangerous sport, Mrs. Pérez."

"Jimmie's name is Pérez. I'm Foster… Mrs. Foster."

"I see." He didn't, but she didn't elaborate further.

"It's just so hard for my son to escape notice. He's so talented."

That did it. This woman was aggravating. Wasn't there a mental disorder where people suffered from delusions?

"Oh, if that's all that concerns you, there's really no need to be worried. I can assure you that Jimmie's simply a run-of-the-mill player."

"You don't know my son!" she shot back, outraged. "You think that because he's just learning how to play. Wait and see! But that's just the point. You can't wait and see. Nobody can see. It's imperative for Jimmie's safety that he go unnoticed!"

David spoke in a deliberately slow, drawn out way: "I'd hate to have Jimmie leave the team. He seems to enjoy it. Don't you think a little exercise and playing a team sport would be good for him?"

"Yes… no… yes… but only if he doesn't stand out. The risk is too high." She wasn't any calmer.

"I honestly think there's no cause for worrying about that…"

She interrupted him, speaking earnestly, "If only you could assure me!"

David shifted his weight awkwardly. Such a strange lady with her absurd concern! "I'm not quite sure what might relieve your distress." He thought to himself, *If there's something that could satisfy her, I'll accept it just to be finished with her now.*

She began tentatively, "Oh, I realize I just seem silly to you but... would you be willing to promise me that my son won't be the captain of the team or score too many goals?"

He laughed in her face and not all that kindly. "Well, the first I can promise, but it's a bit hard to guarantee he won't score goals, isn't it? Do you want me to make him our goalie?"

"No, no... he would be too outstanding there! But you could ensure that he doesn't score too much by taking him out of the game if he starts to get too many."

"Yeah. That's one way." He thought to himself, *She wishes he could score goals!*

"Oh, then I guess it's possible," she said begrudgingly. "Jimmie can stay on the team if you'll promise me those two things: that he won't be captain and you'll pull him out of the game if he scores two goals." She wasn't so happy with this solution. Her eyes were still swimming with worry.

Again, David felt sorry for her and repelled by her at the same time. *Jimmie has her as his mother!* he thought. This made him want to give the poor kid a chance to play on the team all the more... if only to be able to get away from her for a while. It was a strange promise, but needless in any case. And if it did the trick to get his mother's permission...

"Done. I solemnly promise both. Please don't worry anymore." He hoped this interview would end now and that he wouldn't have to run into her very often at the games.

"Thank you." Her breathing calmed and she grew still, although the tide of tears never stemmed. "I'm so ashamed to be seen like this."

He could think of nothing comforting to say, so he remained silent.

"Please let me be the one to tell my son this. He won't understand, but he's such a good boy. It's all for his sake! Now you do assure me that you really are a man of your word?"

He picked up the bag of balls once more and stepped impatiently past her: "Lady, nobody's ever accused me of being a liar. If my word's not good enough for you, there's nothing more to be said."

At that, she turned away from him abruptly and walked briskly to the front, while he headed for the gym, relieved to get away at last.

FOUR

Mrs. Foster's car was in the parking lot in front of the school. She pleasantly greeted her children. "Hello. How was school today?"

The boy in the back didn't look up from his computer game. "Hi, Mom! What took you so long?"

The girl in front had been engrossed with her assigned reader, *To Kill a Mockingbird*. When she looked up at her mother, her jaw dropped and she froze for an instant, and then loudly reproached her.

"Ack! Mom! What have you done to yourself! Please don't tell me you went out in public looking like that! Since when did you ever put on mascara, and so badly?" Mrs. Foster pulled out a wet towelette and cleaned her face placidly. "What did you use to slop on your lipstick: a paintbrush?" As she protested, she slunk down and crouched low in the leg room space. "Quick! Drive away! My friends can't associate me with you like this. You look like a freak! Oh, I can just hear what they're going to say about me! I'll never be able to face anyone again. Drive, Mom, drive!"

Her mother answered pleasantly, "Don't worry. As luck would have it, only one person happened to see me and it wasn't anyone your age."

"Please just drive away! You look like a freak in those clothes.

My whole future happiness at this school is at stake. It's hard enough being new!" As her mother took off her hat, Jackie accused her, "You didn't even wear a hat to Dad's funeral!"

Mikey hadn't stopped playing on his Game Boy in the back. Even with his sister's fussing, he had hardly glanced up to observe his mother's strange appearance and didn't seem concerned at all, perhaps pointedly so to oppose his sister. Besides, being three years younger than her, his mother's odd appearance wasn't as threatening for him.

While keeping his eyes down and still pushing buttons, he commented in a patronizing voice, "Jackie, you're nicely exhibiting a broad array of manifestations typical of the socially maladjusted thirteen-year-old girl that you are: highly emotive; phobia of what your peers might think; both of which contribute to an exaggerated perception of antagonism between you and those in authority, particularly the parental figure."

"Why don't you stick to evaluating your Game Boy more closely? Keep talking and I'm going to shove it down your throat, so you can have the opportunity to submit it to a nice and silent internal evaluation, Houdini!"

The car was now pulling out of the school driveway and heading out of town. Jackie resumed her seat.

"Don't speak to your brother that way!"

"What, Mom?" Jackie responded innocently. "He likes to be called Houdini!"

An answer issued from the back, though the speaker's fingers kept moving at full speed. "While she has sagaciously skirted the real issue at stake, namely her threat to do me bodily harm once more, at any rate she is at least partially correct in affirming my preferred appellation. But the precise name I aspire to answer to is 'Houdini the Second.'"

His sister snorted and picked up her book again, while her mother opted to ignore the interchange. "So how was school today?" she asked instead.

Jackie glared down at her book, still ruffled at her mother's strange dress-up show. "The usual. Boring as anything. I hate school." This wasn't true and everyone in the car knew it. But she went on: "Why can't I be homeschooled like Jimmie?"

Once more the button-pusher piped up. "Duh! Your pathetic insistence on repeatedly asking a question to which you already know the answer is another distinctive mark of your early adolescent phase."

Jackie snapped back, "Hou, get ready to try out your Game Boy buttons on your teeth. But really, Mom, it's not fair! Our I.Q. is just as high as Jimmie's!"

"Jackie, being really fair doesn't always mean treating each child exactly the same. That would be unfair. Jimmie is better off studying at home right now in this place while you two are better off in a school." The girl rolled her eyes and went back to her book.

Mikey suddenly lay down his precious game, caught up by a wonderful inspiration. "Mom, I've got a superb idea! If I were water boy for Jimmie's team, would that suffice to meet your cruel requirement of two team sports per year?"

Now it was his sister's turn to get back at him. "He'll really build up a sweat doing that!"

Mikey ignored the jibe and pleaded urgently, "Could I Mom? Might I remind you that your insistence on sports is merely a means to a higher end: the noble purpose of learning teamwork." Now he softened his tone and pleaded: "Jimmie's only going to be around two more years… and the significance of his male role in my life is heightened now with Dad gone." He knew it hurt his mother to bring up the loss of his father, and he was generally a sensitive, kind boy except for the legitimate jabs at his obnoxious sister. But having a smaller, frailer frame and being so hopelessly uncoordinated at sports pushed him to the point of desperate measures. His tactic worked. He peered into the rearview mirror with a doleful expression.

"Okay," she replied, after a short pause. "That could count for one if the coach will accept your offer."

"Don't worry, Mom. I'm confident of my rhetorical capacities, especially when the stakes are so high."

"Let me interpret that," interjected his sister. "In other words, he's gonna beg like a dog to make the team."

Mikey turned a pained look on her. No anger. In these kinds of matters there was an unspoken agreement that they were supposed to help each other. Jackie relented, since she too had a big heart. She didn't really want to hurt her brother, except of course, for the occasional well-deserved punch.

"Hou, you'll be great at it. I'll help you out if anyone else tries to get the job."

"I'm sincerely gratified by your sisterly offer, but I don't think I'll need to avail of your assistance for now," he responded politely.

Mrs. Foster's eyes lit on Jackie's book. "What do you think of that book?"

"I like Atticus," Jackie answered grudgingly. "He reminds me somehow of Dad. And I like how the story is told from the kid's point of view. I can identify. I just hope I understand you when I get older Mom... because you're pretty mysterious at times. Like today."

She had started out okay, but her voice was petulant by the end. She realized this was as good a moment as ever to break the news to her mom. "Um, speaking of teamwork, today I stuck up for Lily Gomez, a girl in my high school algebra class."

Liz knew her daughter: what she had said sounded good on the surface but that could just be the tip of an iceberg... So she asked tentatively, "How and why did you do that?"

The passion in Jackie's voice betrayed her. "Well, there's this junior boy named Josh, and he thinks he's the best looking guy in the whole world. I mean, he does have these amazing eyes, and he is pretty good looking, but he's so full of himself."

"You don't have to run him down," Liz interrupted. "Remember what I've said about always speaking well of others."

Jackie scowled darkly. "Then I would never be able to say a single thing about Josh because now you already know his sole good quality!"

"So what happened?" her mother prodded.

"Okay, so he and his buddies had been drinking at a party and Josh lost some kind of contest with Nick. So Nick gave him a choice of two penalties: either ask Lily to the spring dance or fall down at the end of Miss Townsend's geography class and do an impression of a fried egg." Mother and brother were entertained so far, though Mikey acted like he wasn't listening.

Liz wanted her daughter to clarify something. "What's so bad about asking Lily out or acting like a fried egg?"

Now her daughter was warmed up. "There's nothing wrong with Lily, only some of the kids call her a nerd. She's really nice, Mom, and smart. But she doesn't wear the nicest clothes or know how to style her hair and she's just a little chubby, though she's really pretty too! Many of the other girls are mean to her, and I think it's because they're jealous of her. But like I said: they call her a nerd."

"And Miss Townsend?"

"You asked me so I'll tell you: she's really pretty and young and knows it too, like Josh, and all the guys…"

"Enough!" cut in her mother. Jackie laughed, knowing that her mother was going to stop her short.

"Well, you asked. Okay, so Josh preferred to take Lily to the dance even though most of the girls would have loved to have gone with him… even the senior girls! And Mom, they called Lily right then and there from the party putting her on speakerphone, though she didn't realize it."

Her mother could guess what happened. She groaned in compassion for the poor girl. "Uh oh!"

Jackie nodded emphatically. "Now you're getting it. Poor Lily! She answered so enthusiastically. When he hung up they spent the rest of the night mimicking her. And she had no clue. So, after two days Josh gets tired of everyone making fun of him for taking Lily to the dance, so he falls down in Miss Townsend's class and does the fried egg, and right after that in the hallway he tells poor Lily that he can't go with her after all because he feels sick. The dance isn't for another three weeks!"

"That was pretty mean!"

"Exactly. So that's why I stuck up for her." It was taking a long time to find out just precisely how, and Liz wasn't about to congratulate her until she found out what she had done.

"So what did you do?" she asked patiently. Now Jackie had to measure her words more carefully.

"I told Josh in between classes that it was absolutely imperative I tell him something urgent right away!"

"And?"

The girl hesitated then went ahead and blurted it all out. "Then, once everyone was in the classroom except us two, I congratulated him for winning the biggest loser of the year award for what he did to Lily, and then I flattened him!"

It was a good thing they were the only car on the road because Liz screeched to a halt in her surprise and dismay.

"You what?" she replied incredulously.

In his enthusiasm, Mikey forgot that he had been pretending not to listen. "Josh must be eight inches taller and weigh about 120 pounds more than you. How did you do it?" he asked eagerly.

While Jackie might have answered harshly that it was none of his business on other occasions, this time she couldn't help boasting a little. Besides, she knew her mother wasn't about to ask for more details, so she had to supply them freely. Moreover, she was really uncomfortable under her mother's outraged gaze which was fixed upon her now that the car had come to a full stop.

"Oh, you know, the typical stuff we've learned in class," she answered breezily. "First I boxed both of his shoulders to wind him, and while he was leaning on one foot to catch his breath, I swiped his foot and he was down."

"Wow! That is just like we learned in class! But it works!" Mikey was momentarily impressed by his sister.

"Yeah, I think I'm actually going to miss our Tai Kwon Do classes now that we've moved to this nowhere town. All those classes were worth it." She was still waiting uncomfortably for her mother to say something, but Mikey had the chance to respond first.

"No worries there! We've already been registered in the nearby town of..."

His mother cut him off, beginning ominously, "Jacqueline Marie Foster... That isn't Christian."

Jackie frowned stubbornly. "Why not, Mom? I was defending someone he had offended real bad! He deserved much worse. Besides I deliberately used moves that didn't hurt him. His head hardly knocked against the ground when he fell..." She wasn't sorry at all for having decked him, but was only concerned about the consequences.

"If we as Christians stoop to do the same things that non-Christians do when they're angry, we're worse off than them because we're hypocrites besides." That stung. The Foster kids had been raised to be honest.

"What's the good of being Christians anyways, if we have to stand by and watch our friends be mocked like that!" Jackie was obdurate.

"I didn't say you have to stand by and do nothing, but you didn't have to throw Josh to the ground! Obviously the boy doesn't lead a very happy life if he can act that way, but your response gives him the wrong idea of Christianity. How is he going to discover Christ, except through the example of kind and merciful Christians?"

She knew her mom had a point, but Jackie couldn't resist trying to get in the last word. "So what do you want me to do about it now? Apologize?" And to her horror, her mother's concerned look evaporated at the suggestion.

"Well, as a matter of fact, yes. That's a capital idea!" She started up the car once more and continued down the road.

"You can't be serious! That's not fair! I won't do it! I mean, what am I going to say to him that would be honest? 'Sorry you're a loser'?"

But Liz had recovered her composure once more. "You and I are both too emotional to speak about this anymore right now. We'll talk again after dinner in private."

They drove on some minutes more in silence, with Jackie reading and Mikey engrossed in his Game Boy once more. The car pulled off the dusty road and over a little bridge. A stream gushed, offering a natural boundary since it was too wide to jump. On the other side, a new twelve-foot-high gate blocked the way. From it ran a chain-link fence topped by barbed wire, which followed the stream up the road. Mrs. Foster pushed the electronic opener and drove through. Though there was no car in sight, she waited for the gate to shut before driving on.

The house wasn't in sight yet. First they had to curve around the hill for a minute on the newly paved road, and then they could see it past the sprawling meadows full of peacefully grazing sheep. A typical big red barn stood nearby the obviously new two-story home. It was large but quite simple in appearance. Certainly not imposing.

Jackie was out of the car and into their home in an instant, but Mrs. Foster remained seated with her car door open. She waited while Mikey got out on her side and then reached for him once he had shut his door.

"Mikey, did you notice that your sister doesn't appreciate being psychoanalyzed by you?" she asked softly but firmly.

"Well... what I said is true, isn't it?" he replied sheepishly under that intent gaze.

"It's true in one sense and not true in another. Your father and I have said we should always speak the truth when we speak, but we don't always have to state every truth. For instance, using words to hurt someone can be worse than telling a lie and is kind of like a lie."

"But Mom! Jackie needs some help with a reality check."

"Christians help others by helping them to carry their crosses, not by making the load heavier. If you find your sister more tiresome right now, that means you need to be all the more understanding and kind."

"Mom, don't you think you're expecting too much of me? After all I'm only ten years old."

"That brings me to my next point. I don't recall giving you permission to delve into developmental psychology."

He looked guilty. "But it's good, Mom. It's not at all Freudian. It's Piaget. Quite fascinating; and he's succeeded very well in identifying Jackie's adolescent quirks."

"You might understand what you've read with your mind; but your own psychology is still only on par with your physical age. That kind of information also needs to be understood with your heart." She tapped him gently on his chest where his heart was. "And you've just admitted that you're not mature enough for that yet."

"Aw, Mom. But it's so interesting. I won't study the part that has to do with her anymore…" He neglected to inform her that he had already read the entire book. He thought it best to leave that detail out for the moment. Perhaps he would get off with the light sentence of being forbidden to read what he was done with anyway.

"The only proper purpose for learning is to do good."

"Okay, Mom," he answered meekly. "But I ardently hope that this current phase of hers will go by quickly!" He gave her a quick hug just to make sure everything was fine and then moved towards the house. After he had gone a few steps, he turned to get permission to take his bath before dinner.

FIVE

Half an hour before dinner, Mikey knocked at his sister's bedroom door. He was dressed only in shorts.

"Go away. I'm busy," she replied without even looking up from her book.

"You'll be interested in this. An opportunity of a lifetime: I'm going to give you a chance to tie my hands behind my back as tight as you can."

"Not again. Don't you think this is getting a little old? Can't you find a more normal way to occupy your time, like stamp collecting?"

"Might I remind you that each time you have gotten tighter and more intricate with your knots and I have never needed help to get out. You should be impressed at my skill and take up the challenge to beat me. I add that the word 'beat' should not be taken here in its literal sense."

He had to be careful with his sister, especially when he was putting himself at her mercy. She smiled despite herself. In fact it was entertaining to tie him up and she was impressed that he could get free on his own.

"What's the big novelty this time?"

"The cord is thinner and this time you are to tie both my hands and feet." She set down her book, which he took for acceptance, so entered the room with his rope. He didn't speak while she worked but took very deep long breathes. Long practice at tying him up had made her quick. In no time she had succeeded in tying his feet tightly together... though not tight enough to leave marks in his skin since she might get into trouble for that. His hands were also very securely tied behind his back. Jackie stood back and admired her handiwork.

"This time you're sunk!" she affirmed.

He smiled enigmatically at her choice of words. "I wouldn't say that yet. Thank you very much. When I reach the heights of fame some day, I shall offer you the first dibs on being my lovely assistant." With that, he hopped out of the room quite cheerfully, still breathing deeply.

Some minutes later there was a large splash in the bathroom. Once more absorbed in her book, Jackie didn't reflect about the significance of that sound until she heard her mother calling from downstairs: "Mikey, don't cause a flood with the bathwater: keep it in the tub!"

No answer came. Jackie suddenly jerked up. She had tied her brother hand and foot. Had he fallen into the bath? If so, would he be able to get out? She called his name tentatively and on hearing no reply or sound at all from the bathroom, went shrieking in. And sure enough there he was, squirming to unloose himself while submerged under eight inches of water. He had a placid look of deep concentration on his face and was slowing releasing little bubbles of air. She screamed and roughly fished him out of the water by his hair.

As soon as he breathed and she was sure he was fine she bellowed, "You freak! Do you want to ruin my reputation forever? I can just see it now in the school headlines: sister cruelly ties up her brother so she can drown him in the family tub! Who would believe me that you set me up, you suicidal maniac!" She shook him some and then let him go only to seize scissors from the cabinet so she could cut him loose. "That's the last time I tie you up! If you try something like this again, I'm gonna kill you!"

Mikey was inwardly relieved that she had rescued him, although he didn't like having the rope cut. The knots were harder to get out of than he had expected, and he wasn't sure after all if he would have been able to stick his head out of the water as easily as he had planned were he to have run out of air. But he wanted to save face, and he was concerned at her threats to stop tying him up. How was he ever going to get this skill down without her help? Jimmie wasn't around enough, and asking Mom was out of the question.

"I assure you that your concerns are most unfounded. I have a decided love for life and I was almost free, as is plainly evident." That part was true… his sister had noticed that the rope was much looser on his wrists. Jackie snorted as she threw the scissors back into the drawer.

"I live in a family of lunatics! First Mom and now you! It's only a matter of time before my friends at school discover the truth. I'm doomed." With these words of desolation she stomped out of the room, down the stairs, and out the front door. There she plopped down on the stairs, hugging their German Shepherd, Shep, who whined softly and sympathetically. Jimmie greeted her when he arrived home shortly afterwards.

"Hey, Jackie. How's it goin'?"

"Do you want the polite answer or the real answer?" came the dour reply. Jackie loved Jimmie immensely. Couldn't get enough of him. But it didn't occur to her how even he could help her in her present distress.

"That's okay. I get the idea… Hard day, huh?" He sat down beside her to see if he could cheer her up some.

"Mom says I have to apologize to Josh for laying him flat. But I'm not going to! He deserved it. It's not fair!" Her brother already knew the whole story because she had called his cell phone and recounted it in detail as soon as it had happened.

"I myself took Josh aside to tell him I was ready to slam him in the guts for treating Lily cruelly, and you know what he answered?" He checked to see if he had piqued her interest.

"What?" Jackie mumbled into Shep's fur, trying to seem like she didn't care.

"He said that you already took care of that and that you had been very effective in letting him see the error of his ways!"

Her head popped up. "He did? Did he really?" She grabbed her brother excitedly by the arm. "He's actually sorry?" The smile and nod from her brother confirmed his words. "But does that mean he's going to take Lily to the dance after all? She told me she'll never go to another dance again." Jackie really wanted justice for her friend.

"Well, he did apologize and ask her, but it turns out that she's already going with someone else!" Jackie was so elated that her friend could go to the dance after all and not be made fun of that it didn't occur to ask who was taking her. Besides, she still had to figure out what she was going to do about apologizing. "Do you think I won't have to apologize to him anymore, now that my correction has turned out to be so beneficial for him?" she asked hopefully.

Jimmie smiled benevolently at his sister. "If you're asking my humble opinion, I guess Mom would say that you still have to apologize for being unchristian…" At that, her head flopped down once more.

"How am I going to get up the nerve to do it? He's always with his friends!" Her brother thought for a moment, then confidently proposed a solution.

"Let's kill two birds with one stone. You haven't made your fudgy brownies since Dad died. How about you make a double batch, so we get some too? And tomorrow at the beginning of lunch you go up to him at his locker, toss him the brownies, and say: 'Sorry about yesterday… I wasn't very Christian.' You can do that, can't you? And I'll make sure some of my buddies are there to help eat them too, so it will be like you're giving the brownies to the whole soccer team, not just Josh."

The prospect of pleasing her brother by baking him brownies was agreeable, as was the idea of the other soccer players getting to eat them too. "That's a great idea. You're my favorite big brother!" She would have hugged him, but he knew her too well and avoided it by standing up.

"C'mon. Mom's calling us for dinner." Only later would Jackie find out that Jimmie was going to be Lily's date.

At school the next day, Jackie slipped out of class early so she could be sure to meet up with Josh. There he was, with his back to her, facing his locker, so she was able to get up close to him before he realized she was there. If he had seen her, he would have pretended he was afraid of her, but as it was, he happened to be gesturing with his arm outstretched and she simply placed the box of brownies on top of his hand. She muttered the words exactly the way her brother had suggested she should and then turned and walked away before he could respond. Josh looked after her with his mouth open, trying to think what he should say, giving Jeff the opportunity to snatch the brownies out of his hand.

"What have you got there, Josh? Yum, homemade brownies! Can I have some?" Jackie was forgotten as he turned to reclaim his prized food, but he was too late. Jeff had already helped himself and tossed the box to Roberto, who gleefully ran down the hall with it while digging out a share. He succeeded in handing it off to Luigi before Josh could tackle him... exactly in front of Mr. West's classroom. And Mr. West was only too happy to give the boy a detention. Josh found the empty box of brownies in his locker.

SIX

Two weeks after the Houdini incident, the same trio again arrived home from school. Jackie was out and running for the barn before the others had unbuckled their seatbelts. To a stranger, it would look much like she was in a hurry to finish her chores as soon as possible. But this was no ordinary barn, though it looked that way from the outside. The right side was just as to be expected: dirt floor with stalls for animals, an open area for storing hay and straw, with a concrete drainage system for animal waste running down the middle. The left side had the irregularity. It was mostly taken up by an office-like structure, enclosed by frosted bank-like windows on three sides, while sharing the barn wall on the other.

Jackie pushed through the big barn door, bounded up the few stairs of the inner building, and entered the room with a flourish. It was a modern science lab. Down the center of the room ran a lower tiled portion, with a drain in the middle. Jimmie, in a white lab coat, was on the right working busily at one of the two long lab tables. Across from him were rows of animal cages, mostly filled with mice, stacked up on each other. A big wooden desk took up the back end of the room, with the sink and storage behind it.

"Jimmie, Mom says to tell you that the visitors will arrive earlier than expected. They'll be here in about half an hour, so you need to make sure everything is set up for them. And guess what!" she bubbled.

Jimmie looked up from his microscope and smiled warmly. "What?"

"They invited me to be on the senior varsity cheerleading team! And I'm the only eighth grade girl on the team!"

"Great! Congratulations. I didn't know you were so good." She knew he was not too moved by the news, but she accepted his kindly attempt to share her joy.

"I didn't say I was so good." She began to list off points with her fingers. "One of their flyers just got injured, and I'm a flyer. I'm small and I already know a bunch of their moves. But I think the real reason I made it is because of you!" She stopped counting to point at him dramatically.

"Me? How could I have anything to do with it? I don't even go to your school or know who your coaches are!" He looked back down at the microscope. At that she drew nearer, still trying to keep his attention. Jackie couldn't get enough of her big brother. She admired him so much and loved to be with him.

"One of the senior girls told me that half of the girls on the squad are wildly in love with you!" If she had expected a reply, Jackie would have been disappointed, because he didn't even look up. "Up until then I had wondered why so many of the high-school girls were so nice to me, when they couldn't be bothered with the other middle-school girls. I should have known better. Anyway, they've got good taste!" Still no response. Jimmie seemed to be engrossed in whatever he was looking at. "C'mon Jimmie! Don't you have anything to say? Don't you want to know who's interested in you? Maybe I could help set you up with one of them."

"Aw Jackie, a guy doesn't want his little sister's help in that area. But thanks anyway." He looked up once more and smiled ruefully at her to soften the rejection, then returned to the microscope.

"But Jimmie, why not? I can help make your life easy, and besides, I'll soon know the inside scoop on these girls and which ones are worthy of you. You could use my help. In fact we could help each other." He didn't bite. "Look, I'll start. I'll tell you who I like on your team if you'll tell me who you like. You just have to promise not to tell anyone…"

Before Jimmie could reply, a disembodied, muted voice responded: "Yes, do tell all! Although the attentive observer could likely determine this on his own without having to lower himself to…" Jackie shrieked angrily and instantly began searching the room for the owner of the voice:

"Hou! How dare you listen in on our private, adult conversation! You're not allowed to be in here anyway! Are you ever gonna catch it from Mom!"

"Well, that would be decidedly unjust if I'm not really there…" His smug tone infuriated his sister all the more. "Perhaps I'm talking by hidden intercom. Perhaps as we speak I'm attempting to crack the combination lock on your diary that will tell me all I ever wanted to know…"

Jackie flew out the door as she threatened, "You're absolutely dead if I find you in my room!" The door shut behind her. A few seconds passed, and then two tiles on the lower edge of the middle of the room suddenly popped out of place.

"To say 'absolutely' in regards to death is redundant: being dead isn't a question of degrees!" Mikey spoke nonchalantly, although he was most intent on witnessing the effect of his appearance on his older brother. Like his sister, he loved his brother dearly. And this was his greatest feat yet. He had secretly spent hours cutting through the tile and wood underneath to gain access to the empty space below the lab. Next he had to quickly fit them back together and plug up the hole he had made so that it would go unnoticed. His big brother was the only person he was planning to let in on his secret.

Jimmie took in his beaming little brother triumphantly holding the glued tile piece and guessed what this moment meant to Mikey. He played along magnificently. First he let out a low whistle, then rose from his chair and knelt down to peer through the hole.

"I never would have guessed there was a secret door. Cover it over again and let me see if I can notice it now." Mikey instantly complied, and plugged up the opening he made.

"Does my light show through?" he called excitedly.

"Not even the slightest crack! What a professional job you've done!" At this warm praise, the lid was lifted once more to reveal Mikey's glowing face.

"I'm not finished because you can only open the door from this side right now. I had to hurry to escape detection..." Mikey only completely relaxed when he was alone with his big brother. He himself didn't realize that with Jimmie his vocabulary and sentence construction was normal. When he was with other people, he used bigger words and more convoluted constructions, as if he wanted to feel more important somehow.

"So, what's the idea, Mikey? Is this all because Mom said she doesn't want you working in the lab until you're older?"

Mikey avoided his eyes. "She never said I couldn't go under the lab.... Just between you and me, I think we should be prepared for the worst in case the ones who killed Dad come after us too."

"C'mon. Don't exaggerate. It could have just been an accident. Besides, we're safe. Nobody's going to find us here."

Mikey didn't look convinced. "Better safe than sorry. Don't you want to see the trap door from this side?" For a split second, Jimmie thought about the slides he still had to prepare for the visitors. But the look on his little brother's face convinced him that this moment was too important to be put off for later. He hadn't spent enough time with Mikey lately. Without another word, the lab coat was doffed, and big brother was squeezing through the hole.

"Oh, good! It's not such a tight fit as I had feared!" crowed Mikey jubilantly. Once Jimmie was through, the cover was fit back into place and for an instant they were in darkness. Then Mikey triumphantly switched on the light of the two homemade miner-type hats and graciously handed one over. Jimmie took in the blankets, big pillow, and book, *To Kill a Mockingbird.*

"So, do you spend much time down here? Does Jackie know you have her book?" he teased as he lay back on the pillow and looked around.

"Jackie's already finished with it. She made me curious because she said Atticus reminded her of Dad... I sure miss Dad!"

"Me too, Mikey. Me too." They were both quiet.

"You know what I've been wishing for, Jimmie? Jackie and I shared our dad with you all these years. So now my dream is that your dad will suddenly show up and turn out to be a good guy after all. Then he marries Mom and you can share your dad with us." These words stung Jimmie to the core, but he kept control of his outward reaction so Mikey wouldn't feel bad.

Instead he responded nonchalantly, "I don't think there's much hope for that. We don't even know if he's alive."

"Mom does. Won't she tell you anything about him?"

"Not yet. She keeps telling me that she will soon. I don't even care if he's not a 'good guy' like you're hoping. I just want to know who he is." End of topic for him. Looking around some more, Jimmie asked, "Where's the escape route?"

Mikey scrambled along on all fours towards the barn wall. He unlatched the low secret door, swung it up, and crawled through, with Jimmie right behind him. Mikey reached under the door with his finger to latch it once more from the inside while Jimmie got to his feet and brushed himself off.

"Now we have two things in common, Jimmie. We both know the secret entrance to the lab, and we're both on the same soccer team."

"Right. And you're not bad as a water boy." He offered his hand for a high five. "Coach David seems pretty happy with you anyway." Mikey liked helping Coach.

"Yah, we get along great! He lets me help in planning all the tactics while we're sitting on the bench together during the game."

Jimmie leaned down to admire Mikey's handiwork and was commenting that this door too was unnoticeable when they heard a car pull in.

"Quick, brush the dust off of my back. I have to run and finish setting up." He did his best to shake the dirt from his body with Mikey helping from behind. One last congratulatory high five, and he headed off for the normal entrance of the barn to beat the visitors there.

It was the same old routine for new visitors, three or four at a time. First they were shown slides and offered detailed explanations. Liz did most of the talking, but Jimmie could hold his own and helped out here and there, filling in key details. The visitors were always impressed by the wealth of his knowledge, given his youth. But no explanations were offered on his account. Strictly business. Each of them received packets containing specimens and compact discs with instructions and guidelines.

The lab demonstrations over, they would retire as usual to the main house for delicious home-cooked food served on the family china. The visitors were astonished at the close of the meal when sons, daughter, and mother took up piano, violins, and flute to entertain them. It was impressive to see how they played so expertly.

Normally, it was Jimmie who saw the guests to their car, but he excused himself early to go back to the barn. Liz found him there once she had seen them off by herself. He was feeding the animals in their cages. She came up beside him and started helping.

"Is something wrong, Jimmie?" He didn't answer right away. Liz waited quietly by his side, opening the cages and inserting the sweet-smelling seeds.

At last, he demanded, "When are you going to tell me about my father?" He didn't look at her. The topic was too painful.

She knew she would have to choose her words well. Jimmie

hadn't broached this topic in a long time. "When you're ready, Jimmie."

He wheeled towards her abruptly, tensely. "Whatever it is I have to do to 'be ready,' I'll do!" he declared emphatically. "Just tell me what I need to know!" It was uncharacteristic of Jimmie to express tension, impatience, or much emotion at all.

Liz took a breath, then reached up and tenderly brushed back a lock of hair on his forehead, something she did to show affection to Jimmie. "You'll be ready once you're convinced your heavenly Father is your true father."

He grimaced. "Okay, great. I know God is my true father. Now please, tell me who my earthly father is! You've kept me waiting so long!"

"I think you'll be ready soon, Jimmie," was all the comfort she could offer. He went back to feeding the animals, as did she.

After a good stretch of time he commented morosely, "I'm so afraid that something will happen to my real father or to you before you tell me who he is, and that I'll never get a chance to meet him."

Liz answered by embracing her son from the side while he stood there motionless. "There's no need to worry about that. Your father is in heaven," she assured him softly. Jimmie looked away, heartbroken. He hadn't expected to hear that. He cried very rarely, but he did now, though he made no sound and hoped his mother wouldn't notice. Of course, she was observing him closely. She wiped away his tears tenderly. "You've been so patient up until now. Just wait a little longer and you'll know everything. And then you'll see why your dad and I waited to tell you. Just keep in mind for now that the captain of a boat can forget where he came from, but he can never afford to forget where he's going. You don't need to know your past to know that this life is a voyage to our heavenly home."

He stood stiffly, mutely. Gazing at him now in his sorrow, it occurred to her that he needed to be distracted from so much work alone in the laboratory. She had been driving him too hard. After all, he was barely sixteen… he needed to be doing something engrossing with other people that would keep him from brooding about himself. "Tomorrow I'm going to go with you to Father Matthew, to see if you can do some volunteer work in the parish once in a while. C'mon. Let's go to bed now. We're both tired…"

Once outside the barn, Jimmie pointed out Mars in the sky. While gazing up at the sky, Liz veered to the right as she walked. Without warning, Jimmie suddenly pulled his mother back to the left while exclaiming that she should be careful.

"What's the matter, Jimmie? There's nothing there."

He chuckled. "Then you haven't found out about Houdini Junior's latest invention. He's set up what he calls the Lilliput spider trap all along this side of the barn. If you walk in there, you'll be trapped by bunches of thin, sticky cords which are fastened to the ground. And the harder you fight, the more they'll stick to you! Mikey demonstrated just for me with one of the biggest sheep: the poor thing got really stuck and plenty scared! It was impressive. But don't worry: he's already trained Shep to keep away when he sets it up at night… He begged me to try it on Jackie, but I put my foot down and gave him a stern warning. You know Hou can go overboard sometimes…"

"He's been like this ever since Henry died. I'm hoping it's just a passing phase…"

Jimmie nodded. "Yeah, let's hope."

The next morning, with the first pleasantries over, mother and son were seated across from Father Matthew in his parish office. He peered at them with benevolent interest: she seemed so young to be this boy's mother… but women are good at hiding their real age. Both were handsome but not alike in appearance at all: she with golden blond hair, blue-eyed, milky skin, finely chiseled features, and such a petite frame, and he darker, tall, big-boned, with brown hair and eyes. Even their manner was at odds. He had an affable smile on his face as he leaned back comfortably in his chair, while Mrs. Foster was severe looking as she sat ramrod straight in her chair, awaiting the priest's invitation to begin the conversation. He was curious to know why she had asked to see him.

"Well, how can I help you, Mrs. Foster?"

That was enough for her. She launched right into the proposal, maintaining a low, businesslike voice all the while. Jimmie looked down silently while his mother went on. His stillness betrayed his acute embarrassment at his mother's words. She emphasized again and again that her son was very special and so needed to follow his own private academic program at home. No school was good enough for him. But he lacked the opportunity to think about the needs of others. In addition to playing soccer, she wished him to do volunteer work in the parish. But he must remain low-key. Attention and praise wouldn't be good for him at all. It would go to his head. It was imperative that Father keep that clear. This was all in confidence of course, for foul play was suspected regarding her husband's recent death.

She lost her breath at this point and turned her eyes away, but soon rushed on. All this was very trying for her and her children. They had moved away seeking peace, privacy, and safety. Jimmie must not stand out in any way, but he was to be at Father Matthew's service five hours a week. He could mow the lawn. He's very good with gadgets, fixing things, painting… He's fluent in Spanish so he could help give catechism to the children as long as this wouldn't attract too much attention.

At the end of her monologue, she concluded, "I do hope that you appreciate the importance of my son maintaining a low profile?"

"I don't see any problem with what you're asking, Mrs. Foster, but before answering I would like the chance to speak to your son alone for a few minutes if I could, please." She acquiesced, smiled significantly at her son and left the room. As the door closed, Jimmie looked up with a rueful smile.

"My mom's a little overprotective… especially with Dad's death and all… I just try to humor her and not get too annoyed. I'm almost seventeen: I'm not fragile. But I know she means well." Father Matthew returned an understanding smile then launched into his own proposal.

"Look, Jimmie, you just might be the answer to my prayers. I'm young and don't have a lot of experience yet. This is my first assignment as a priest, and I only beat your family here by a couple of months. I'm eager to work in this parish, but it hasn't been easy so far. For one, I barely succeed in saying the Mass in Spanish for our Hispanic community, and I can't really hold a conversation in that language. Many don't speak English. You speak Spanish, so I could really use your help, or rather the Lord could put your talents to good use in our parish. But I need to know if you yourself are willing to lend a hand."

Jimmie looked square into the face of this young, good-hearted priest. "Are you kidding? I'm happy to get out of the house and do something for others! Mom and Dad were missionaries in Mexico when I was younger, and I helped too."

"Good! Because that's the only way I'll take you." Both of them intuited that they were going to get along well. Jimmie stood up to leave. "There's just one thing more." He sat back down. "You're only going to be of any use if you're able to do more than merely humanitarian work. What people really need is to know Christ." Jimmie stared back blankly. "Do you have a prayer life?"

"What do you mean?" He was taken aback and somewhat abashed by the question. After a pause he went on: "Mom taught us to say our night prayers, and I sometimes still say them. We pray the Rosary together on Sundays…" His voice trailed off uncomfortably.

"That's not enough. Now that you're practically an adult, you need to relate to Our Lord as an adult. If you're going to give Christ to others first, you have to possess him. To do that you'll need to get to know him personally through prayer." Again a blank look. "We'll talk more about this next time. In the meantime, I'll tell your mom that we're set, but that you're going to be doing more than mowing the lawn around here."

"So what do you think of Father Matthew?" asked Liz in the car on the way home.

"He's okay, Mom," he replied noncommittally. That's all he would say on the matter, and she knew better than to push for more.

SEVEN

For the next four weeks, Jimmie was surprised that Father Matthew had him spend so much of those five service hours learning how to pray. But it wasn't boring or weird. When the priest discovered what an advanced reader Jimmie was, he had him read the section on prayer in the Catholic Catechism as well as classic works by saints on that theme. He had taken Mrs. Foster at her word that Jimmie was especially gifted, so he got him to employ his intellectual capacities to learn about prayer while prodding him to employ his heart and will as well.

More importantly, he would spend time with Jimmie in the chapel, kneeling beside him and quietly, fervently directing him in the art of real Christian meditation. They spent long hours in dialogue about the heart's deepest aspirations for God. Father Matthew offered convincing answers for why God permits evil in the world; how he could still be a loving God although he seems to let the innocent and weak suffer unjustly; what heaven is like, etc. Jimmie also came to appreciate the sacraments, particularly the Eucharist and confession, under the tutelage of this holy priest.

But it didn't end there. Father Matthew insisted that knowledge of Christ flows over into daily life, into a person's words, attitudes, and actions... into a living prayer. The goal was to become another Christ. Over time, Jimmie grew to look forward to these conversations and times of deep, silent prayer before Christ in the Blessed Sacrament. He told Father Matthew once that God had gifted him with the capacity to master all kinds of talents quickly: sports, studies, musical abilities, and more. But knowledge of Christ was something where he was just on par with everyone else.

"I can't become an expert in Christ the way I can master other kinds of knowledge. Knowledge of him only comes to those who are humble and seek him with a sincere heart. I can't master Christ, but I need to ask him to make himself known to me. This is the biggest challenge I've ever faced!"

"And the most important," replied the priest. "That's all that really matters in a person's life: to get to know the person with whom we hope to spend eternity. So many people are wasting away with hunger for him, but filling their bellies instead with the husks of noise and sensual pleasures."

As the weeks went by, the priest also drew him more and more into his parish work. They would go together to the parishioners' homes, with Jimmie acting as translator. The people grew to trust their priest and would open their hearts to him. He in turn would offer them the help that he could give: words of consolation, advice. He would encourage them to go to Mass on Sundays. When they were in financial need, he would look for ways to help them, even giving them money out of his own paltry funds. At first, Jimmie felt awkward, remained aloof, and merely translated. But over time, he grew involved as well and would offer his own words of comfort and material aid. He would return later on his own to the more dilapidated homes, showing remarkable ingenuity and skill in fixing up the buildings. He only asked that the owners not let others know what he had done. But they let their parish priest know.

Father Matthew was amazed to discover that Jimmie also spoke other languages fluently. He found this out by chance when they came to a door where only the German-speaking grandmother was home. Later, there was an Italian immigrant family. On both occasions, Jimmie spontaneously translated without offering a word of explanation. The second time this happened, Father Matthew had asked Jimmie point-blank afterwards if he knew any other languages. Jimmie only shrugged his shoulders enigmatically and asked the priest not to let his mother find out that he knew Jimmie spoke other languages… Father Matthew wondered about this boy, but he never pushed to know more nor let on that he knew about all the good

Jimmie was doing for others. He just kept encouraging him to widen his horizons and open his heart to help as many people as he could, both humanly and spiritually.

In addition to his work with Father Matthew, Jimmie also kept tutoring some of his fellow soccer players. Right away, he had seen how they were mostly low-level students in school. Many of them needed a big break if they were to get anywhere in life. Some had to hold down jobs to help support their families. In all, they gave little thought to going on to university. This concerned Jimmie and he spoke to Father Matthew about it, but he didn't quite know what he could do to encourage them to hope for something more in life and go about obtaining it.

Then one day, with the season half over, it came to Jimmie in a flash. If they worked hard, some of them could become good enough players to get scholarships... but their team would have to be scouted and they never made playoffs. Long before joining the team, he had mastered the sport, but he had hidden his talents so his mother would let him stay on the team. But couldn't he quietly coach some of the more promising players? As long as they promised not to make him known, there was no reason why he couldn't help them a little...

EIGHT

Father Matthew chose a cool, pleasant afternoon to visit the parishioners' homes that were close enough to walk from one to the other and which also provided a good amount of time for conversing on the return stretch. Soon after they had headed back, he sucked up his courage to launch his plan. Out of the blue he declared melodramatically: "Self-complacency does in many a fine soul!" They had been keeping a companionable silence, so Jimmie looked at him in surprise.

"Excuse me, Padre, are you talking to me?"

Father grinned apologetically. "Sorry. I was mulling over a talk I need to give and these words just sallied forth of their own accord." He paused. "You know, it might help me to speak out loud. Do you mind?"

Jimmie's affable grin was typical. "Go ahead." Then he added teasingly: "Maybe I can give you a few pointers."

Father Matthew had been counting on just such an easygoing reply. He cleared his throat. "Self-complacency keeps good souls satisfied with the kiddy pools of good they do when they're really meant to be diving into the great white ocean of mercy through their deeds." He turned to his young companion eagerly. "How's that for starters?"

Jimmie's face registered confusion. He ventured a noncommittal though ever-polite reply: "Hard to judge so far."

The older man insisted, "But have I succeeded in grabbing your attention? The first words are crucial, you know."

Jimmie felt hard pressed to be encouraging. "I guess."

Heedless of the evident skepticism of his one-man audience, Father Matthew blustered blissfully on with his imaginary talk.

"These well-intentioned but self-complacent folks are like Red Cross doctors who wend their merry way through the trenches, offering band-aids and aspirins to dying soldiers. It wounds the sensibilities to consider their amazing capacities and yet witness how satisfied they are with doing pipsqueak!"

Narrowed eyes fixed upon the offending speaker, Jimmie asked, "May I ask who exactly this talk is meant for?"

Father Matthew lifted his brow archly. "A very select audience."

Jimmie laughed pleasantly, then bantered back, "Well, just in case you're thinking of directing it at me, may I remind you that I volunteer at least five hours a week at your parish?"

The priest was unruffled. "No need to get defensive about it…"

Jimmie's jaw dropped in mock outrage. He rejoined playfully but pointedly, "That's way more than anyone else my age, and you know it."

Father Matthew kept his gaze forward. "Self-complacent people like to brandish their good deeds and compare them to others' as a way of anesthetizing their consciences."

Jimmie dug his hands into his pockets and looked away thoughtfully. "I'd say your talk lacks realism."

Father Matt smiled graciously at the boy. "Now, as long as you're applying it to yourself, I would have to agree: it's an understatement."

Jimmie shook his head in consternation before answering playfully: "What more do you want me to do? Move into the rectory?"

"Certainly not! I'm thinking of the tremendous good you could do by reaching out to others."

"Maybe I do and you just don't know about it."

"Do you imagine that my parishioners don't tell me about your return visits to their homes?" Jimmie tried to hide his surprise. "That's where your particular strain of self-complacency is most lethal!"

Jimmie couldn't decide whether to laugh or give into a sudden sharp impulse of annoyance. He chose to satisfy his curiosity. "Now I'm really lost."

"You're responding to your do-good desire with a bunch of humanitarian type stuff: plumbing, carpentry, and whatnot. Personally I'm delighted that you're fixing up peoples' homes; but I wish you would also work on a higher plane, the spiritual level."

The answer was wry: "Oh I see. You expect me to preach to them."

Father's lips turned up slightly at the corners. "Evidently you don't see at all. I don't want you to preach. That's not very effective for getting anywhere with a bunch of uppity teenagers. Just turns them off."

"Teenagers? Aren't we talking about the people in the homes we've been visiting?"

"I've been speaking about your peers all along. They're the ones who need your help so desperately. Take your soccer buddies, for instance. A sorry lot indeed! Are you aware every single one of them is Catholic? Wouldn't know it by their Sunday attendance, or rather the lack thereof."

Jimmie was silent for a moment. When he did speak it was in earnest. "Padre, what could I possibly do to help them with their faith? They wouldn't listen to me: I'm their age."

"That's where I disagree," Father Matthew countered energetically. "It's you more than anyone else who stands the best chance of bringing them around!"

"You don't know them," Jimmie responded, trying to reason with him. "Most of them have no interest in their faith whatsoever. They don't care about anything but girls, drinking, drugs, and skipping school." He added, "What's more, to be honest, I've got my own issues to sort out before I would feel ready to be a spiritual leader."

Father Matthew stopped dead, raised his eyes to the heavens, and gestured soulfully with his hands as he continued on with his talk. "Self-pity seals the sad fate of the self-complacent. When these two form a pact together, it's difficult, nay, nigh impossible, for people to broaden their horizons beyond their own backyard."

Jimmie shuffled uncomfortably as the priest's words hit home. He softly protested, "Isn't it legitimate for me to be on standby mode until I discover who my father is?"

"Says who?" the priest countered strongly. "Who says it's good to mope around feeling sorry for yourself, imagining the sun will shine once you find out a nasty bit of information? After all, you're not duping yourself into believing you'll hear good news one day, are you?"

The boy's face darkened. This was his sore point, which he rarely discussed. "How can I try to be a somebody for someone else when I don't even know who I am and where I've come from? That's a huge bit of information for me!"

Father's tone softened. "You're setting yourself up for a big let-down. When you find out who your father is, you won't have solved your real question."

Jimmie gave him a searching look.

"What I mean is, you're not alone in your quest. Everyone seeks to solve the problem of their own identity, especially people your age. And the answer isn't to be found through knowledge, but by giving yourself to others. At least, that's what the Holy Father says, and he's a wise man. He keeps quoting a phrase from Vatican II: 'A person will remain a mystery to himself until he learns to give himself to others.' God is your Father, and he created you with infinite love. Your life is a gift. You won't understand what fulfills you until you learn to give yourself to others. If you want to discover the meaning of sonship, then be a son to God the Father by reuniting him with his lost children. I'm taking that straight from Scriptures, you know: 'Blessed are the peacemakers, for they shall be called sons of God'. My emphasis is on the word 'son'. Isn't the best kind of peacemaking the kind that brings about reconciliation between a sinner and his creator?" Father Matthew walked along quietly while Jimmie pondered his words.

At last Jimmie remarked regretfully, "I wouldn't be able to get anywhere with them. They would only laugh at me."

"Are you being fair to them? Have you ever tried?"

Jimmie shook his head. "It's useless. And if it did occur to me to try to help them, I wouldn't know where to start."

His companion observed drily, "Many people would say the same thing about fixing up broken-down old homes. You, on the other hand, have had remarkable success there. Now, if only you would direct your genius towards the very needy souls of your soccer mates...."

Jimmie sighed. "Where would I start?"

Father Matthew's heart leapt inwardly, but outwardly he only shrugged his shoulders. "I have no idea. You're the genius!" Smiling, he added, "But I do have one piece of advice to offer: remember basic physics." Holding one hand in the air and the other a foot underneath, he went on, "You want to help bring them up to this spiritual level, 'point B,' from this spot, 'point A,' here below. You just need to figure out the formula, with a little inspirational help from Our Lord on how to connect the dots."

He brought his hands together and returned them to his sides. "Oh, yes, one more elementary physics lesson. If an archer wants to hit a bull's-eye, he needs to point his arrow higher than his target because of the law of gravity. So remember to aim high!"

NINE

Coach David scanned the crowd: there were a lot more fans than normal! Of course, this was the first time the school had come so close to making it into the playoffs. The season had started out poorly, as usual, but then in the last four weeks some of the players had made remarkable improvements. It was uncanny. He'd been coaching this same group for three years and never suspected they could get so good so quickly. He wondered what had made the difference. Were they eating better or drinking less? Hard to tell. In any case, here they were: if they won this game, at least they were in. Wouldn't even matter if they were knocked out in the first round. It would be an incredible achievement to get in, a real boost for the morale of these kids.

He spotted Jimmie's mother making her way through the stands and sitting down. *How could such a crazy dame be the mother of such great kids?* he wondered once more to himself. Their paths hadn't crossed at all since their first meeting, which was fine with him. She came to the games but was in the car ready to leave before they were over. Mikey and Jackie always had to run as soon as the game ended. He noticed the vast improvement in her appearance, which was now classy and dignified, but he didn't waste time trying to figure her out. He was content that she kept out of his way.

Mikey appeared at his side. "Anything I can do for you, Coach?"

Good kid, David thought. *Very bright, happy, attentive, helpful... just not very athletic.*

"The ref's just about to start the game. When he blows the whistle, you can help collect the balls."

"I think we stand a good chance to win, Coach." Mikey began enthusiastically. "Jimmie taught two more new moves to Carlos, Andre, and Jorge and..." His voice trailed off as David snapped his head around to stare fixedly at him.

"What did you just say, Mikey? So it's Jimmie whose been teaching them on the side?" The young boy clapped his hands on his mouth in horror at what he had let slip out. He grabbed David's arm earnestly.

"Is there any possibility you would consider forgetting what you just heard? Please! Jimmie won't teach them anymore if he finds out that you know, and even worse, he'll never trust me again!" The ref blew his whistle and the players began to run in from the field.

"Don't worry, Mikey," was all Coach had the chance to say. He had half guessed anyway. After the pep talk, the players headed out to their positions, and David pulled Jimmie to the side. "I want you to play your true best today, Jimmie."

Jimmie greeted his intent gaze calmly. "I want the team to win as much as you do, Coach."

Straight out, Jimmie scored the first goal of the game. The crowd cheered. Liz was annoyed, but smiled grimly and clapped perfunctorily so as not to draw attention by her lack of joy at her son's good play. From there, the score went back and forth between the two teams, with Jimmie melting into the background as was customary for him. It was his protégés who shone. In the fourth quarter, with their team down by one goal at 4-3, Coach David once more pulled Jimmie aside and insisted on another goal. He complied almost immediately, making it look like a fluke. He seemed to almost trip as he knocked the ball through the goal. Again, the cheers. Liz moved to the edge of the field and signaled for Mikey to come to her.

He returned with a message. "Coach, my mom wants to know if

you're a man of your word?" He glared across the field at that neurotic woman. Did she have no sense of how important this game was for the kids? Meanwhile some of the players were helping Jimmie off the field. It seemed he had twisted his ankle in making the shot. With the substitution made, the coach sat down beside Jimmie.

"I would have taken you out. You didn't have to fake the injury."

"Wanted to make it easier for you and me…" Jimmie wasn't about to go back on his mother's "two-goal only rule," but he didn't like it either. With him out, the team lost its momentum and the other side pulled into the lead once more.

Only then did it really dawn on David how much Jimmie meant for the team. He normally didn't play so outstandingly, but he was there encouraging the others from the background, quietly holding the players together as a team and making the great majority of the assists. Now it all made sense. David made a mental note to try to recall later what Liz had said about her son in that ridiculous meeting. At last it was apparent to him that it might be true: Jimmie just might have been a phenomenal player from the start. He was just so good at hiding his talent. But why? What were they trying to hide? These kinds of questions occupied his mind for the few minutes that remained of the game.

When it was over, Coach gathered his team together for the end of the season pep talk. He was just getting warmed up when Mrs. Foster interrupted all smiles.

"Boys, my congratulations. You played the best you've ever played! I want to celebrate the success of your game by taking you all out for pizza." They brightened up. Good food when you're down can be consoling.

However, Coach David cut her off irritably: "Ma'am, I'm sure you have the best intentions. But we don't celebrate losses around here." The two stared each other down, she smiling innocently, he cold and unyielding. She turned and began to walk away amidst the groans and protests of the players.

But when she had gone fifteen feet, she turned back and called out to Jimmie in a bantering tone, "Jimmie, I commiserate with you for your terrible loss. So I'd like to invite you to come drown your sorrows in a pizza! Invite as many friends as you like to Papa Gino's." Coach saw the mutiny in his players' eyes and threw up his arms in exasperation.

"Go!" They were gone in an instant. Mikey hurriedly scrambled about to collect the water bottles and equipment for David. Only Jimmie remained standing before the irate coach.

"I'm really sorry Mom interrupted like that." The loss of the day rankled David. They could have won if it wasn't for that woman's interference and now she had butted in again. Jimmie, the son of that woman, happened to be standing there. The player who had secretly been outsmarting him all this time! He was better than he had let on. He had been coaching his players without his permission.

Out of the blue, he demanded, "Just what was your problem with providing your birth date so we could provide the full roster in case we had made it into the playoffs? Jorge told me you said you needed to talk to me before you could state your birthday. Don't tell me you've been hiding that you're too old!" He knew it wasn't right to take out his annoyance on the kid, but in that moment he couldn't hold in his anger.

Jimmie's face became expressionless, soldier-like. "Sir, it's kind of awkward for me to explain…" David was already regretting his outburst. Nevertheless, he didn't try to make it easier for the boy to answer. "You're aware that my mother's somewhat overprotective of me…"

"Somewhat!" snapped David.

"She's told me for years that I need to wait until I'm older before she'll explain about my father. I don't know a thing about him. Not only that, but she says it's not safe for me to be found and so she hasn't even acquired my Social Security number. Without that I can't get my driver's license. That's why I bike everywhere: it's my freedom."

This was interesting and pitiable, but it didn't explain the part about his birthday. Coach stonily insisted on the point. "And your birthday?"

"My mom has given me a day for me to celebrate it like everyone else, but she's always let me know it's not my true birthday. That's part of the hush-hush business about my birth... I can't figure why that has to be secret too. I think perhaps she doesn't want me doing any checking on my own..." His voice trailed off. "Anyway, my real birthday hasn't mattered until now...I didn't want to give you a fake date, but I didn't want to explain this to my teammates either."

David exploded. "That's completely exaggerated. It's mad!" He waved his arms back and forth to emphasize his words. "You need to stand up to your mother, Jimmie! Soon you'll be going off to college. It's about time she filled you in on your background! You've got a right to know!" He spoke roughly, again from the wrath he felt toward the mother and not the poor son.

Jimmie's eyes glinted back, a fire enkindled. "Do you know who my mother is?"

Coach blinked at the answering anger. "Who?"

"She's my mother. That's enough for you. I ask you the courtesy to speak respectfully of her in my presence at all times. This is a private family matter, and I'll thank you to keep out of it." The two glared at each other.

Mikey had been watching the two nervously. It was time to act! He opened the ball bag up and held it with one hand, then grabbed as many water bottles as he could cradle in both arms. Then the water boy headed quickly towards his brother and Coach, chirping brightly: "Here's everything, Coach."

Just as he reached them he stumbled and fell sprawling at their feet, bottles flying everywhere and balls rolling free of the bag. Mikey groaned and gripped his ankle in pain. Anger momentarily put aside, the two bent down in concern by Mikey's side. "Ooh, that smarts! What did I trip on?"

Jimmie smiled reassuringly. "Nothing."

Coach conjectured, "Perhaps you lost your balance from the way you were carrying all that stuff."

"I'll give you a ride over to the restaurant on the seat of my bike," said Jimmie as he stood up.

Mikey perked up. He had been hoping his brother would offer to do that anyway. Jimmie rolled his bike over, straddled it, and held it steady for Mikey to climb on the back. He managed with David's help.

That done, David calmly remarked to Jimmie, "You have every right to ask me to speak well of your mom. I'll do as you ask. But keep my advice in mind."

Jimmie inclined his head slightly. "Coach, Mom said I could invite all the friends I want. I'd like you to come to Papa Gino's more than anyone else. You're a great coach!"

No reply.

"We'll be waiting for you," Jimmie called out as he cycled off with Mikey waving somberly from the bike seat.

When they were out of David's earshot, Mikey inquired roguishly, "Who do you think faked his fall better today: you or me?"

TEN

The boys pushed a bunch of tables together at the back of Papa Gino's so they could all sit together. However, Mikey insisted that his mother leave them alone.

"Mom, it's elementary that these adolescents have a decided preference for being left to themselves. In any case, Jimmie has been the recipient lately of far more attention from you than me. I lament to admit that I've been experiencing an unwonted jealousy against my elder sibling!"

It was so unusual for Mikey to be jealous of Jimmie, and her youngest son did have a point about the boys probably preferring to be by themselves, so Liz complied. They took a booth together at the entrance. "If you sit here you can at least keep a maternal eye on the team." Mikey gallantly indicated for her to sit facing the back of the restaurant. Then he took the seat he had planned for himself so he could watch the door.

When Coach David finally entered, Mikey acted swiftly. Before Liz even realized who was at their side, Mikey had slid in beside her and was announcing to Coach David that he and his mother had saved a seat for him. Liz's blush belied his words. She looked like she wished to leave then and there, but of course she couldn't because her son was blocking her escape. However, she was too polite to say otherwise.

David felt a certain satisfaction at her obvious discomfort. His anger had dissolved already, but hadn't she been unreasonable with her demands? He was also suddenly intrigued about her real character: she seemed so different from their first encounter. If she were wearing makeup at all today, it wasn't noticeable. Classy clothes as always, but hair down around her shoulders, pearl earrings, and a small cross around her neck. She really was strikingly beautiful.

"Mikey, I came to join my team but you've convinced me that the two of you would be hurt if I don't join you, and I wouldn't want that." He was careful to keep the sarcasm out of his voice. Mikey was ecstatic but didn't show it. Wishing to leave them alone in conversation he reached into his mother's purse, pulled out a file of newspaper clippings and appeared to become engrossed with them.

"I wouldn't have recognized you from our first meeting," David remarked conversationally. She blushed a deeper red, which encouraged him to continue in the same vein. "Tell me, are you an actress for a living?"

Mikey snorted. "My mom an actress? She can't fake anything! The instant she tries, she starts crying or blushing..."

David was amazed and delighted to see her skin take on yet a deeper hue. "So that's why you wore so much heavy makeup that day: to cover up your real skin tone," he observed.

She laughed a little and replied laconically: "Coach Johnston, everything I said that day was true. And if you happen to judge a person by their appearance, that's your affair."

"Fair enough..." he replied, smiling. He ordered his food while she ate hurriedly. As he sat watching her, it occurred to him that she might be eating fast in order to get away soon. Since it had been fine with him that their paths never crossed, it hadn't crossed his mind until now that she could have been avoiding him. She blushed once more under his attentive gaze, then at last mustered up something gracious to say.

"I would like to thank you for the way you've helped my sons. They both admire you a lot. I'm very grateful for that."

Mikey interrupted her. "Utterly preposterous! Look at this article. Britain's Royal College of Obstetricians wants to permit euthanizing seriously disabled newborn babies. Mom, why do they want to kill them just because they're not perfect? That's positively beastly!"

David reached out for the article. "You're reading pretty heavy-duty stuff there, Mikey!" He glanced over the article then handed it back. "Don't worry. It's not going to happen. Normal people wouldn't put up with it."

At once, Liz responded passionately. "Really? And why are normal people putting up with so much right now? That kind of proposal is just one more step down a long stairway."

David was taken aback by her ardent response and even more so when she stretched across the table to set his hand upright on the table like it was a wall. On one side she brandished the knife she had been eating with. "For years now, behind the cover of a very thin wall, a knife has been cutting away millions of lives. Now those same doctors just want to move the knife's action to the other side of the wall and into the light." She moved the knife over the wall of his hand to the other side. "It could be a difference of hours or days. Same child, same knife. The only thing stopping them for now is an extremely fragile wall of public opinion!"

David sat back, appraising her. *This woman's got some gumption!*

For an instant, she seemed abashed for having reacted so fiercely and then composed herself and returned to her food.

David reached out for the file. "Can I see these, Mikey?"

"Sure… they're Mom's…"

He leafed through the articles, reading two of the titles out loud: "Woman Who Lied to Get IVF at Sixty-Seven Seeks a Younger Husband to Help with Twins"; "Human-Cow Hybrid Embryo Planned." All of the articles had to do with recent medical cases from around the world.

"Mrs. Foster, I've forgotten—what it is you do for a living?"

She put out her hand for the file, then stored it away in her purse.

"Normally for a person to forget something they need to have heard it before." A slight smile and the gentleness of her tone took the bite out of her refusal to answer.

Undaunted, David turned to Mikey.

"Mikey, what does your mom do?" He was now engrossed in his Game Boy, but he looked from one to the other. His mother was smiling with a raised eyebrow.

"My mom works with animals in our barn," he affirmed.

David snorted in disbelief and looked pointedly at her hands. "No calluses. What kind of animals allow farmhands to stay so soft?" She only smiled enigmatically, sure of herself, or at least certain that there would be no leakage of information on that matter.

"Would you like to come see for yourself?" piped up Mikey eagerly.

David glanced at Liz, who pursed her lips. "I appreciate my son's desire to entertain you, Mr. Johnston, but I'm afraid that wouldn't be possible right now. With the death of my husband, I don't entertain guests."

Mikey objected, "What about all those men in suits that come all the time?"

Liz remained unperturbed. "Mikey, that is strictly business."

"Well, I'm thinking strictly business as well, Mrs. Foster. In fact, it's a practice for me to visit the homes of each of my players once a year. I'm interested in helping them as persons, and not just on the playing field." He made a mental note that he had better begin this "practice" right away…

"As I said before I'm grateful for your noble dedication to your players." She pointedly changed the subject. "You know, Mr. Johnston, you seem to me to be more suited for the city than a small town like this. How long have you been here?"

He responded candidly: "Three years. I was in Houston before that as the CEO of Head Hunters International. I had worked my way up the ladder pretty quickly. So had my wife in her own firm."

"And what happened?" she asked with interest, visibly relieved to be asking questions and not vice versa.

His voice was toneless. "Janice liked to drive fast. She was in a collision. Her own fault. Died instantly."

"I'm sorry," Liz responded compassionately.

"Dad died in a car accident, too." offered Mikey solemnly. "Or at least it seems that's what happened. But my father never sped…"

Liz put her arm around Mikey and hugged him.

"She was pregnant with our first child. I wanted that little son so bad! Made me rethink everything. What does success in life really mean anyway? I came here to figure out things for awhile, and time keeps passing."

Liz was listening attentively. "Have you found any answers?"

He looked away, lost in thought, his chin resting on his hands. "I know I would do things differently if I had it to do it over again. Mikey: it's essential that you get your priorities straight in life before you marry and when you choose who you're going to marry."

Mikey leaned into his mother and hugged her back. "Your words are unnecessary, Coach David. I've determined that already. I'm going to marry someone just like Mom!"

Liz prodded him to go tell the players to make their last orders since she was about to pay the bill. She herself began sliding out of the booth, but David halted her with a gesture of his hands.

"Mrs. Foster, do you mind my asking if I could be released from my promise to you for the next soccer season? The captain of the team graduates this year, and it turns out that Jimmie would be the best fit for that role. He really is outstanding, although he avoids the limelight…"

Liz broke in on him energetically, "I'm sorry, Coach Johnston, but the conditions for Jimmie need to remain in force. I would much prefer that he didn't play at all. Only my confidence in your being a man of your word gives me peace."

David's earlier annoyance returned. "Don't you think you need to cut your son a little more slack, Mrs. Foster? He's a big boy now. Just today I found out why he bikes everywhere. Isn't it a little exaggerated to keep him from getting his driver's license? By any chance, does his father happen to know his whereabouts?"

She looked right through him, as she fired back in icy tones, "I would thank you to keep out of our personal family matters! Good day!"

With that she paid and left, Mikey trailing behind. Coach David remained rather pensive as he watched her car pulling away. When he had entered the restaurant, it hadn't crossed his mind that he might find this woman attractive, and yet here he was with mixed feelings for her. There was something charming about her. She was poised, full of spirit, and yet somehow fragile too. But was she completely balanced? Was she honest? He had his doubts, but how could he possibly find out? It certainly wouldn't be easy to get near her… but perhaps there might be a dinner down the road.

At the back of the room, he pulled up a chair to join the players. After finishing the end-of-the-year pep talk that had been interrupted by Liz, he made some announcements. There were going to be two new captains for the new season. Carlos would be the titular captain, meaning he was the official captain in the eyes of the referees, parents, and fans. But the real, undercover captain was to be Jimmie. The players cheered, Carlos included, and whacked Jimmie on the back. He was the obvious choice. As Carlos was a close friend of Jimmie, he understood better than anyone else why Coach had done this: he knew there was no other way they could convince Jimmie to be publicly what he already was anyway, the heart of the team. Jimmie said nothing. He just smiled.

"My other announcement is that I have a new policy. From now on I'm going to pay a home visit to each of your families every year." The boys looked around at each other, taken aback.

"Coach, you've never set a foot in my home before!" observed Roberto. "Why the interest now?"

"Roberto, it's about time. It will help me coach you better."

When he had gone, Jimmie made another surprise announcement to the team. "We're going to have a special soccer practice this Saturday for next year's team, including the new players."

They all shouted at him at once.

"The new position has gone to your head!"

"That's too early for next year!"

"Forget it."

He calmly insisted. "You'll understand when you come. I have a surprise for you. Just don't tell anybody." They rolled their eyes and continued protesting, but they all knew they would end up going.

ELEVEN

Two days later, Coach David stayed put when the last bell of the day rang. Now that the soccer season had ended, at least for his team, he had no need to head out to the field. Mikey tapped respectfully at the door. Coach smiled and warmly beckoned the boy in. He liked the kid.

"What brings you to the high school, Mikey?"

"Sir, I have a formal proposition to make to you."

David raised his eyebrows and responded playfully, "Oh, some kind of business proposition?" He pointed to the chair in front of his desk but Mikey remained standing.

"I heard that you have the ability to concoct root-beer floats within these four walls," Mikey began. "It's hard to talk business on an empty stomach."

Coach David complied by opening his little fridge and pulling a vanilla ice-cream cup out of its freezer. Next, he snapped open a can of root beer, poured it into a tall cup, added the ice-cream, stuck in a twisty straw, and handed it over. Mikey received it eagerly and sipped it down with gusto while David patiently watched him. When he was done, Mikey thanked him profusely, then asked point-blank whether Coach ever offered seconds. The whole procedure was repeated.

At last, satisfied, Mikey unfolded his plan. "Earlier this year, my mother forbade me to read any more from an excellent text on developmental psychology until I grow in maturity. I neglected at the time to inform her that I had already completed a thorough study of the aforesaid material. Regrettably, she was correct in her assertion that I was not prepared to confront what I encountered there."

So far, Coach David could not determine where this was going. He mustered up a question to help Mikey get to the point of the matter. "What did you find there that bothers you?"

"First of all, I was delighted at the uncannily precise description of adolescent girls, which fits my sister to a 't.' This has therefore heightened my preoccupation with what it claims about boys. The author underlines the importance of a father figure for young, adolescent boys to be able to mature and develop in an optimum fashion."

Mikey peered at Coach seriously and pronounced solemnly: "Coach David, in less than two years I will be one of those adolescent boys. Most likely, Jimmie will be gone by then. I might therefore be deprived of any close male father figure for the most trying period of my life! And I do not think my intellectual precocity will make any difference."

David carefully controlled his facial features so that he wouldn't smile. He was finding Mikey's melodramatic concern very amusing. "That would certainly be a hardship, Mikey."

"I'm glad you concur with me, sir. That's where my proposition comes in. I wouldn't have to be deprived of a father figure if my mother remarried…"

David chuckled, but inside he thought how much he would like being this young boy's dad. His feelings for Liz were more ambivalent. The attraction was there, but he didn't know what to make of the woman. Of course, he wasn't about to share his feelings with her son.

"I would say most kids are *against* their parents remarrying!"

Mikey remained unruffled. "Perhaps that's because they don't experience having a say in the selection of the new spouse. However, you would be the perfect choice for a father, next of course to my real dad!"

David was inwardly moved at this mark of appreciation. He tried to respond in the same reasonable tone. "You've got it all worked out, Mikey! I'm flattered that you would like me as a second father. To tell you the truth, I sincerely would love to have you as my son. But that's not enough of a reason to marry your mother."

"Certainly, sir, but in addition my mother is well worth marrying for her own sake! She's the best mother in the world, and she was a wonderful, loving, supportive, kind wife to my father!" Mikey was in such earnest that David kept his mirth in check.

"Mikey, to be honest, speaking man-to-man…" Mikey leaned forward expectantly. "A solid relationship of love between a man and a woman needs to develop over time. Now it's very possible that a guy could find your mother attractive. But that's only the first step in starting a relationship. From there, it's fundamental for the two interested parties to be able to spend time getting to know each other." He paused and leaned back in his chair thoughtfully. "However, that's practically impossible when it comes to your mother…"

"I've considered that daunting feature already, sir. In sizing up the matter, I concur that my mother systematically avoids propitious occasions for establishing a friendship with the opposite gender that could bloom into a long-lasting relationship of love…"

"So there you go, Mikey. Sorry there's nothing we can do about it." David was convinced the matter was closed and indicated so by pushing his chair back as if he were going to stand up. However, Mikey, with all the dignity and assurance of an adult, politely and calmly motioned for him to wait.

"But sir, my whole purpose in coming to you today is to offer to help 'arrange' just such occasions. All we have to do is capitalize on the statistically verifiable odds of people haphazardly running into each other in a small town. You would be free to stop anytime, of course. I'm convinced, however, that the more you get to know my mother, the more you'll want to spend time with her. In the meantime, you're also welcome to send root-beer floats my way as a token of your appreciation for the inside tips."

David didn't respond right away. He sat considering the proposal. To his own surprise, he found himself accepting a trial run on the following Saturday. Of course, Mikey could hardly contain his excitement.

"Sir, in the same vein, I also recommend that you agree to be the coach of my volleyball team. This would provide ample opportunities for friendly interchanges with my mother, since she likes to stay after games and practice with me."

"That'll be the day, Mikey! I'm head coach here… and coaching little tykes doesn't even appear on my list of priorities! Besides, your class has a notorious reputation for no-win seasons."

"I shall not reduce myself to groveling, but please do it as a personal act of mercy for me! Mom makes me sign up for two team sports a year, and my water boy duty for your soccer team unfortunately only counts for one. Of the remaining sports, volleyball is the least torturous for me: no body contact and less endurance training. Nevertheless, the scorn and humiliation I must endure for my poor athletic skills is agonizing. You would make the difference for me if you were the coach!"

David was careful not to offer Mikey any hope. He spent enough time at school for other "necessary" sports. When Mikey had gone, David wondered to himself what had moved him to agree to the scheme. *Since when does an adult man connive with a ten-year-old boy to win a woman's heart?* he chided himself. But Mikey was no ordinary kid, and his mother was no ordinary woman. It was worth trying at least once.

TWELVE

It was the first time all three could ride into town together. A "family biking trip," they told their mother. Jackie had sometimes tagged along, but until today Mikey hadn't been permitted to go that far, even with Jimmie. In any case, he was only going one way, since he was to meet up with his mother at the grocery store later on. If Liz had realized what they were up to, though, she never would have permitted any of them to leave the house that morning. As it was, she was blissfully unaware as she saw them out the door.

Jimmie was nervous and excited about launching the big plan that could potentially make a huge and lasting impact on the lives of his teammates. For her part, Jackie was also thrilled at the chance of hanging out with her big brother and the other boys on the team. On any other occasion, Mikey would have been ecstatic at getting to help his brother and being included in on the secret, but today of all days he was preoccupied with the grocery store "event." So much was at stake. He had already reminded Jimmie several times that he simply had to leave on time, even if the practice wasn't over yet. Jimmie was too lost in his own plans to ask what the urgency was, but Mikey wouldn't have told him anyway.

If they'd been asked, each of the players would have given the same reason for showing up for this mysterious meeting: they owed a lot to Jimmie. When any of them had needed help he had been there for them. So if Jimmie wanted them out of bed early on a Saturday morning just after the season had ended, they were there. But that didn't mean they wouldn't give him a hard time about it.

"Here's the Nazi commandant, ready to start torturing us." Roberto was always the first one to mouth off.

"Start! It's torture enough just to be here," Jeff growled.

"Shut up! Or at least keep your voices low. I've got a hangover."

"Jimmie, this better be good, or we're gonna hang you over!"

Jimmie took it in stride. "I assure you all, it's going to be well worth your while."

Once the motley group had fully assembled, Jimmie sat them down to watch a live presentation of his "vector theory." With Louie, their goalkeeper, in place, Jimmie whispered some instructions to his brother and sister, who moved to the goal line, then carefully measured their steps out from the line to their places. There they awaited Jimmie's corner kick. As Jimmie ran towards the ball, he counted out loud rhythmically: "1-2-3-4..." and on "5" he lofted the ball into the air.

Up to this point, none of the players seemed impressed. They barely paid attention. Jeff was laying on the ground, head covered. Mikey and Jackie continued the count, and on "8" Mikey moved forward effortlessly. Lo and behold, he was exactly on time to tip the ball into the goal. Roberto derisively suggested to Louie that he open his eyes.

Jeff lifted his head up. "What did I miss?" Raymond shoved it back down again.

Ignoring Roberto, Louie shouted to Jimmie, "That was nothing but a fluke. Just try that again!"

He obliged right away, counting out loud once more as he ran. This time, Jackie got the goal by bumping her knee against the ball on the count of "9." Josh and Jeff joined Roberto in mocking Louie for letting a little girl beat him.

Jackie protested, though it was obvious she was enjoying being in the limelight, "Hey! Who are you calling a little girl?"

Louie ignored her, insisting once more that they go again. Now they had his full attention and all his concentration. Mikey and Jackie took up different positions, counting once more from the goal line to find their new place. On "8," Jackie popped the ball past Louie with a gentle kick. The players hollered with delight, mercilessly ribbing Louie as the demonstration continued; time after time, brother and sister regularly shot the ball past him. He was able to stop the ball sometimes, but the success of the two younger siblings was remarkable, particularly because their moves were so effortless: each one was completely calculated in advance.

After a while, the two new freshmen recruits, Miguel and Juan, got up to help defend the goal. But even then, the duo all too often succeeded in knocking the ball through. When everyone was convinced that there was something promising here, Jimmie huddled the team together and launched his sales pitch.

"I asked Mikey and Jackie to help me out today so you could plainly see that my vector theory is not about brawn or talent." Jackie made a face at him, while Mikey grinned from ear to ear. "Not physical strength, but the laws of physics and geometry: you know, hyperbolas, etc."

Blank looks all around. So he reached into his pocket and unfolded a 3-D computerized color print marking the path of a soccer ball, with players standing along its path.

He traced his finger along its course as he continued. "I've succeeded in determining the curve and time interval for the trajectory of the ball from my 'base kick.' By that, I mean a kick I've been able to perfect so that the ball goes pretty much the same way each time. Using simple mathematical formulas, I then plotted out the time and place where the ball will pass by. From there I made my calculations: first, where Jackie and Mikey needed to place themselves; second, exactly when they needed to move; and third, what body part and how fast. You saw the results! But that's just a sample of what the vector theory can do. Just picture it now on the grand scale!"

"You mean to say, we can figure out the exact time we need to move our foot or knee or head to hit the ball into the goal? Forget it, man. I'm failing Algebra."

"The game would be over before I do a single calculation."

"I'm not only saying it, Raymond, you just witnessed it for yourselves. Have you seen how Mikey ordinarily plays soccer?" All eyes turned to Mikey. He beamed once more and shrugged his shoulders. In another situation he might have been embarrassed at being singled out as a klutz; but in this moment, here on the team where his brother was captain and he was the official water boy, he was proud that he got to help show off Jimmie's brilliant theory. Louie gave the young boy a high five, and Carlos ruffled his hair affectionately.

"Each one of us can perfect his own base kick and plot out its trajectory. With that, we won't have to limit ourselves to corner kicks. We'll be able to move the ball all over the field based on the vector theory."

He sounded convincing, even if most of the players didn't quite get how it could be done. They were hanging on his words by now. Jimmie was only warming up. "But there's more to the vector theory than just hitting the ball. It applies to our lives as well. We're young. The possibilities of what each of us could accomplish are incredible… but some of us here haven't been doing too much projecting of our lives up until now. How many of you have thought about going on to university?"

No immediate answer. Carlos responded first. "It's too expensive Jimmie. I'm just gonna help my dad with his business when I graduate."

Jimmie objected, "You could do better than cutting lawns the rest of your life, if you want to."

Roberto cut in. "My grades are too low to go anywhere worth going."

Jeff added cheerfully, "Too much work for a lousy piece of paper."

Jimmie's voice grew intense and passionate. "You haven't been projecting yourselves outside of this little town until now. But this vector theory makes topnotch universities a realistic goal for all of you. If my little brother and sister can learn it, so can you. Nobody has anything to lose. In fact, you're losers if you opt to do nothing with your lives. What a waste when you could go so far!" They mulled over that silently, none of them liking the term loser.

"What do we have to do?" asked Josh noncommittally.

Jimmie brightened. "You need to take Physics, Algebra II, and Geometry next year."

A volley of protests followed.

"I failed that class twice."

"Mr. West kicked me out. He says I'm unteachable."

"No way! Those are the toughest classes. You only need Algebra I to graduate."

Jimmie's voice somehow prevailed above everyone else's: "I'll get you through with flying colors!"

"How, by getting us the final exams in advance?" Everyone laughed at this.

"No! I'll tutor you, and you'll be shocked at how easy it is to learn since you'll already be applying the knowledge on the soccer field. It'll be a cinch, as long as you're committed to attending my sessions. Imagine the consternation on Mr. West's face when you not only pass, but you ace his silly exams!"

The prospect amused them, and Jimmie's enthusiasm and assurance were catchy. However, Jimmie was still only warming up. He had something more to demand of them if they truly wanted to learn the vector theory.

"Wait. There's something more to the vector theory, which is the biggest challenge of all. Aren't you sick of the fact that we call ourselves Christians but don't act that way?" They looked at each other, shrugging their shoulders and laughing. None of them seemed too concerned.

Roberto replied with a smile, "No."

"Aw, c'mon Jimmie. We're not monks or anything," added Jorge.

"Hey, what y'all saying? I go to church every Sunday!"

"Right, Nick!" Jeff gave him a playful punch on the shoulder. "I'm not sure Jimmie would count standing outside church talking to the girls as going to Mass."

"Or what you do the night before," quipped Raymond.

Nick grabbed for Raymond's head, putting him into a headlock while protesting, "You know what I do the night before only 'cause you're usually right there with me. And everyone knows you're just jealous because you can't hold as many beers as I can."

"Depends on what you mean by hold…" sputtered Raymond, as he fought to get out of the headlock. Josh and Jeff jeered at Nick's boast as Jimmie took up his cause again in a more earnest tone.

"No big deal if one of us cusses, gets drunk, messes around with his girlfriend, avoids church, and does nothing to help out anyone else. You know, the poor and needy… This is a Catholic school, but you'd never guess it by the way we act. Doesn't it bother you that we're just a bunch of hypocrites?"

"Hey! Watch who you're calling names!" protested Roberto. The others looked back mutely. The urgency of his voice and the word "hypocrites" caught their attention.

"We need to help each other out to be real Christians! We're supposed to be aiming at heaven with each one of our acts. And not just heaven for ourselves—we're supposed to be bringing others along with us! That's the rest of the vector theory." Jimmie pulled out another colored computer printout showing the trajectory of an arrow. "You see how the archer, if he wants to hit a bull's eye, needs to aim much higher into the air? Well, we need to aim higher than heaven if we want to get there with a whole busload each."

Louie cut in, "But Jimmie! Who says I need to bring so many with me? I was just planning on a pass/fail to get in there myself. More fun that way!" This remark was met with guffaws.

Jorge added, "Hey, my mom does enough praying to get my family and our whole team into heaven!"

There was fire in Jimmie's eyes as he shot back: "If you live only for yourself in this life, you'll never find real happiness now or in the next life. The two go together. And that's just what I meant by saying we're all a bunch of hypocrites. True Christians care about others and want them to get to heaven too. There are so many people in our town who are in real need and really suffering, and we're not doing anything to help them! We're not doing anything to make ourselves better either."

Since this was Juan's first practice with the team, and he was also the youngest, he had said nothing up to this point. But now he couldn't contain himself any longer.

"I'll do something for others, Jimmie, but what? Maybe I could help old people with their grocery shopping." Raymond rolled his eyes.

Jimmie eyed the whole team gravely. "It's all or none of us, Juan. Either everyone agrees to employ the entire vector theory, or none of us do it. It was designed for the whole team."

"We're in, Jimmie," stated Carlos firmly. "What do we have to do?"

"Hey, man, speak for yourself! I want to hear the entire plan first. I ain't gonna be no monk!" protested Roberto.

Jimmie pulled out thirteen small cards and handed them out, keeping one for himself. "Besides taking the classes I've already mentioned, we also have to commit to working together as a team to become real Christians. Each week at the beginning of practice everyone has to show they've gained fifty points during the last week.

"Practice?" asked Louie.

"Each week? asked Josh.

"Points?" added Jeff.

"Points for what?" insisted Nick.

"Read the card and see for yourselves," answered Jimmie evenly. Roberto announced that he would read the card out loud, and then did so in a fake British accent:

Attend Mass/service on Sunday: 30 points

Have fun but stay sober at a party: 20 points

Help out at the weekly mission: 20 points

No cussing all day: 5 points

Help a teammate with any of the above: 20 points

"I ain't doin' this!" He contemptuously flipped the card to the ground.

Carlos scooped it up, challenging him energetically, "Roberto, what have we got to lose? You got a better plan to make it out of this town, or do you want to keep helping your dad when you grow up?" Their fathers worked together doing odd jobs around the town, mowing lawns, helping on the sheep farms during the busy season, etc. Carlos turned to them all: "Jimmie's right! Who here had any plans for going on to college besides Jimmie?" No response.

"We'll keep on having soccer practice on Saturday mornings through the summer so we can learn the vector theory," he said, ignoring the grumbles. "The trick is for nobody special to shine. You'll all be outstanding, except for me. I'm just the mastermind..."

Louie broke in, "Now I get it. You were already teaching this stuff to Jorge, Andre, and Carlos, weren't you? That's why they got so good all of a sudden!" They nodded and looked expectantly for Jimmie to go on. They were willing to go along with Jimmie's plan, but were waiting for the more outspoken guys to get onboard first.

"Part of our pact is that nobody can know who's behind the theory. In fact, I'd rather we don't even mention that we have a special trick. It's best for us to keep low-key at the beginning of the season, but we'll win enough games to make it to the finals, and then we'll go on to win the state championship. From there, the scouts will see you and you're set. Those who don't get offered scholarships will get them from their grades, or as merit scholars!" Nobody scoffed now. Jimmie had convinced them it was possible, even though it sounded incredible. "So, is everybody in?"

Carlos, Jorge, Andre, and Juan were the first to commit. Miguel was the next to comply. Roberto showed his acceptance by asking for his card back from Carlos.

"But I'm gonna do the easy stuff. I'm gonna get twenty points for keeping Nick from getting drunk!"

That was enough to egg Nick into assenting. "I'm only joining so that I get chance to keep Roberto out of trouble."

As his sign of agreement to the plan, Ross told Jeff, "Every time one of us cusses, the other one gets to slug him in the arm."

Jeff agreed and slugged him right away, saying that was his advance pay. Jackie beamed with pleasure that they all agreed to her brother's plan. Mikey would have too, but he had already quietly left to make sure he got to the grocery store early.

THIRTEEN

Mikey reached the grocery store fifteen minutes before his mom was due to arrive. He made sure that she hadn't gotten there early, and then he popped into the store and hurried to the end of aisle nine. He was relieved to see that the Jello display was still there, exactly as it had been the week before. Next, he pulled out his cell phone and double-checked the two text messages he had prepared. It would only take an instant to send them. With everything set, he went outside to await his mother.

Liz arrived at the store right on time. She and her husband had always done the shopping and then gone out for lunch together afterwards, just the two of them. It had been their weekly date, which they had both enjoyed. Their kids knew this and were only too glad to respect it. Ever since the death of her husband, Mikey had nobly offered to be her grocery companion and always did his best to be cheerful and helpful. Liz found this particularly comforting and was grateful for his childlike goodness of heart.

On this particular occasion, she waved a greeting as she approached Mikey, asking if he had been waiting long. He shook his head and smiled. They went in together and began their usual routine. Mikey tried to act as normal as possible, though inside he was beside himself with nervousness. Whenever Liz looked away, he checked his watch. They started with the fruits and vegetables section and then walked methodically up and down each aisle, starting with aisle one. Mikey usually liked to time how long they spent in each aisle, and today this information served him well. At the end of aisle seven, he surreptitiously sent off his first text message to give the five-minute warning. Aisle nine was the easiest to calculate because it was the cookies aisle, and Liz rarely even looked at the items, let alone bought anything. To Mikey's dismay, she normally would briskly lead the way without stopping. Counting on her typically depreciative attitude towards what she called "junk food," he secretly sent the second text message at the beginning of the aisle. When Liz hesitated halfway down, remembering that Jackie's birthday was coming up soon, Mikey sprang into action. Every second mattered.

"Oh, c'mon, Mom. Why give in now to temptation? You always bake something for us on our birthdays… remember? That's much better for us than this junk food!" Liz was surprised at his change of tune. Mikey gently took the cart from her and picked up the pace just a little, trying to make up for lost time. They were seconds behind the carefully calculated time allotment. As they neared the end of the aisle, Mikey turned back to say something to his mother while he continued walking forward quickly.

"Mom, is it too late to change my mind? Maybe we could buy some cookies after all…"

"Watch out!" was all Liz was able to get out as he ran into both the Jello display and the front of a shopping cart that was just coming around the corner. Jello boxes went flying everywhere, including at David's head and into his cart. Liz gasped in dismay. Of all people to run into like that! Acutely embarrassed, she apologized profusely and scrambled to pick up the Jello boxes.

"Coach Johnston, I'm so sorry! My son can be careless at times."

Mikey chimed in woefully, "The onus of apologizing falls fully upon me, Coach! Once more, I must lament my ineptitude!" He reached dolefully for the Jello boxes on the floor. Inwardly, however, he was delighted to see how many he had succeeded in knocking down and how far they had scattered! This was his personal application of his brother's vector theory.

David kindly assisted with the cleanup. He was in a good mood, teasing both Liz and Mike as he went.

"Do you often demolish grocery store displays, Mikey?"

"No, sir. Hopefully this is my first and last attempt at the matter."

"I really am sorry, Coach David. Mikey can be a bit clumsy at times!"

"Say no more! We'll have this fixed in no time."

With the last package back in place, David turned to Mikey and announced, "Mikey, we need to do something to make you feel better after this jarring experience!"

"Ha ha, Coach!" replied the apparently subdued Mikey. He was trying hard to appear mortified at his clumsiness.

"I do believe I owe you a root-beer float, don't I?" The boy visibly perked up.

"Well, as a matter of fact you do, though I didn't feel it proper to pursue my claim. It's good of you to remember that, sir!"

Liz frowned. She was trying to avoid this man, and yet she was hesitant to rebuff his thoughtful invitation especially after helping them to clean up the mess her son had made.

She made a weak attempt, "I try not to feed soda and such to my children. It's not good for them."

With a confident smile, David rejoined, "Would you keep me from being a man of my word? I owe this to Mikey!" Turning to Mikey, he continued: "Mikey, I formally invite you now for the float you have coming to you… and you can invite all the friends and family members you want."

Liz laughed in spite of herself. "Touché!" There was no way out of it.

Mikey couldn't believe that everything was going exactly as planned. "We're almost done, sir. We'll meet you at the Dreamery Creamery in fifteen minutes."

A short time later, the three of them sat at the counter on revolving stools, Mikey between the two adults. Liz just asked for water, so David ordered two root-beer floats and a coffee. The waitress set one float in front of Mikey and the other in front of the coach. He ignored it, drinking the coffee instead. Both adults watched Mikey as he guzzled down the first float. Then, without a word to David, he stuck his straw in the other one and pulled it towards himself.

Liz gasped in horror. "Mikey! How could you be so rude?"

David and Mikey smiled at each other. "Mikey knows full well that I never drink the stuff. I ordered both for him."

That cleared up, Mikey proceeded to work away at the second one with a deep air of satisfaction. His mother never would have allowed him to order two! He forced himself to drink this one much more slowly. No conversation had started. He needed to get them talking before his drink was finished, or his mother would be ready to leave in no time.

"Coach, were you married for very long?"

"Ten years. We married as soon as we graduated from college. Not too common nowadays."

"Don't you like kids?"

David gave him a funny look. Liz was visibly mortified by her son's impertinence.

"Mikey! That's no kind of question to be asking Coach David!" Her discomfort amused David.

"Don't worry, Mrs. Foster. I don't mind Mikey's questions. In fact, I love kids. But Janice wanted to get her career straightened out first. We met through debate club in high school..."

"Oh really? Mom and Dad met in a club too! It was a genius club!" Liz poked her son, and he said no more.

David looked thoughtfully at the boy. "A genius couple? Wow. Well, Janice was pretty smart too: valedictorian for her class. And she had a lot of ambition to go far in life."

"How far did she have to go before she was ready to have kids?" piped up Mikey.

Liz poked her son again, making Mikey squirm.

He protested out loud, "Mom, Coach already said he doesn't mind my questions!"

David continued on as if there had been no interruption. "I wish there was a clear-cut answer to that. I don't think she knew. It can be a tough decision."

Mikey snorted. Evidently, he didn't think the decision was so hard. But he was distracted by the woeful level of his float. He was a little over halfway done, but he was at its tastiest point since just the right proportion of melted ice cream was now mixed with the soda. He longed to down the rest, but he held himself back for the sake of his plan.

"Sir, I too am concerned about confronting challenges: those of young adulthood! It seems that kids lose some of their wits during their teen years, and they stay lost in adulthood. For me, the best thing in life is a happy family which includes kids."

Mikey then excused himself, ostensibly to go to the bathroom, and remained there for a long time. When he finally came out, he slipped unnoticed into the empty booth by the bathroom door and pulled out his Game Boy.

Once Mikey left, David remarked with sincere admiration in his voice, "You've done a wonderful job with all three of your kids. They're all outstanding, and not just because they're smart."

"Thank you. I enjoyed listening to you talk to my son" Liz responded, favoring him with a genuine smile. His evident friendship with her son had disarmed her.

"I've been trying to figure out what's special about them, and now it's suddenly come to me after listening to Mikey. Your kids are pure—something not very common these days. Jimmie goes to the school dances, but he treats the girls respectfully. He's decent. Then there's Jackie. Sure, she's boy-crazy like the rest of the girls her age, but she wears modest clothes and keeps her dignity around them. As for Mikey: he's still a little angel!"

"In some ways! He knows how to get his sister going, and he's always up to something!"

"Yeah, yeah, but you know what I mean. They're special! What have you done to make them this way?" His appreciation for her children touched her. After all, they were her soft spot.

"Henry and I worked this out together long before Jimmie was old enough to be taught anything. We decided that the best way to teach them how to love others the right way was for us to love God, love each other, love them, and love others. We've also been extremely vigilant over what they read and see... they don't watch a lot of television or go on the Internet very much. We keep them busy learning and doing good things. That's pretty much it."

"Wow! And is that how you were raised?"

"Not at all! I was an only child of agnostic parents, though my mother's parents were devout Catholics. I was put into a magnet school when I was young, and no expenses were spared for me to develop all my talents and skills. But I wasn't taught any values. I owe my outlook to Pope John Paul II. My Catholic grandmother gave me a collection of the audiences he had delivered on the theology of the body at the beginning of his pontificate. I read them during a lonely moment in my life, when I didn't have much to occupy my time. His teachings changed my whole outlook on life, love, and real happiness. I was blessed though, because Henry converted to the Catholic faith with me. We were so happy together!" Her smile was bittersweet.

"How long has it been?" David asked compassionately.

Her voice became soft and tremulous. "Almost a year, but it feels like only yesterday that he was at my side." Liz was chagrined to find tears suddenly flowing down her cheeks. David offered her his handkerchief, gazing compassionately at her. She wished that he wouldn't—it undid her all the more. Minutes sailed by as she remained weeping silently. Every once in a while she would glance at him in discomfort at her weakness, but he kept the same sympathetic, still gaze fixed on her. She found it comforting. When she was able to speak again, she apologized.

"I'm sorry. I haven't cried in a while. I wouldn't have mentioned his name if I had thought I would carry on like this!"

"Don't be so hard on yourself. It's good to grieve," came the understanding reply.

"Do you still miss Janice?" David recognized her question as a ploy to take the attention off of herself. He complied, although he skirted her question.

"Our marriage wasn't the happiest. We were faithful to each other, but our lives kept growing more and more distant with each passing year. We were both so busy with our careers. But we didn't know what arguing was until she got pregnant. I know men can often pressure women into having abortions, but ours was the opposite situation. She still wasn't ready to have a child yet and so she was considering having an abortion. I couldn't believe it, since I had been longing for children from the start! To have your wife seriously thinking about taking the life of your own child: I don't think hell can get much worse than that."

To her relief, Liz's tears dried up as he spoke, but now it was her turn to show compassion and his turn to look away. "I'm sorry."

He changed the topic. "Your kids seem to have their heads on straight about what's important in life. Hopefully they'll stay that way!"

"That's my hope and prayer!" she replied.

"So far, so good. You've done extremely well, especially considering that you must have been a mother at such a young age. You're so young to have a sixteen-year-old son!" As soon as the words were out of his mouth he knew he had said the wrong thing. What had begun as a compliment ended on the topic that she was so sensitive about: Jimmie and his origins. Inside he kicked himself, while she sat up straight, her face once more taking on that cool, impenetrable look.

"I prefer not to talk about that, Coach Johnston." Turning in the direction of the bathroom door where her son had disappeared, she spied him sitting in the corner. His heart sank as she called out, "Mikey, we need to go now."

She said to David perfunctorily, "Thank you for being so gallant!" With that she nodded and was out the door. Mikey dashed back to the float, gulped it down, looked searchingly at David for an instant, winked victoriously, and was gone too.

Once inside his own car, David pulled out his cell phone.

"Hey Davie-boy! It's been a long time!"

"How ya doing, Buzz?"

"The same, the same. You know. So what's up?"

"Look. You remember that you owe me a big one, right?"

"C'mon Davie, you don't think I'd forget, do you?"

"I need you to run a top-of-the-line security check on Liz Foster, her son Jimmie Pérez, and her other children, Michael and Jacqueline Foster. She was married to Henry Foster who died about a year ago in a questionable car accident, at least according to her ten-year-old son. I need whatever you can come up with, especially who Jimmie's father is."

Buzz hesitated. "Hmm. Yup, that's a big favor. You know that when we run those kinds of checks the Feds sometimes want to know why."

"If you get any flak, just give them my name and tell them to come after me. Can't you tell them I'm a big client interested in making a private deal with Mrs. Foster? I am a big client, aren't I?"

"Alright. You're on! Get back to you as soon as I've got the info."

"Thanks, bud!" David remained sitting behind the wheel, thinking about Liz. She provoked such a mixture of feelings within him. Such a lady. So feminine. So beautiful. Seemingly strong, yet somehow alluring in her poignant solitude. And aloof. Mysterious, if not suspicious. He couldn't decide what to think about her. But he did know that he wanted another chance to spend more time with her. Was he going to have to rely on Mikey again?

FOURTEEN

Buzz called with the information a few mornings later.

"Here you go, Davie boy. You've hit on quite the interesting family! First of all, Elizabeth Smyth and Henry Foster met in a Canadian genius club of all places. They're both from the upper echelon of society: his dad was a multimillionaire."

"They don't appear to be wealthy."

"It's all a façade then, because they're rolling in the stuff. They were also both involved in a highly classified scientific project for the Canadian government in 1989."

"What kind of project?"

"You're asking too much. The key word is 'classified.' The funny thing is that each of them bailed out of the program early and moved to the States, where they got married the following year. Wonder how the Canucks liked that."

"You don't have any records of a previous marriage or love interest of Elizabeth?"

"Look, this is a high-level security check, not a tabloid! Anyway, she married the guy when she was barely eighteen. Within months of their marriage, they legally adopted six-year-old Santiago Pérez from some Mexican immigrants, Manuel and Maria Paz Pérez, in the town of Fort Lancaster, Texas."

"What? Adopted? Are you sure she herself wasn't married to Mr. Pérez? Just one boy? If he was six at the time, then he must be twenty-two right now. What about Jimmie Pérez? He's sixteen years old."

"Hold on, hold on! Like I said, Elizabeth's only been married once. And there's only one record of a single adoption. Nothing about a 'Jimmie.' And nothin' more about the immigrant couple. Elizabeth gave birth to Jacqueline in Florida, '92, and Michael in South Carolina, '95." He paused. David heard a slight rustling of papers.

"Anything else? Give me whatever you've got on them. Do you know anything about their education? I'd like to know why Jimmie is being homeschooled, while the other two aren't."

"Let's see here. Santiago graduated from an online Canadian public school called Lord Worchester in 2001 and from Michigan State University through their online program in 2005. He's currently studying for a Masters in Biochemistry through Princeton... again online. Meanwhile, his younger brother and sister are registered in the private online Canadian genius school, Prince of Wales. Jacqueline is about to graduate from there and Mikey is in his junior year." David whistled appreciatively.

"You mean to tell me that the youngest two kids are geniuses?"

"I guess it makes sense that if both of their parents are geniuses those two would be as well... I'll settle for someone of normal intelligence any day!" David was too focused on Jimmie to think about anything else in that moment.

He insisted: "You sure you have nothing at all on a 'Jimmie'? I didn't even know there was an older brother, Santiago. They never talk about him."

"Nope. That's all I could dig up on 'em."

"Can you tell me anything about their house?"

"Sorry. Don't even have an address for any of them, not even a post office box. It must be registered under a different owner's name."

"How can they have no address? Don't they have to declare it somewhere?"

"Like I said: they've got the dough. So a private management firm, Infinite Horizons Group, takes care of all their financial matters and other affairs, including registering for school... which is online anyway. So their personal data isn't ever disclosed."

"But Mikey and Jackie are registered here at St. Patrick School."

"Not according to our data..." David felt lost. His mind went back to Jimmie.

"I thought Liz was Jimmie's mother. Doesn't Jimmie think that too?" He was thinking out loud rather than asking a question. "But she and her husband adopted his older brother... How could there be no information at all on him? Has she been married more than once?"

"We're starting to get redundant here. I already answered that one. Negative." Buzz was starting to get impatient. "The Fosters stayed married until he kicked the bucket. Seems his death is still under investigation. Rolled off a mountainside and the car burst into flames. Burned to a crisp. If you want my opinion, I would avoid any business deals with this family. Sounds Mafioso to me. Well, anyway, consider yourself paid back. Whaddya bet the Feds really do get on my case for this one?"

"Thanks, Buzz. And like I said before: send them to me. I'm the customer who requested the security check. So your back's covered."

"Yeah, yeah. Keep in touch, Davie-boy!"

David's head reeled over what he'd just heard. What about Jimmie? Why did they officially adopt his brother and not him, although he had his brother's last name? Buzz hadn't solved anything for him—he had only confused him all the more. Where could he turn to get answers? At least he could find out whether Mikey and Jackie were registered at the school. Even there, though, he needed to be discreet. He didn't want to stir up any trouble for Liz, especially when she was so concerned to stay under the radar.

He made sure to enter the main office late in the afternoon when nobody would be around. That way, Mrs. Evelyn Rorke, the school secretary, would be sure to ramble on freely about any topic he happened to broach. She had held that position now for twenty-two years and knew everyone and everything that was going on. David normally avoided being alone with her since she was a notorious matchmaker and constantly bombarded him with offers to set him up with someone.

Mrs. Rorke always wore old-fashioned schoolmarm-type dresses over her well-endowed figure. She kept her gray hair back in a bun. Bifocal glasses hung around her neck and were removed as soon as she was finished with them. She made it her business to keep people well informed about everybody else's business.

"Why, Coach David, what gives me the pleasure of having you in my office? Funny thing, we were just talking about you earlier—that is, two of the most attractive single teachers and me. They were both saying that—"

He cut her off politely but firmly.

"Good afternoon, Evelyn. I'm just here to do my good deed for the year. You can stop making all of those desperate or threatening phone calls: put me down to coach the sixth grade boys' volleyball team in the fall."

"Don't tell me! Is this the same man that said he would coach that particular group of boys over his dead body? Have they suddenly become more athletic?"

"That was three years ago. Now that I've got a better grasp of the situation, I'm not going to fight a losing battle, or rather I'm determined to demonstrate that this team can do okay. Once I get them in shape, the parents will be begging me to take over the coaching!"

"How proactive can you get!" She smiled slyly. "In fact, that's one of the things Sharon told me she admires most about you. Now that's one woman who's not interested in money, but in a good man!"

David ignored her words.

"Oh, there's one more thing. Have you got the sports eligibility list handy? I want to make sure my athletes are keeping up their grades."

"There you are, being proactive again! These kinds of qualities are ingrained in a person. Here you go. Now, both Sharon and Ronna also have some outstanding qualities…" She began enumerating them, but David tuned her out as he perused the list for the Foster kids' names. After a minute, he interrupted her:

"The Foster kids didn't make the list? Did they get left out because they're new, or are they poor students?"

"The Foster kids? There are two kids you don't ever have to worry about for eligibility." Her eyes narrowed in disapproval. "Boss' orders are for them to be kept off of any list in the school."

"Now, that's odd!" he said as nonchalantly as possible—just enough to prompt her to offer an explanation.

"I'll say!" Evelyn pointedly looked around to make sure no one else was around. He didn't seem to pick up on her cue, however, since he turned his back on her and began photocopying as if he thought their conversation was over. Never would he be so far ahead of schedule in photocopying if he got through the large stack of papers he had brought in.

Evelyn wasn't daunted by his apparent lack of interest. She lowered her voice, rushing on in a more confidential tone: "But the odd one is their mother! She came in here during the summer all draped out in black from head to toe. I thought to myself: 'She's a fine beauty, but cold as ice!' I wouldn't trust her as far as I could throw a stone."

David tried not to manifest his rapt attention by keeping his gaze on the papers shooting out of the printer, but Evelyn needed no encouragement.

"So I'm sitting with her in the principal's office for the new parent interview, like I always do, and she mentions that she is looking to make a substantial financial donation to a Catholic institution, and why not here if her children turned out to be happy? I say to myself: 'She's barking up the wrong tree. She doesn't know how fair Mr. Jackson is, and that if she's looking to get some kind of fancy treatment because she waves her checkbook around, she's going to be disappointed!' Sure enough, Mr. Jackson doesn't bite. I know the man. I've worked for him these past ten years. Of course, I go further back here than he does.... Then comes the punch line: she says that of course she expects that her children will receive the same treatment as everyone else, but that there's just one matter in which she needs his help. 'Here it comes!' I tell myself. He invites her to state her concern frankly, but she replies that it's a most delicate matter and glances in my direction significantly. Of all the nerve! I didn't expect Mr. Jackson to order me out, but that's just what he did! He stands up and walks me to the door and shuts it tight after me. Next thing I know, I hear sobs coming from his office. 'Nothin but alligator tears!' I say to myself. 'She's a fine actress if ever I saw one. But she's not going to take in Mr. Jackson.'"

David couldn't help smiling. The scene sounded all too familiar to him, and he had caved pretty quickly.

"Then I hear them speaking in low, hushed tones. The door opens, and there he is telling her: 'I'm sure your children will be very happy here. Rest assured that everything will work out fine.' Once she's gone, he turns to me with this order: 'Evelyn, neither of her children are to appear on any roster in the school. I will personally instruct her teachers to call their name in roll call like any other student, but not to record any details about them.' 'Why Mr. Jackson,' I protest, 'Is this legal? You've never been one to shirk the law to get a donation!' I shouldn't have been so forthright, I know, but I was astounded at how he gave into this woman!"

Once more David smiled to himself. At least he wasn't the only one to fall for her tactics. "'No need for worries there, Evelyn, everything is perfectly in order, but it's to help her with a private family matter. I've got her personal information in my cabinet that proves we're perfectly in line with the law. Incidentally, I'm also going to instruct their teachers and appropriate staff members that they're not to speak at all amongst themselves or with others about the Foster case.' Of all things! We're not supposed to talk about them!"

David stopped his photocopying to turn and raise his eyebrows at her. She had the grace to look somewhat abashed, but quickly recovered herself. "Of course I can mention this to you, Coach David, because somehow you got overlooked. I'm just saving you from getting a serious warning from the higher up!"

"It's a good thing I know now, Evelyn, so I can be sure not to talk about them." He carefully kept any irony out of his voice as he continued. "Wow, look at the time! I better fly! Have a good afternoon." He escaped before she could make any more offers to set him up with Sharon or Ronna.

As he headed for his car, David considered what he had just gleaned from Evelyn. Only Mr. Jackson knew why the kids were kept off of the school records. That explained why Buzz's information didn't show they were here. For some reason, Liz wanted her kids in a regular school even though they were formally registered at their genius school at much higher grade levels. They were already fulfilling the law that way, so Mr. Jackson was free to let them stay off the lists. Here in this backwater town, her kids could lead apparently normal lives and escape detection. But he wondered what she was hiding. Buzz mentioned the Mafiosa. He had also corroborated her sob story (literally speaking) that she suspected her husband had been killed. Wasn't that enough to make her want to go undercover: for her own sake and that of her children? But who had wanted to kill her husband, and why? Perhaps they were guilty of something underhanded and this was revenge. Perhaps the Mafiosa idea might not be too far-fetched.

In any case, David was looking forward to his next personal encounter with Liz. Mikey had already arranged with him. A "cinch," he had said.

FIFTEEN

Mikey had primed his sister over breakfast Sunday morning when his mother was out of the room. Next, he uncharacteristically dillydallied at home in his room, making them a few minutes late for Sunday Mass, something that happened only rarely. He got out of the same side of the car as his sister so he could add another jab under his breath.

"It's really too bad you're only a girl. And they were so delicious." Then he rushed inside ahead of his mother and sister to ensure they took their regular Sunday morning place, three seats back from the front on the left hand side. He was afraid his mother would have motioned them elsewhere when she saw that David was right in front of them. Jimmie had arrived earlier by bike and was already sitting at the back of the church with his soccer buddies.

This was the first time David had shown up to the 8:30 morning Mass: usually it was too early for him. But Mikey had promised it would be worthwhile. He further fanned the flames he had been stoking all morning by leaning back out of his mother's view and catching his sister's eye. He made a motion between David and himself, grinned triumphantly, and gave the thumbs-up signal. Then he made a motion between his sister and David, grimaced, and gave the thumbs-down signal. Jackie glared back furiously.

During the sign of peace, David turned to greet the three Fosters. Mikey shook his hand heartily, and Liz did too, though with much more restraint.

But when David offered his hand to Jackie, she pulled both her hands away with disgust, whispering fiercely, "I don't shake hands with male chauvinists!" David raised his eyebrows in surprise and faced forward again without a protest, while Liz stared at Jackie in disbelief at her rudeness.

"Jackie! That's no way to treat Coach Johnston!" Behind his mother's back, Mikey gloated triumphantly at his sister. She tried to ignore her brother, but inside her heart the fire of resentment fanned higher.

"But Mom, it's true! He's not being fair!" Acutely embarrassed, Liz decided to wait to correct her daughter until Mass was over and they were out of David's earshot. David had other plans, however.

As soon as Mass was over, he turned around in his pew and addressed Jackie contritely. "Young lady, I wish to apologize for anything I have done to offend you. I just need a reminder about my particular misdeed since I've searched my conscience and come up dry."

Liz started to interject, "Please Mr. Johnston, there's no need for you to apologize at all! It's my daughter—"

Jackie cut in accusingly, "Mikey says you took him to the Dreamery Creamery for two root-beer floats in gratitude for his service as water boy, but that you would never do the same for me because you don't like girls. He says you look down on cheerleaders."

Mikey's eyes widened in surprise. He was the picture of innocence. Inside he was congratulating himself for his expertise in the field of psychology of young adolescent girls.

He replied with a wounded air, "Anyone who knows me well will certainly realize that you're misquoting me in a most deplorable fashion."

David spoke up before Liz or Jackie could respond.

"Rather than waste time determining if young Mikey has been misrepresenting me, I prefer to assure you that I have a high opinion of the opposite sex and in particular of you, Jackie."

She crossed her arms defensively, looking sullen and very much unconvinced, so David continued: "The best way of redeeming my tarnished image is to offer you the same treatment I gave your brother." He bowed slightly, making a flourish with his right hand while Jackie's face brightened with sudden hope. So did Mikey's heart, although he only permitted himself to smile moderately at David's suggestion.

Jackie exclaimed, "You mean…"

"Would you please do me the honor of accompanying me to the Dreamery Creamery for as many root-beer floats as you can stomach or as your mother will permit, whichever comes first."

Liz attempted to protest. "I'm afraid I cannot permit my daughter to importune you in this way, especially after having insulted you!"

In reply, David held up his hand in mock seriousness and fixed his eye on her gravely. "Madam, do you mean to condemn me to remain as an object of scorn in your daughter's eye? I'm not prepared to suffer the consequences throughout her high-school career. Shakespeare had it right when he said 'Hell hath no fury like a woman scorned,' or even a woman who thinks she is. I demand the right to prove my good will towards the feminine gender!"

Despite herself, Liz smiled. That was enough of a go-ahead for the expectant three.

Mikey grabbed David's arm, saying ""I'm riding in your car!"

Jackie quickly added, "Me too!" She was in no hurry to receive the talking to she deserved for her behavior, and she was well aware that no amount of root-beer floats would stave it off. At least it could wait until later.

The foursome sat in a booth. None of them noticed a short, balding stranger with soft-soled shoes slide into the next booth, with his back to Liz's.

David ordered four root-beer floats, a coffee, and a water. Jackie seized hers with glee and quaffed both of them down as fast as her brother normally did.

Mikey was still on his first when Jackie suggested, "Coach, if I have four root-beer floats while Mikey sticks to two this time, then I'll have caught up to him." Mikey calculated rapidly that it would likely take her a long time to drink two more.

"Might I suggest that you have five? Then you can be one ahead of me," Mikey answered.

Liz put her foot down. Her two children were familiar with the warning note in her voice. "You've had enough already! Two is more than sufficient. Any more than that would be gluttony."

Mikey told himself this was the moment. He tore himself away from his second float to challenge his sister: "Bet I could beat you at pinball!"

She took the dare readily. "Bet you can't!" Mikey had raided his piggy bank that morning and filled his pockets with quarters. He figured his sister would play with him as long as he paid and kept beating her. He was right.

When they were left alone, Liz tried to apologize for her daughter's bad behavior.

"I'm glad I have this chance to apologize for Jackie's attitude at Mass this morning. She's ordinarily not like…" David cut her short with a wave of his hand.

"Please, Mrs. Johnston. You have wonderful kids. Seems like it was just a matter of sibling rivalry or something like that. But it doesn't matter at all. Forget about it." Mikey had given him some safe topics to bring up. He tried one of them now. "Can't believe the summer's upon us once more. Less than a week of school. Got any plans for the summer?"

Liz shook her head. "Not really. We'll be staying at home. But of course we'll spend lots of time together as a family, hiking and swimming. What about yourself?"

"I'll be gone the entire vacation. Never done that before. I promised to spend the time with my parents at their cabin up in Michigan. I've got a bunch of nieces and nephews to spoil. It seems their parents also have issues with junk food. That's fine with me: it makes me a popular fellow among the little tykes."

She smiled. "I bet you're their favorite uncle! Speaking of which, please don't offer to buy my children any more floats…"

The request was made gently, but he saw the glint in her eye. David nodded his acquiescence sheepishly. He was happy the same scam had worked twice. He was pleased to observe how she visibly relaxed when he agreed.

Perhaps to show her good will, she leaned back and looked reflective. "Mr. Johnston, ever since you mentioned you worked for a 'head-hunting' company, I've been curious to know what your job entailed."

Another safe topic. Basically, anything that didn't center on her or her children, especially Jimmie, was safe.

"My company finds people to fill top executive positions worldwide. I was in charge of finding, interviewing, and narrowing down the candidates."

"It sounds challenging. I suppose mistakes would be costly and even detrimental."

"I avoided making mistakes..."

"There's a lot of con men in this world. They can disguise their activity for years."

"So far, nobody turned out to be a dud, at least as long as I was there. I took my time in the selection process."

"What did you look for?"

He thought for a moment. "You have to take each person as a whole and observe a heck of a lot. I looked for personal integrity above all. Of course, competency goes a long way too. That's easier to spot."

"But a person's own assurance of their integrity can't count for much." She seemed sincerely interested. He warmed up to the subject.

"If you really want to know, I took my time with each candidate. I would try to be with them in a variety of situations so I could observe their reactions, attitudes, and consistency."

"But people can go to great lengths to present a certain image of themselves that doesn't necessarily match reality," Liz said.

"To tell you the truth, I paid just as much attention to what they most wanted to present about themselves as to what they didn't say or show about themselves. Silence can speak volumes."

She pursed her lips. "Oh."

He saw the cloud in her eyes. Her interior wall was going up. He realized he was somehow treading again on thin ice. She glanced down at her watch, then turned to regard her children. He could tell she was about to stand up.

He thought to himself: *What the heck! I might as well press on.* Then he commented out loud, "Take you, for example."

Her eyes were inscrutable. "I'm afraid, Mr. Johnston, that I wouldn't make the eligibility list. I'm too much of a private person, as you've noticed."

At least she responded to me, David thought.

He answered playfully, "Oh, that's where you're dead wrong. You could easily be one of the finalists for a number of positions. Though I must say, I have found myself wondering whether you're a partial lunatic, or involved in some shady business, or merely mega-overprotective given the untimely death of your husband."

In spite of herself, Liz inquired, "And what have you concluded?"

He said lightly, "I haven't, for lack of data. That's what made me so successful at my job: I'm circumspect."

"I would think you had enough acquaintance with me to conclude all three," she answered, trying to seem uninterested.

He bantered back, "Is that what you would like me to conclude?"

She stood up. "Any of the above, or all three: it's a matter of indifference for me. Thank you, Coach, for your kindness and patience with my children. I wish you a good summer." She beckoned to her children and was gone.

Jackie swooped by. "No fair! I haven't beat him yet! Thanks a lot for the floats, Mr. Johnston... and sorry for being so rude to you!" Mikey flew to the table and gulped down his second float without taking the time to suck it through the straw. He looked expectantly at David for a signal. He gave the boy a thumbs up, ruffled his hair affectionately, and Mikey was gone.

No sooner had the Foster car left the parking lot than the stranger sitting in the next booth closed his newspaper and stood up, coffee cup in hand.

The man fixed his piercing eyes on David and asked, "Do you mind if I join you with my coffee?" David was taken aback by the request, but before he could reply, the man had seated himself across from him. "I couldn't help overhearing your conversation with Mrs. Foster. I too am a headhunter of sorts."

David frowned at the mention of her name. This man knew Liz but he hadn't greeted her. He wondered if the man had deliberately been using the newspaper to cover his face, since he had it open the entire time.

"How could I be of service to you?" he inquired coldly.

The man grinned cheerfully. His hand dove into his pocket for his wallet from which he extracted a card. He handed this to David as he stated: "Hugh McClury, FBI. You'll note that's two 'c's.' People spell it wrong all the time."

"Am I in trouble for something?" he asked in measured tones. Hugh shook his head emphatically.

"Not at all. Not at all. We're hoping, rather, that you can help us out." He lowered his voice, although he was already speaking quietly. "It's the company you keep."

David understood then. He tried to keep the emotion out of his voice but didn't succeed. "Is Liz in trouble?"

Hugh shook his head as he clucked his tongue.

"Wish I could have warned you in time! That dame's trouble. If I were you, I would keep my distance from her."

David frowned. "What do you mean? What has she done?"

"It's not that she's 'done' something precisely. We agents don't just look for the bad guys, you know. Big time trouble is looking for her... a heap of big trouble if you know what I mean."

The conversation was exasperating for David. "I don't know what you mean. Please explain."

Hugh took a long sip of his coffee. "Sorry. Can't tell you. It's all classified."

David banged his fist on the table in frustration. "Then what are you talking to me for?"

The man made a quieting gesture with his hands and said, "Shhh. This is an undercover operation. I'm only making myself known to you because you could help us."

David waited impatiently for the man to go on. Hugh took another sip of his coffee and smacked his lips appreciatively. "Nice flavor. It's got something in it, but what? Almond extract? Vanilla? Hard to say."

David crossed his arms to keep himself from hitting the table again.

"You would do a great service for your country by keeping us informed about the comings and goings of Elizabeth Foster and her kids."

"Why are you asking me?"

Hugh smiled knowingly and answered as if he were talking to a buddy in a high-school locker room.

"Who are you kidding? I can guess what kind of business transaction you're interested in when it comes to Mrs. Foster. She's a nice-looking dame. I can assure you, by the way, that's she's not a)off her rocker, and she's not exactly b) doing underhanded stuff. She's definitely c) big league over-protective, but then I can understand why."

"Buzz Sweeney gave you my name."

The man nodded appreciatively.

"You're sharp. He said you told him to contact you if we showed interest in why you were running a high-level security check on her. So here we are. No need for explanations, though. Seems obvious to me."

David didn't like the insinuation, although the man had guessed right. He chose not to respond.

"We want to thank you, by the way. We've been on the lookout for her since the death of her husband. She took off directly after her husband's funeral. Didn't even go home. We hadn't banked on that."

David couldn't help asking, "Why didn't you force Infinite Horizons to tell you where they were? Didn't you say you belong to the FBI?"

Hugh shook his head emphatically. This seemed to be a characteristic gesture. "Been there, done that. You can only subpoena a company so many times before you run into big obstacles. In fact, once was enough. They took us to court! You know what happened when we tried to throw our weight around? We succeeded in locating the Fosters, but then Mr. Foster inconveniently died a week later. We want to help protect people, not lead killers to them."

David sucked in his breath. "So her husband really was killed?"

Hugh abruptly made a stop sign with his hand. "Now I didn't quite say that, did I? That would be classified info, you know. Let's just say the coincidence of Mr. Foster's early demise to our discovering their whereabouts was too close for my own comfort. So we're very much obliged to you for helping us find her again."

"If Liz is in so much danger, you need to warn her!" David responded anxiously. "You need to do something!"

"Tell me about it. That's why we're talking to you. The more information you can supply about her the more we can help her."

"But why don't you just talk to her yourself?"

Hugh made more clicking noises with his tongue. "The minute she finds out we've succeeded in locating her, she's outta here! So if you're really interested in the woman, I'd advise against your telling her about our presence. I guarantee that you would never see her again. She's so good at hiding that she must be part hobbit."

David gazed back in dismay. He didn't know what to think or do.

"But as I said before," Hugh continued, "my advice would be for you to keep away from her. She's trouble." He finished off his coffee, gave one last smack of appreciation for it, then rose from the booth. "I haven't tasted coffee like this in a long time! It's my weak spot, you know." Hugh tossed some bills down on the table and gave one last nod in David's direction. "Call me any time, day or night."

He started to leave, but then checked himself and returned to David's side. "Incidentally, I want to apologize for any inconvenience our association may cause you. I've got a guy with me who's in training. He's still a little rough around the edges. I mean, he leaves traces of his presence. I'm working on him though, so don't worry. He'll be up to snuff soon: top notch."

David sat glassy-eyed for a while, trying to process what had just gone on. Perhaps it was good that he wouldn't be seeing Liz again for several months. He realized his heart was already too involved. The break would provide him time to distance himself emotionally from her and determine whether or not it was wise to pursue her any further. Perhaps he should take Hugh's warning. Maybe she would only bring trouble and heartbreak to him. Anyway, hadn't she just assured him that she didn't care what he thought of her? And yet, he told himself, she blushed deeply when she said it, and he had thought he had detected a hint of regret in her eyes as she spoke. Was he imagining it? Could be.

Hugh's parting words made sense as soon as David reached home. Someone had gone through his apartment. It wasn't too messy, but some furniture and papers were out of place. And on Monday morning, he discovered that someone had also gone through his office. David put it down to Hugh's apprentice. No big deal, since he had nothing to hide. But he wondered if Liz's house had received a similar treatment and how she would take it. The summer break would do him good. He was glad to get out of Ft. Davis for a while.

SIXTEEN

The Luciotti's were from the wealthier end of town and could afford to give their sons the best, but up until now Louie seemed to have no drive, no interests, and therefore matching low grades. They had been at their wits end until now, so they were overjoyed at this sudden desire of their middle son—and, in fact, his whole team—to excel scholastically. They didn't need to understand why; they were only too willing to promise him they wouldn't talk about this in town if that would somehow help him to keep his interest up. As long as he was applying himself, they would support him completely. It was astounding, however, to witness firsthand the intense weekly gatherings at their residence throughout the summer and into the fall.

Mrs. Luciotti delighted in plying the players with homemade pizza and other specialty Italian dishes while they plugged away in the basement at their subjects. The large open room was perfect for their purposes. They would sit or sprawl on the plush carpet, observing Jimmie's demonstrations. When it came to geometry and physics, he constantly used examples that they would then apply during their Saturday morning vector theory soccer training.

Recruits were summoned from the other parts of the house to help with the individual tutoring, including English and writing. Jackie was called from singing lessons with Mrs. Luciotti—ostensibly, that's why she was there—and Mikey from Stefano's room, where he was building model airplanes with Louie's younger brother. Though Mikey often found it hard to get along with boys his age, he didn't mind Stefano too much and actually enjoyed building planes with him. Both Mikey and Jackie had a complete understanding of the material, and their explanations were just as good as Jimmie's, so the trio of tutors succeeded in giving one-on-one help to each person.

Of course, it felt strange and seemed humbling at first to have such young tutors, but when the boys realized both of Jimmie's siblings were geniuses, it didn't matter. Besides, Mikey was a great kid —they all liked him; and Jackie was cute, like a sweet little sister. By mid-June, the plan was running smoothly. On Mondays and Wednesdays, all the players arrived at Louie's house at 4:00 p.m. sharp. Jackie and Mikey were dropped off by their mother at 4:15. Sometimes Liz would stay for a quick cup of tea, but she never suspected the soccer team was down in the basement studying, of all things. She returned to pick them up an hour and a half later. By then, the soccer players had already left.

Come fall, all of them did fine on their first exam. Bolstered by the evident improvement and now piqued by a healthy competition among them, the team players now strove to outdo each other and get the highest score on their next algebra exam. On the Monday morning following the exam, the nine players taking Mr. West's class sauntered into the classroom with high expectations. Mr. West had strongly objected at first to five of them even enrolling in his class, insisting that they would hold back the rest of the group. But their parents had prevailed, and he had begrudgingly agreed at least to a trial period. As he went through the room handing out the graded exams, he uttered a word of praise here and there. When all the exams had been handed out, he turned to the nine players and coldly bid them to see him after school. None of them had received their exams back. They eyed each other uneasily, guessing that he suspected them of cheating.

Only Roberto was amused. From his freshman year, he had been the ringleader of the childish pranks played on Mr. West behind his back. Of course, Mr. West suspected Roberto, but he hadn't been able to catch him yet. His teacher was inwardly glad that at last he had such evident proof of cheating and was only too happy to throw the book at them all.

As they entered his classroom en masse that afternoon, they spotted their exams neatly spread out on his desk.

"Boys, would you care to tell me if you see any similarities between your exams?" His voice was dripping with irony. Obediently but leisurely, they gathered around his desk and studied them together, leaning languidly on each other's shoulders, making a point to take their time about the matter.

"Hey... you did your answers exactly the same way I did mine," Jeff noted conversationally to Josh.

"Yup. Only you put it wrong. You did your answers exactly the same way I did mine," he retorted.

"Look how well our way of calculating matches: it's uncanny!" replied Nick.

"We were all so neat with our columns! And we all worked our answers out in the same methodical way. What's come over us?" declared Raymond.

"What I want to know is if I got the highest grade!" added Andre.

"That'll be me! I didn't get any wrong!" exulted Louie.

"Neither did I!" crowed Jorge, giving Louie a high five.

"Hey, don't go thinking you're special. Looks like we all tied for the highest grade!" announced Roberto. Carlos was the only one to keep his mouth shut the whole time.

"You certainly tied for the same grade, but the one you deserve: zero. And your fine little mockery of innocence will only get you a stiffer punishment," Mr. West informed them indignantly.

"Mr. West, you're mistaken. We really are innocent this time. I swear: none of us cheated!"

"Well, at least you've spoken a partial truth, Roberto, in saying 'this time.' I can see I'm not going to get anywhere with you, so you can all march right down to the principal's office to receive your suspensions or expulsions, depending on your past 'achievements,' shall we say."

"Just make sure you bring 'the evidence,' Mr. West."

Their teacher gave them a withering look.

"No need for concern on that point."

In the principal's office, the outraged students and Mr. West all tried to speak at once. The boys would normally have been amused, but now they had suddenly realized they might not get to prove their innocence. It's a good thing Mr. Jackson was a clear-headed man. Naturally he was inclined to side with the teacher against these boys, given their checkered past, but he also knew this situation had the potential for getting really messy. He was the one who would ultimately have to face the angry parents, so he was also prepared to listen to the boys' side of the story. Carlos, the most even-tempered of the boys, spoke for all of them, while several of the others elbowed Roberto to keep quiet.

"There's another logical conclusion that can be drawn from why our answers look so similar: it's because we have the same tutor."

Mr. Jackson asked expectantly, "Namely?"

Carlos hadn't figured on being asked who. Given that they had promised not to divulge the Foster kids' names, he wasn't sure what to reply. He looked to his fellow players for help. Louie glared at Carlos for being tongue-tied at such an important moment.

He offered confidently, "It's my father's work associate, Larry." Louie couldn't think of a last name fast enough so he left it at that. Although they were caught by surprise at first, the others understood that he was faithfully keeping their true teachers a secret. They immediately chimed in with a "Yeah!" or a "That's right!"

Carlos continued, "Mr. Jackson, it's easy for us to prove our innocence if you'll give us half a chance!" There was an expectant silence. Mr. Jackson could read their earnest expressions. "Have Mr. West give us different problems like the ones on the exam to figure out right now in front of you."

The others seconded the motion emphatically.

"Yeah! Give us a chance."

"We can do it!"

Roberto decided to push it further by threatening, "I'm going to ask my parents to make a complaint to the school board that Mr. West is harassing minorities..."

Mr. West glared at him, but Mr. Jackson decided to give them a chance.

"Mr. West, kindly give each of these boys three different problems to solve right here and now in front of us. We'll separate them and bring them into the office one by one so there's no chance of them helping each other out."

"Make them even harder, if you can!" taunted Roberto. Again, he received elbows in his side from his buddies. Once they saw they would get the chance to prove themselves, all of the boys visibly relaxed, a telltale sign for both of the adults that they really were innocent. One by one, they were called separately to solve a problem alone, under the suspicious gaze of Mr. West and the curious and then admiring eye of Mr. Jackson. The latter was ready to let them go after the first three students effortlessly solved their problems, but Mr. West insisted that each student demonstrate his capacity. When even he couldn't find any further pretext for claiming they had cheated, he glumly admitted defeat.

"I can't believe it. It's simply uncanny that they all know the material!" Mr. Jackson thereupon called all the boys back into his office.

"Gentleman, you are to be highly congratulated for your outstanding scholarship! You deserve to be publically praised!" His tone was warm and conciliating, motivated by the fear that he might have nine sets of furious parents down his back for unjust treatment of their sons. This was pure damage control.

"I, on the other hand, will only be fully satisfied once I understand better what made you improve so fast..."

Mr. Jackson curtly cut off Mr. West. "None of that, Mr. West. As long as they're achieving, we have no questions at all, just praise and admiration. Boys, in honor of your outstanding work and to make up for this little misunderstanding I'm going to give all of you early dismissal for the next three days. Let's put this distasteful moment behind us and keep moving forward."

With that, he respectfully ushered the boys out of the office, and then turned resolutely to Mr. West. "We can't afford to make a mistake like that again, Stewart, or you and I both will be offered a mandatory early retirement."

This event served as a catalyst for the boys to improve even more. If they proved to be top students, they would make Mr. West look even worse and shock everyone else. It was also the origin of three related nicknames for the secret young tutors: Mikey was "Little Larry", Jackie was "Larrita" (she liked the name), and Jimmie became just "Lar."

That afternoon, Mr. West sat at his desk brooding. Mr. Jackson had strictly warned him to stay off their case and not question them anymore, but he was determined to solve this puzzle anyway. The janitors came and left while he continued to leaf through their exams and reflect. Suddenly he recalled that he had seen that someone else made similar types of columns as these boys. That Foster girl, the one who was taking Algebra I although she was still in middle school.

He pulled out a folder to look for one of her tests. Yes, she had the same style as the others, even though she made too many sloppy mistakes in her arithmetic. He wondered what the connection meant. At last, he stored them away in a separate file for further perusal. The only common denominator was that Jackie Foster's brother played on the same team as the other boys.

The next day, he paid a visit to Coach Johnston and relayed the incident. David was surprised and just as clueless, but at least he came up with his own game plan. It was time to start visiting the homes of his soccer players as he had told them he would do at the end of last season.

SEVENTEEN

He was nervous again, just like he'd been about the grocery store, but he assured himself that it was all a matter of timing. If things had gone without a hitch the first time, why shouldn't the same scheme work again? Mikey felt in his pocket for his cell phone and gripped it tightly. He was sitting in the back corner of the library, deliberately out of sight of the entrance, with the three books that he was going to "remember" on his left side and the two books he was going to "forget" on his right side.

"Ready, Mikey?" That was his mother calling for him to come. He scooped up his "remember" books with his left hand and felt for the button with his right thumb. A moment's hesitation merely to ensure she was truly headed for the door, and then he hit "send." Next, Mikey rushed to the first set of double doors to hold one open for his mother. As Liz reached for the second set, David began to enter, saw her, and held the door for her instead.

Simultaneously, Mikey exclaimed, "Oh no! Wait, Mom! I forgot two of my books. I'll be right back!" Before Liz could say anything, he ran back into the library and headed for his corner. Out of sight, he settled down comfortably at the table, checking his watch first to see how long the conversation would last.

Meanwhile, Liz greeted David politely as she passed through the door and then stood on the other side waiting for her son to reappear. David let the door shut behind her instead of going through it himself and stood with his arms crossed, smiling at her benevolently. His right hand, folded under and out of sight, held his cell phone, and like Mikey, he had his thumb on the send button. This would be Mikey's signal to come running.

"Good morning, Coach David. I wouldn't have expected to see you here!"

His eyebrows went up, giving him a roguish expression. "What? You think coaches are illiterate?"

Liz blushed, and then laughed pleasantly. "That didn't sound quite right, did it? But to be honest, I didn't expect to see you here."

David knew this was his one chance to draw her into a conversation.

"Why, as a matter of fact, not only do I like to read, but I happen to make a point of promoting it among my players." This was true, although he ordinarily obtained his books through the Internet, not the public library. "And look: this is no comic book either!" He held out his book for her to see: *Man's Search for Meaning*, by Viktor Frankl. His faithful little informant had observed his mother thumbing through this book lately. Again, she looked shocked.

"What a coincidence! I was just going over that same book at home a couple of days ago." He feigned surprise. "I first read it as a teenager. It made a deep impression on my life. What did you think of it?"

David was delighted that she took the bait. He was also relieved that he had already prepared a well thought out answer to that exact question. "I was inspired by the whole thing. It seemed incredible to me that someone could come out of the Nazi concentration camp and describe what he experienced in such a detached and balanced way. He witnessed and suffered so many horrors and yet wasn't bitter or broken by the experience. On the contrary, he's offering a psychotherapy that by now has already helped thousands of people find real meaning in their lives."

Liz nodded agreement. She added, "And he was a prophet, too, in predicting that today's society will opt for euthanasia in the same vein as Hitler's 'mercy killing' program of all those he didn't find useful in society: those who were incurably ill, the mentally handicapped, etc."

David wondered at her passion for matters that involved protecting life. "Is that what made you pick it up again after so many years?" he asked.

She shook her head and looked reflective. "No. I wanted to go over the three different ways that Viktor Frankl says a person can give meaning to life. The first aspect was what inspired me as a youth: 'by creating a work or doing a deed.' His book led me to throw myself into scientific research so I could achieve something great in life. But then I discovered the second way: 'by loving someone.' I found three different fulfilling loves for a man and God and a child all about the same time." She paused, debating whether or not to go on.

David read her look of sadness and intuited why she was hesitating. "And now you're discovering the third way: 'by the attitude you can take to unavoidable suffering.'" She said nothing, but her eyes told him he had guessed rightly. He would have liked to reach out his hand to her, but he didn't dare. Instead, he spoke without thinking about how she would receive his words. "Liz, I'm sorry you lost your husband." Her breathing became heavy and her eyes filled with grief. "But you're suffering from something else as well, aren't you? I would like to help you if you would let me." No surprise at her response: the wall was back up. David pressed the send button.

There was diffidence in her tone as she turned away. "Excuse me, but I need to go see what happened to Mikey."

David stepped aside and began to open the door for her just as Mikey came bolting out. Before his mother could reproach him for taking so long, he greeting Coach David happily.

"Hey, Coach!"

David smiled down at the boy. "Hi, Mikey. What's up?"

"My birthday's this Saturday, and we're going bowling."

"Bowling! What a great idea! I've been meaning to get over there myself lately."

"Why don't you join us? We'd love to have him come, wouldn't we, Mom?" Mikey looked up eagerly at his mother. He was playing this for all it was worth, which was easy, since he really did wish Coach David would join them.

Liz objected, inwardly surprised at how strident her voice sounded. "Mikey! You shouldn't imposition Coach David like that. I wouldn't think of taking up his valuable time!"

"Why, Mikey," David cut in amiably, overriding Liz's protests, "I'd be honored to accompany you and your family on your birthday. Thank you for the invitation. It's not often I get invited to birthday parties anymore." Mikey beamed with pleasure. "Like I said, I've been meaning to go bowling soon anyway, so I'll be grateful for the de-lightful company."

Mikey quickly provided the details before his mother could get in another word: "Great! This Saturday at 5:00."

"You're on! See y'all later." David gave Mikey a high five, nodded to Liz, and entered the library. Mikey hurried off to the car to avoid further discussion on the matter, leaving behind a bemused Liz. She was both pleased and uneasy that David would be joining them, but she didn't really want to delve too deeply into the reasons for either of those feelings.

EIGHTEEN

Mrs. Luciotti audibly gasped with surprise as she opened the door for Coach David. She still had some last minute preparations for their guest and here he was, fifteen minutes early! Immediately, however, she tried to cover over her reaction by smiling graciously and beckoning him in. David stood hesitantly in the doorway, wondering at her initial response: after all, he wasn't *that* late.

"Mrs. Luciotti, I'm so sorry for arriving late! I do normally try to arrive right on time, but..."

At that, she laughed warmly.

"Don't tell me! You think you're late, but we thought you were coming at 6:30, so you're really early."

Consternation and then dismay flashed across his face.

"No!" He made as if to turn and leave. "How about I come back then, in fifteen minutes or so?"

"Nonsense!" she kindly insisted. "Come in! I wouldn't hear of you leaving now! Unfortunately, I sent my husband out to buy some fresh ingredients for tonight and he hasn't returned yet... and I need to be in the kitchen for a few more minutes. But I'll have Stefano show you around in the meantime."

She shouted for Stefano to come quickly and give David a tour. When he didn't instantly appear, she called again in her native tongue while freely waving clenched fingertips back and forth in the typical Italian fashion to express impatience. That did the trick. The short, rotund figure appeared, making little effort to mask his annoyance at being called away from his project. The two looked so much alike in their portliness, although he hadn't yet learned to imitate his mother's hospitable manner.

But at least he was willing to start the tour, beginning with the most important place first: his own bedroom. Model airplanes had long taken over the room. Some WWII fighters hung by strings from the ceiling, while a set of modern fighter jets were lined up on top of his bookshelf. Still more were displayed on shelves apparently installed for that purpose. When David noticed Stefano closely watching for his impression, he obliged.

"Wow! These are some planes you've got here! Look at the neat paint job on each one." Stefano glowed from the praise. Having singled out a few more planes with some mark of respect, David spotted his current project in the corner, on a low table, still mostly unassembled in tiny pieces. "Now, that one looks pretty intricate. What's it called?"

Stefano grimaced. "Mission Impossible. And it is!"

David sat down at the table and picked up the small part of the plane that was already partially assembled. "Hmm. I used to do model airplanes myself when I was a boy. But I've never seen something this hard. Can I help?"

Stefano happily agreed and plumped down on the floor beside him. They worked together for a few minutes in a companionable silence. "Do you work on them all by yourself?" David asked.

Stefano frowned slightly. "Well, I did until this year. But now Mikey Foster's been helping me some," he answered morosely.

"You don't sound too happy to have his help. Does he just get in the way?"

Stefano's frown bloomed into a full-fledged glower. This was a sore point for him. "Are you kidding? He's the best! I need his help, otherwise I'll never finish this plane! Look at all those little pieces! I only took it because he promised to do it with me, and because he also promised we could make it fly once we get it together. But that's never gonna happen." He glared down at the pieces as if they were to blame.

David was puzzled. "So if he's really good, then what's the problem with him helping you?"

"There's no problem with him helping me. The problem is with him *not* helping me!" This seemed to make full sense to Stefano, so he didn't offer to elaborate further.

David prompted him. "Well, how often does he come?"

"Twice a week," Stefano said. His voice was flat.

"And for how long each time?"

"Just because he happens to be in the house for an hour and a half doesn't mean a thing. I only get him for the first twenty minutes! And he's *my* friend!" he added emphatically, as if some personal injustice were being perpetrated against him.

David found a piece of the model airplane, showed it triumphantly to Stefano, and then glued it in place. "What happens after those twenty minutes?"

"Jimmie and Louie call him downstairs, and I don't get to see him again until it's time for him to leave."

David's heart leapt. He was on to something. He spotted another piece of plane and nudged Stefano to make sure he saw it.

"What do they want him for?" David asked nonchalantly.

"I'm not allowed to say!" responded Stefano sourly.

David's mind raced to come up with something that would move the boy to say more. "Oh, I get it. The whole thing is a big secret!"

Stefano rolled his eyes with disgust. "It's gotta be the stupidest secret in the entire world! Secrets are supposed to be interesting. But who cares about what they're doing?"

"I guess that means they're not having any fun."

"The only thing even closely connected with fun is that they're keeping me from having fun with my friend!"

"Poor Mikey! He must be pretty bored with them too!" David tried to commiserate with him.

"Mikey? Nah! He doesn't mind… He's a Larry! That's why they want him." Stefano knew he wasn't supposed to give away what they were doing, but it never occurred to him that this name would mean something to David.

"A 'Larry'? Is that his middle name?"

"That's only what they call him. He's 'Little Larry' and Jimmie's 'Lar.' Their sister's 'Larrita.' How dumb can ya get?"

"She comes too, huh?" David asked, reaching for yet another piece.

"She's supposed to be here for singing lessons, but she goes downstairs too when Mikey's called," Stefano answered bitterly.

It all clicked for David. He tried out his deduction on Stefano. "Yeah, those three make great teachers. They're the reason why the whole soccer team is suddenly doing so well in school!" he observed calmly.

The boy gasped in surprise and fright. He jumped to his feet, evidently flustered. "I didn't say that!"

He rushed on nervously. "You can't say that because they'll say I told you, and I didn't!"

David smiled reassuringly. "Don't worry Stefano. Nobody will know I know anything. But I just need to know if this is also a secret from Mrs. Foster."

"I just know that they especially don't want her to find out!" Stefano replied urgently. At the sound of approaching footsteps, he fell silent, fixing a worried gaze on Coach David.

Mrs. Luciotti poked her head through the door. "Stefano, didn't you show Coach Johnston the rest of the house? There's more to see than your model airplanes!"

David enjoyed the dinner immensely. Louie's older brother, Marcello, was there too, adding to the lively atmosphere. Both Mr. and Mrs. Luciotti and their two eldest boys knew how to hold interesting conversations involving their guest. Everyone felt free to state their opinion candidly, and then defend it intelligently, accompanied by vivacious hand gestures and a sense of humor. Only Stefano sat mutely, mainly because he was concentrating on the food. David could see that this was a close-knit, happy family where there was lots of love to go around. All throughout the dinner, Mrs. Luciotti plied him to take more of her homemade pasta, wine, Italian pizza, etc.

The table only grew quiet at one point, when David said to Louie: "I've been hearing big things about you and the whole team regarding your grades. Congratulations!" Louie and his parents smiled pleasantly enough, while Stefano rolled his eyes and wriggled uncomfortably. "Yeah, you've stumped Mr. West. He claims you're all hiding some big secret," David continued.

Stefano glared at David, while Louie cut in calmly, "Aw, there's no secret, Coach! We just decided to try harder, you know, to be more mature."

Stefano screwed up his face with a pleading look for David to drop the subject.

"We're so proud of our son, Coach David!" Mrs. Luciotti added. "And we think it's partly due to the good influence of his teammates. You know, Louie's father and I, we've always been hard workers. We emigrated from Italy together when we were only in our twenties. He had a good job opportunity and told me that either I married him and came along, or he was going alone. So I went with him…"

She launched into their whole family story, effectively turning the attention away from the reason for her son's success. As she went on, David wondered to himself at the capacity of the Foster family to convince others to keep their secret. All of the Luciottis were in on it!

Late that evening as he headed home, he reflected on how fortuitous it had been to choose the Luciotti family for his first home visit and then accidentally arrive early. His time alone with Stefano had supplied him with a clue to deciphering the enigmatic Fosters. Now he puzzled over why the three kids were keeping their tutoring a secret from their own mother. In any case, he had confirmation that the younger siblings were geniuses. He determined to keep up with his family visits.

NINETEEN

Jimmie smiled in satisfaction when he heard the sounds of hammering and sawing. He remarked smugly to his sister, who was biking at his side, "You hear that?"

"What? You mean all that banging?" She was unimpressed. "So what? Isn't that why we came?"

"Don't you get it? They beat us because they came by car, but only by a matter of five minutes or so… and they're already hard at work!"

"Oh, that's right. And they call you their slave driver, but you're not even there to make them work yet!" She beamed at him now. "You were right, Jimmie! You said that as soon as they got a taste of helping others, they wouldn't want to stop."

"Well, Mr. Luciotti is there, so that's got to be part of it; but still…" His mind drifted back to the first voluntary sessions.

The first time they had to declare how many points they'd earned for the week, Ross, Nick, and Jeff manfully owned up that they hadn't made the fifty-point mark, so when the early Saturday morning practice was over, they were sentenced to a "service tour" with Jimmie, amidst the jeers of the rest who even pummeled them for coming up short. Roberto rubbed it in the most.

From where he was sprawled on the ground, he commented languidly, "Now, if you were farsighted like me, you would have taken young Juan to Mass with you, and not cussed that day or the next, and you would have been free the rest of the week."

Nick objected, "Juan, wouldn't you have gone to Mass anyway?"

"That's not the point," Roberto countered complacently. "I 'helped' him."

Jeff leaned over and punched Nick, then motioned him silently to shut up. He was willing to accept their Saturday sentence, but he didn't want to give Roberto any fuel. Nick didn't understand what was going through Jeff's mind, but Roberto did.

"Nick, Jeff's telling y'all to shut your mouth in hopes that I'll shut mine," he drawled, "but this is too good to let go. After all, y'all are convicts."

He realized that he should have been wary of retaliation the moment he saw Ross nudge Nick and Jeff with his elbow, then jerk his head back in Roberto's direction. He sprang to his feet and started running, but the other three boys had already lunged towards him. Jeff tackled his feet, Nick sat half on his head and half on his back, while Ross twisted his right arm behind his back. Jimmie and Louie headed off together for Louie's house, while the rest of the players laughed at the plight Roberto had brought upon himself.

Ross gave the order: "Apologize before we give you the full treatment." Amid groans and shouts of protest, Roberto finally managed to spit out an acceptable apology. "Okay, already! I'm sorry. Mightily sorry. Let me go: you're breaking my arm!" He lay there on the ground nursing his sore arm as his assailants calmly followed after Jimmie and Louie.

Roberto waited until they were far enough away that he could make a run for it. "I really am sorry… sorry, that is, that y'all are convicts!" They chose to ignore him, while the other players grinned and shook their heads at his obstinacy.

With the exception of Jimmie and Louie, none of the players knew that the "volunteers" first got to go to the Luciottis' for a fabulous brunch. The rest of the week, these three boasted, especially to Roberto, about their incredible feast, going on and on about how much they had enjoyed helping repair the little old lady's back porch. The next time, out of curiosity and a desire for good food, Miguel and Juan volunteered to join the same three who had come up short again.

At last today, for the first time, the entire team had turned out.

Mrs. Luciotti had been in her element, delighted rather than daunted by the amount of food they could consume. Their stomachs full,
they had begun working on their next project, that of adding on two
rooms to a house that was much too small for a immigrant family of
seven. Next, Jimmie was going to launch a project of collecting food
and clothing to fill a truck and drive it across the Mexican border for
those who had been left destitute from recent floods. As they pulled
up to the little house, Jimmie dumped his bike on the front lawn,
which had foot-long grass.

"I'll be right back, Jackie. I'm just going to see if I can borrow a
mower from the next-door neighbors to cut this grass." Mr. Luciotti
had generously offered to supply the material and to oversee the construction work on the house. Jimmie was more than happy to stay in
the background.

Jackie, on the other hand, hurried to where the action was, determined not to make this a one-time deal. Permission to accompany
Jimmie had to be cajoled from both her brother and her mom, so she
had to show everyone she could do just as much work as the boys.
Right away, she picked up a hammer and eagerly began nailing according to Mr. Luciotti's specifications. When Jeff observed that she
was able to pound in a nail with a single blow, he turned to Nick and
Josh in awe.

"Man, look what our lovely Larrita can do. She's not just a brai-
niac!" It took a while before she became aware of their fixed attention. When she did, she lowered the hammer and first checked her
clothes and hair to make sure they weren't staring because there was
something wrong with her appearance. Her confusion made them
laugh.

"Why are you staring at me?" she demanded self-consciously. All
three of the boys were going to be seniors and she was just an incom-
ing freshman, so she felt intimated by the sudden attention. That
made them laugh even harder. But when her face grew stormy, Josh
responded admiringly: "Don't you realize that not everyone can get
the nail to go all the way in with just one hit? Who taught you how?"

Jackie relaxed. "Oh, is that all? That's just something I learned in Tai Kwon Do. It's part of learning coordination and patience."

Nick moved over to her side. "Can you teach me how to do that?"

"Yeah, right! Do you know how many times I banged my thumb before I got it down? I don't need anybody blaming me because they hit themselves." She thought to herself that this would probably ensure she would never get to join them again.

"You sure have a lotta talents for a little girl!" remarked Jeff.

"Well, you're not allowed to tell anyone about this talent either!" she responded heatedly, still flustered at the attention.

"We're not allowed?" repeated Jeff teasingly, as he eyed the other two boys significantly. That sounded too much like a challenge to them.

"Why not? What's wrong with people finding out you could beat up any boy in the school?" This was the first time Josh had referred so explicitly to what she had done to him. After all, she had apologized to him so sweetly and it wasn't something he was proud of, but he couldn't resist teasing her now.

She pursed her lips. "I didn't beat you up," she countered testily, "I knocked you flat. That's different! And I was very careful not to hurt you."

Josh chuckled, while Jeff and Nick turned to him in disbelief. "Whoa! When did that happen?"

Josh didn't mind explaining to his buddies under these circumstances. "It was last year after I broke off my date with Lily to the spring dance. Jackie said she had something to tell me just before class, so I hung around like an innocent lamb. Once the hall was empty, she chopped me here with her hands, sudden like, knocking the wind out of me." He pantomimed the motion on Nick. "Next thing I knew, I was lying on my back on the ground, I'm not quite sure how..."

The other two hooted in delight, offering Jackie a high five.

"Way to go! Just let us see you do it next time," was Nick's hearty commendation.

"That's why you've been acting nicer to all the girls, not just the pretty ones! He learned his lesson, Jackie," added Jeff.

Nick asked wistfully, "But didn't anybody get to see?"

Josh was enjoying himself immensely. "Yeah, of all people, Mr. West. Through the window on the door of his classroom, he must have seen her come flying at my shoulders. So he comes out, looks at me on the ground and Jackie standing over me, then grins and goes back into his class as if nothing had happened! So much for equal justice for all!" The three boys laughed heartily, but Jackie didn't even smile. She wasn't comfortable with the whole conversation.

"C'mon, Jackie, do it again to him now so we can watch," urged Nick.

"Do it to me… just promise not to hurt me," begged Jeff.

"Yeah, good idea: do it to Jeff!" Josh like the idea of a demonstration as long as it was on someone else. But Jackie shook her head vehemently.

"All the guys in the high school are going to be afraid to go near me now!" she whined. Once more, the three boys exchanged significant glances.

"Don't worry about that at all, Jackie," said Jeff, "because no boy is going to get near you anyway."

This made her exclaim in shock, "But why not? I'm not ugly, am I? And I'm nice, aren't I?" Her discomfort shot up while the three boys delighted at her naivety.

"Because I will personally beat the tar out of any guy who even stands too close to you," assured Josh with a big grin.

"Not if I get to him first. There won't be any tar left!" declared Nick.

Then it was Jeff's turn. "You'll both have to fight me to get the first swing at him."

"But you can't do that! You wouldn't!" protested Jackie, her mouth and eyes wide open at such a terrible prospect.

Josh patted her arm reassuringly. "Don't worry, the warning will go out the first day of school, so all the guys will know they're taking their lives into their hands if they so much as look at you."

That was too much for Jackie. She dropped her hammer and went to ask Mr. Luciotti for another job further away from those three. The wonderful afternoon had been ruined for her. Not so for Josh, Nick, and Jeff. They went back to their work laughing together at their joke. They admired and liked Jimmie's little sister a lot, but it was just too tempting to give up the chance of somehow getting the better of her. Besides, what they had said was close to the truth anyhow. They all felt as protective of her as if they were her big brothers.

TWENTY

By late afternoon, the players departed in good spirits. They had done something noble together, and they felt the deep satisfaction that only comes from reaching out to those in need. Brother and sister leisurely biked side by side as they headed for the bowling alley. Observing that Jackie was unusually subdued, Jimmie probed: "Are you glad you joined us today?"

She looked at him morosely. "Jimmie, I can't do anything else with your soccer team ever again, including tutoring."

"What's the matter? Did something happen today?" he asked in a concerned tone. She didn't look at him, but tears started trickling down her cheek. At that he braked his own bike.

"Stop!" There, on the side of the road, he asked kindly: "What's up, Jacks?" It was a nickname that she permitted just him to use as long as nobody else was around.

The tears were flowing even more liberally now. "It's just that hanging around your team is going to destroy my social life for my entire high-school career!" she exclaimed. Her big brother barely succeeded in not smiling at her melodrama, knowing that she really felt that way, and that she would be hurt if he didn't seem to take her seriously.

"What? Did someone insult you?" He didn't know quite what else to say.

"No. It's not that. They basically assured me that they would beat to a pulp any guy who tries to get near me!"

Jimmie almost exploded with laughter but refrained. "I guess they see you as their little sister and want to protect you. That's something good. They know how many guys just use girls, and they don't want that to happen to you." He hoped that would calm her down, but she grew even more agitated.

"You think it's good that no boy is even going to be able to talk to me for the next four years? It's just not fair! I've been helping them, and that's how they're going to show their gratitude! Thanks a lot!" She didn't have any Kleenex, so she wiped her face on the arms of her t-shirt. Scowling, she straightened up her bike and started pedaling disconsolately down the street once more. Jimmie drew up beside her and tried to say something comforting.

"Aw, Jacks, they were only teasing you. It won't be so bad. Besides, Mom doesn't want us dating until we graduate, anyway."

For an instant, Jackie forgot her own plight. "Just tell me one thing: why are you obeying her? You know you could get away with it if you wanted to, and most of the girls in the school are crazy about you!"

Jimmie fixed his gaze ahead for a while, pondering whether to answer or not. After all, this was a matter he guarded deep in his heart, and he felt neither the need nor the desire to share it with anyone. But Jackie was his little sister, and perhaps his words would help her. Meanwhile, Jackie kept glancing over at him, wondering what was going through his mind. At last, he sat up straight, letting go of the handlebars, stretching out his hands wide. They were on a quiet back street, so it didn't seem reckless of him.

"Jacks, if this length here—" he turned sideways, facing her with his arms still spread out, "—stood for the eighty years that we might live, then show me what proportion would the four years of high school be?"

"One-twentieth."

"Sure, sure. But show me. Measure."

Jackie also sat up gingerly, letting go of her handlebars, and began more or less dividing up the length between his hands into portions. She didn't have the same dexterity as him sitting sideways while still biking forwards, but she wasn't about to act nervous. The one-twentieth part was small enough for her to show with her thumb and index finger. He nodded.

"Look how little that is in comparison to a lifetime!" All the while, he had kept his arms spread wide, facing her as they biked along. If it were anyone else, Jackie would have been quick with a sarcastic remark. Since it was her hero, Jimmie, she merely communicated that she didn't get his point.

"So?"

"Jacks, we teenagers have our whole life in front of us, but we seem to think we have to do everything worth doing right away." Her face still registered puzzlement, so he went on patiently. "When I get married, I only want to get married once. And I want to raise a happy family. Mom and Dad were so happy together."

Jackie's face indicated that she was getting more confused by the minute. "I still don't get it." Here they had to cross a street that had some traffic, so both sets of hands went back to their respective handlebars. Jimmie continued with his explanation on the other side, once more sitting up and spreading his hands. Jackie kept her hands down so she could concentrate better on what her brother was saying.

"So many people our age make mistakes in dating, doing things they shouldn't with each other, looking for happiness. But they're not going to find it by experimenting on each other."

Jackie rolled her eyes. "You're starting to sound like Mom and Dad," she warned.

Jimmie laughed good-naturedly. "You're right. I've heard this from both of them... But they had the best marriage I've ever seen, so their advice is worth listening to, isn't it? Anyway, I myself have thought and prayed about it, and I've decided on my own to wait to date until I'm really ready for the fullness of love, the kind that ends, or rather blooms, with marriage—that is, with a happy family and great kids like us!"

He tried to be amusing with that last line. At least he got a smile out of Jackie. "True love is worth waiting for, and I'm not going to waste my time on relationships that could get too physical too quickly, because that might tarnish the complete love I want to give my future wife down the road."

Jackie burst out, "You must be the only guy your age to think that way!"

He raised his eyebrows at her. "Maybe that's why my soccer buddies aren't going to let anyone near you!" Jackie's laughter showed his point hit home. "Besides," he added mischievously, "who says there'll be anything left of the guy for them after I get through with anyone who tries something on you!" He spoke lightly enough, but Jackie knew he meant it, and was inwardly pleased to know she had a big brother like him looking out for her. Glancing at his watch, Jimmie urged: "We're going to be late and it's Mikey's birthday! C'mon, I'll race you." Crisis over, the two raced furiously down the street.

On arriving at the bowling alley, they were surprised but pleased to discover Coach David there with their mother and little brother. David had brought lots of pizza and two root-beer floats for each of them, along with tons of chocolates and candy... foods that were not ordinarily present in the Foster household. Mikey was already having such a great time that he barely reacted when his siblings arrived. It turned out that David fit right into the intimate family gathering: he patiently gave the almost hopeless Mikey lessons at bowling; he teased Jackie in a way that made her laugh and not get angry, and he competed heavily with Jimmie to see who would get the highest score. At one point, when David was ahead by a little, Jackie proudly whispered to him that she thought her brother was holding back because he usually did much better!

For brief snatches of time, David was also able to converse with Liz companionably enough. Though she didn't show it, she was enjoying his presence. She was touched by how well he interacted with her children and was struck by his goodness of heart. He for his part admired her ladylike poise, even while bowling, and her gentle but firm manner with her children. She was at ease with him in that setting. Her warmth buoyed his heart.

Wisely, he chose not to stay the whole time, using the excuse that he had a previous appointment in response to Mikey's disappointed protests. He was going to leave while he was ahead, before he put his foot in his mouth. As he pulled out of the parking lot, David wondered to himself what it would be like to become a permanent member of that happy family. Well, at least four of the five interested parties might like the idea, and after this afternoon perhaps the fifth might too. In any case, he felt ready to set the stage to launch out on his own: he was going to look for the right opportunity to ask Liz out.

TWENTY-ONE

Normally the small lake was like a limpid mirror that early in the morning. But the water had already been disturbed by the busy crowd of mallards pushing in around the white-latticed gazebo, which jutted out into the water from all sides. The quaint little bridge connecting it to the land was only wide enough to let one person cross at a time. No wonder this cozy spot was a favorite of couples in the evening.

Even the lone swan had been enticed from her quiet roosting spot to join in the flurry of feeding. David was seated on the low bench that lined the inside of the gazebo, generously flinging duck feed into the water. When he saw the swan approaching, he threw out even more, delighted at the presence of the majestic newcomer. The other ducks instinctively opened a pathway for her, and she gracefully assumed the choicest spot as if by right.

Mikey had given him the Internet address for obtaining the magical brand—"Winston Special Gourmet Duck Food"—and David had meekly complied, not even wincing at the exorbitant cost for something so mundane. However, he hoped this would be the last time he needed to rely on his young genius friend to "bump into" Liz. Today he was going to muster up the courage to ask her out, precisely when they reached this romantic corner. She would stoop down to feed the swan, and he would nonchalantly invite her to try out the pasta with him at a quaint Italian restaurant he had discovered.

Once more, the scheme went as planned, or at least Mikey's part did. He was accompanying his mother around the lake, Liz jogging and Mikey on skates. As they drew near the bend closest to the gazebo, he contritely announced he had forgotten his watch by the clumps of mesquites where they had stopped to feed the squirrels. With the assurance that he would quickly catch up, he skated back in the direction from which he and his mother had come, leaving her to jog on alone. A minute later, David "happened" to come huffing around the bend and gallantly offered to accompany her for a while. Liz gave him her customary gracious smile, and they walked along together.

When they neared the gazebo, Liz exclaimed in delight at the sight of the swan. "He's normally hidden in the rushes on the other side at this time!"

That was David's cue. He pulled out his Winston Special, while noting to himself that it was worth the ridiculous price.

"Here, would you like to feed it?"

Liz nodded readily. She stepped across the little bridge, entered the gazebo first, and then did just as David had pictured she would: she crouched low, stretching out her palm full of seed for the swan to come eat from it.

It's now or never! he thought to himself, only to discover he had lost his courage. Annoyed with his own weakness and knowing Mikey would appear at any moment, he fought to gain control of himself so he would sound casual. Taking a deep breath, he surprised himself by blurting out his request in schoolboy fashion.

"Is there any chance you would accompany me on a real date, Liz?" He knew that he had botched it even as he finished the sentence. She started visibly and then, with a slight frown, turned an accusing gaze upon him, the swan forgotten.

"A real date?" she replied slowly, questioningly, and then more suspiciously still. "A real date?"

Helplessly, he witnessed the light dawning in her eyes. Then she scrambled to her feet while his mind whirled unsuccessfully for something to say. At least he had the presence of mind to block the way out of the gazebo with his body; by now he knew her tendency to bolt.

"So, is this present encounter some kind of a date, even though it certainly couldn't be classified as a real one?" His avoidance of her eyes and his discomfiture confirmed her deduction. "Coach Johnston, have you been using my son to plan all of our chance meetings?" she demanded, outraged.

Things had certainly taken a turn for the worse, but David had great presence of mind. He knew it was useless to pretend innocence. Instead, he was thinking about what to do next. One thing was certain: he couldn't let her storm off in anger. He would never get another chance like this to get near her.

For her part, Liz was considering whether she should try pushing past David in order to leave.

"I'll thank you to keep away from my son from now on," she commanded icily. Then she stepped towards his side, aiming for the doorway. David acted quickly. He reached out and caught her by both shoulders, then held her lightly but firmly at arm's length. He spoke before she could order him to let her go.

"Liz, I'm sorry. I'll do as you say. And I'll leave you alone from now on if you'll just tell me one thing." She stood there, full of tension and not looking at him. "Only tell me you could never be interested in me as a man, and I'll be sure to avoid you from now on."

Surprised, her eyes found his for an instant, and then she broke free of his grasp and gaze by stepping backwards and looking away once more. To his delight, she remained silent, confirming his hunch that her apparent anger might be a cover. Why else would she be angry? If a woman cared nothing for a man, she wouldn't necessarily be angry that he showed interest in her.

Her mind was racing too. She wanted to get as far away as she could from him, but he blocked the way out. Ready to press his sudden advantage, David took a step towards her. She did care for him! Liz responded by taking another step backwards. He took another step forward, and she took one more backwards. This time, she felt the low bench against the back of her leg.

"Please stop!" she pleaded weakly, then sank down onto the bench. He sat down close beside her. When she spoke next, her words poured out in a jumble.

"You mustn't pursue me. You mustn't! I'm in a weak moment. I'm so alone. I'm so vulnerable right now, it wouldn't be fair. If you pursue me right now, I might give in. I might let you catch me."

He raised his eyebrows quizzically since that prospect appealed to him, so she hurried on, trying to make him understand. "If you catch me right now, you'll only have the shell of me. It would only be a cheap, shallow love—if you could even use the word. I couldn't possibly belong to you right now! So if you do insist on pursuing me, my only choice is to run. We'll have to move again." The anxiety in her voice reached its peak, and she had to stop speaking for the moment.

At that threat, David protested, "No, Liz—"

But she motioned for him to be silent as she struggled to gain control of herself once more. Then, in a steadier tone, she went on.

"It would be terrible for all three of my children to move right now. They're all happy and settled here, and I don't have another home prepared yet, so we'd be constantly on the run. It would make them bitter. And they've already suffered so much recently with the death of their father."

He tried to interrupt, but she kept talking, her voice becoming louder and shriller. "I'm not safe for you, David! You might get killed as well, like my husband! I would never be able to forgive myself!" Once more she broke off, tears streaming freely down her cheeks.

David offered her a handkerchief. He couldn't grasp her reasoning nor understand her fears. This much was obvious, though. He had to assure her that he wouldn't push a relationship that might possibly bloom in the future. He needed to wait patiently and not frighten her away.

"Liz," he began softly and reassuringly, "you're safe with me. I won't push." He rose and offered both hands to help her rise, and then enfolded her gently in his arms. She didn't protest, and they stood like that for a while in silence, her shoulders heaving. "I'm not going to chase you. And you're not going to run away." Gradually the violent shaking subsided. "Nobody around here is going to do any chasing, and nobody is going to do any running," he said again. "We'll just be friends for now, okay?" When at last she was calm he released her.

With a barely audible "Thank you," she turned and made her way out of the gazebo, not looking back. Mikey appeared suddenly. He must have been there, hidden, watching for some time, but he gave no indication of having observed anything. Together, the two went back up the path.

Once they were gone, David heard an annoyed honking at his side. The swan had entered the gazebo and appeared to be glaring at him.

"Sorry!" he muttered and then dumped out all the rest of the "Winston's Special" at her feet.

TWENTY-TWO

On the same day as the "Winston Special" incident, Jackie appeared at the doorway of David's office and abruptly announced:

"Mikey says to tell you he's busted, and that you would know what he means. I sure don't. I promised to come tell you because I've never seen him so sad—except of course when Dad died!" She poked her head further in and gazed around his office curiously.

"Jackie! I've never had the pleasure of you coming to see me! Come in." He waved her in warmly with his left hand, while reaching automatically for a root beer and ice cream with the other hand. She hadn't come for anything else so she debated about entering, but when these ingredients materialized before her eyes, she exclaimed:

"That little stinker! He never told me you made root-beer floats here in your office!" Coach David smiled at her capacity to express outrage and delight simultaneously.

"You only get this if you promise not to do Mikey any bodily harm for withholding vital information," he replied teasingly.

Jackie plopped into the chair next to his desk. "How many have you already given to him?" Her question was framed in accusing tones, as if she had somehow been wronged.

"You're going to have to change your tactics if you want to compete with Mikey," came the placid reply. She received the drink graciously and sipped at it appreciatively. David gazed at her amiably, then went back to his papers to avoid making her feel self-conscious. He was right that she would soon have grown uncomfortable otherwise, but she also didn't appreciate the feeling of being ignored either. She searched her mind for something interesting to say to him.

"You know what the latest gossip is in school?"

He didn't even look up. "No, and I don't want to know, thank you."

Undaunted, she observed, "Well, you should, because it's about you. It usually is because everyone thinks you're so good-looking." She didn't mean to imply the opposite, but she realized by his good-natured chuckle that this was the impression she had given.

"Sorry. I don't mean to say that you're not... but you're old!" He chuckled again. "Oops. I mean you're not *that* old, but you're too old for us students. But anyway, if any of the teachers liked you too, they've all been frustrated—that is, until you and Miss Townsend became an item."

Caught off guard, he responded without thinking, "Ronna?"

Jackie was pleased that he answered *and* that he was surprised.

"So it's not true, after all!" she chortled. "And everyone was so sure!"

David couldn't help but ask her where they got the idea. In a businesslike manner, Jackie proceeded to enlighten him. As she listed them off, she kept tally with her fingers. "There are many pieces of evidence. First of all, you went to the school picnic with her."

"No, I didn't. I sat at the same table with her at lunch..." In his mind, David completed the sentence, *because Evelyn insisted I sit there*. "I didn't even know Miss Townsend was at that table when I sat down."

Jackie was unconvinced. "But you also left with her."

David shook his head. "Yes, but that's because the one who drove her there had something come up and wasn't able to give her a ride home after all..."

Jackie went on: "Okay, but then you were also her date at the formal teacher dinner the parents' club put on for you last week."

"It was assigned seating," he replied with annoyance. "I had nothing to do with it. Anything else?" He kept to himself that it was probably Evelyn who arranged the seating chart.

"Well, yeah. You share a classroom with her. No other teachers in the whole school do that."

"Her room just happened to be assigned to me because I only teach one class, so I don't merit a room of my own... I have my coach's office, as you can see. And my one class just happens to coincide with her spare. Is that it?" he asked tersely.

At last Jackie seemed convinced, although she had to get in one last remark.

"Well, that sure is a lot of coincidences, if you ask me. Anyway, I'm gonna make sure that everyone knows the truth. You're obviously not an item, or you wouldn't have made such a point of denying it."

For any other person David wouldn't have bothered. He wasn't going to worry about clearing up idle gossip. But he wanted to set the record straight with Jackie, just in case something got back to Liz.

"Hold on now. Just what do you mean by the 'truth'?" Jackie squirmed under his probing gaze.

"Obviously, Miss Townsend is crazy about you, Coach. So I'm going to tell everyone how she spends hours of her time devising ways to get near you."

He banged his desk with his fist emphatically. "You better not!"

Jackie jumped in astonishment, and then, taken back, she asked tentatively: "But why not? Then you really do like her?"

David glared at her. "You're missing the whole point. You shouldn't be gossiping about anyone! You can really hurt people that way. Would your Mom approve?"

Jackie shook her head meekly. To show her there were no hard feelings, David prepared her another root-beer float, which she accepted readily.

"Wow, Coach, you sound just like my dad!" That was a big compliment coming from Jackie.

David went back to his papers, while she worked on her second drink happily enough. She didn't mind that he had corrected her. He had made her remember her dad by his words and passion. In that silence, her mind wandered back to the news of his sudden death and the trials that had followed. It was such a relief to come to this town where they seemed to be safe. All except for those phone calls, of course. To Coach David, her wistful statement came out of the blue, though it followed the train of her thoughts:

"I wish we could stay in this town, Coach David. I love it here."

He looked up questioningly. "What's keeping you from doing that?"

Jackie hesitated, since she knew her mother didn't want them talking about their family situation to anyone.

"If Mom gets scared, we'll be on the move again. But I don't think that will take too much since she's already nervous about the phone calls."

If she had been looking for his undivided attention, she had it.

"From whom?" he asked gently.

Jackie snorted in exasperation. "Do you think Mom will tell me? When it rings in the car, she sees who's calling and won't answer it. Once it rang just as we got in the door, and she went into her bedroom to answer it, shutting the door. But I lay down on the floor and put my ear against the crack to listen in."

David thought about correcting her for this, but let it slide. She went on: "Mom was telling the person to leave her alone, that she didn't want their help, that she didn't trust them. It scared me. We're just three kids and a mother, with I don't know how many people out to get us. And we don't know who we can trust."

At David's look of compassion, her eyes welled up and overflowed. He offered her a Kleenex while reassuring her. "You can trust me."

At being able to unload her burden on someone so much like her dad, Jackie cried harder. "But can you do anything to help us?"

They both considered the question on their own, but nothing occurred to either of them for the moment.

"You couldn't get me the phone number of the person calling your mother, could you?" David asked.

She sniffed, blew her nose, and then replied, "I already have it. Once, when the phone rang in the car, I snatched it up and studied the numbers long enough to memorize them before Mom could stop the car and get it back. She was really mad…" He passed her a slip of paper, and she wrote down the number.

"That's a pretty good trick to be able to memorize a ten-digit number so quickly…"

"No big deal… when you're desperate," came the perky reply, belying her own words.

"Look, I can help you. Stop worrying," David reassured her. "You can call me any time, anywhere, if you think you're in trouble, and I'll come running."

Jackie blew her nose one last time for good measure. "Thanks, Coach. Only don't tell Mom I gave you the number, okay?" She stood up. "I better go, but really, thanks."

Seconds after she had left the office, she popped her head back in the door. "Oops—I forgot: do you have any reply to cheer up Mikey?"

"Tell him this old saying: 'Sometimes you have to lose a battle to win a war.'"

She made a face. "I guess he'll understand. I don't. But that's okay—I got two root-beer floats out of it."

Once Jackie was gone, David carefully shut his door, dialed the number, and left a message:

"Hello. This is David Johnston. I received your number through a mutual acquaintance and have a personal matter to discuss with you for our mutual benefit."

His phone rang a few minutes later. On picking it up, he recognized Hugh's distinctly nasal tone. Somehow, David wasn't surprised.

"So you're still mixed up with the dame, eh David?"

"Is this your phone, then?"

Hugh began conversationally, "No, it belongs to a mutual acquaintance of Elizabeth's and mine—" but David cut him off angrily.

"And is it part of your method to strike so much fear in your quarry's hearts that you put them on the run?" A low whistle came from the other end of the phone.

"Oh-oh, David. Sounds like you've got it bad. I warned you to stay away from her. She'll bring you nothin' but trouble."

"You didn't answer my question! Is she going to be safer somewhere else if your acquaintance sends her packing because of his threatening phone calls?"

Hugh attempted to calm him down. "Let me remind you that we're the ones on the side of law and order, and she's the one who's messing with trouble big-time. My acquaintance merely wishes to warn her about the real danger she is in, whether she stays here or moves on. But so far, she won't listen long enough to get the idea. It's only a matter of time before they close in on her, and by then it'll likely be too late to help her."

Hugh's matter-of-fact tone and the seriousness of his warning gripped David's heart. How could he help her if he didn't understand the root of the danger?

"Would you please tell me who 'they' are?" he asked beseechingly, attempting to sound patient and in control of himself.

"Yeah, but then I'd have to kill you. Ha ha, just kidding..." David was not amused. "Look, you're not going to find out from us, and I still highly recommend that you drop any personal ties you might have with your lady friend before it's too late for you, too. This is the big league..."

David made one last attempt. "You're an intelligent man. Find some other way to reach her besides threatening phone calls!"

There was a pause on the end of the line as if Hugh were considering. "Maybe you're right. Perhaps there's a better way to get in touch with her. Remember to call me if you notice anything fishy." The line went dead.

David remained lost in thought, wondering if he had helped Liz or not by intervening. It was terrible to be in the dark.

TWENTY-THREE

Of all the soccer team families he visited, Louie's and Carlos' were by far David's favorites. Though Carlos' family was much poorer than Louie's, the Lopez family showed a similar warm hospitality, and it was obvious there was a lot of love to go around. With three younger siblings at the table, the conversation was animated and amusing. When Mrs. Lopez could get a word in edgewise, she extolled the benefits of her son belonging to the team. She admitted that at first she had been concerned about the Coach requiring them to have soccer practice once a week throughout the entire year, but later she came to value how the boys devoted many of their Saturdays to works of charity. David shot Carlos a quizzical glance but kept his mouth shut for the time being. When dinner was over, David indicated that Carlos should see him to the car.

"Carlos, as the coach of this team I should know about the year-round practices..." he began as soon as they were alone.

"Aw, we were just having unofficial scrimmages, Coach. They're not really practices. I just say that to Mom so she'll let me go."

David was nonplussed by this and called him on it. "That's not what Mr. West says. He gets up at an ungodly hour every Saturday morning and sees you all out there. He says you're all pretty intense and that you're doing some amazing moves. Pity I should have to find this out from the math teacher and not the team captain..."

Carlos bit his tongue instead of observing that, after all, he was only the "titular" captain. He looked back uncomfortably at David, not knowing what to say. "Your team has done a complete turnaround, Carlos, in grades and attitude. All the teachers are talking about it. Nobody can figure out what the cause is. But I can pinpoint it right down to Jimmie Pérez!"

Carlos exclaimed, "Don't. You can't! Jimmie's gotta stay under-cover or everything will be ruined!"

David's eyes gleamed. Now he was getting somewhere. "Funny that you're so concerned for Jimmie's welfare, when he's threatened by being on your team. It seems that he's the only one not getting any personal benefit from your secret projects."

"We're not doing him any harm, Coach!" Carlos objected.

David came back strong and hard: "That's what you think! He's risking his life by his plan to improve all of your lives."

Carlos frowned. "What do you mean, Coach?"

David pressed his point. "Are you aware that Mr. Foster was murdered?"

Carlos' eyes grew big. "Wow! No, I didn't know."

"And are you aware that the same people who killed Mr. Foster would do the same to the rest of the Fosters?"

Carlos shook his head. "But how do you know?"

"It doesn't matter, does it?" David countered sharply. "What matters is that their lives are endangered, and you and your team are only making matters worse.

Carlos responded nobly, "Honest, Coach, we didn't know. What do you want us to do? Call everything off? Break up the team? I'll support you if it'll help the Fosters."

This kind of statement was just what David was waiting for. "No, I don't think we need to do that, at least not for now. But there is a way you could help me help Jimmie."

The boy's eyes lit up. "What? I'd do anything for him. He's my best friend."

David leaned forward, lowering his voice. "Jimmie doesn't know it, but I think he's adopted by both parents, not just one." Carlos looked shocked. "At least the Fosters adopted his older brother, Santiago, from Manuel and Maria Paz Pérez in Ft. Lancaster. There's no record at all of a Jimmie, although he's got the same last name."

"Um, Coach? Your Spanish isn't too good, is it?" Carlos tried to say this politely but couldn't resist a big smile.

"Why do you ask?"

"It's just that Santiago is James in English, and Jimmie is short for James..."

David inhaled sharply. He hit his forehead in annoyance.

"Well, that raises even more questions."

He thought to himself that Jimmie couldn't possibly be twenty-three years old...

"All the more reason to find this Pérez couple so they can tell us something about their child and why they gave him up for adoption. Can I count on you to help me locate them? Obviously, I don't think we should tell Jimmie anything until we find out more, because his mother likely wouldn't approve of our investigating his true parents. You know how she is."

The boy nodded emphatically to both questions. He struggled to be tactful with his own request. "Only I think you should let me handle this, Coach. I bet I would have a much better chance of finding out something than you."

David's face registered surprise. "Why?"

"We're looking for Mexicans. I'm Mexican, and I know my people. It would be easier to hide something from you than from me. We don't always give truthful answers to gringo strangers who come asking nosy questions about fellow Mexicans, especially if they're poor and maybe in the country illegally. Trust me. I know. Just give me time, and I'll find them. I'll start making trips over there on the weekends."

"Trips? Wouldn't one be enough?" David couldn't imagine what Carlos would do there.

"Coach, if you want to find out the answer, you have to be patient. Trust me. Just give me time and I'll find out."

Ft. Lancaster's parish hall of St. Francis left much to be desired: poor lighting and paint chipping from yellowed walls. It was furnished only with plywood tables on rickety, folding metal legs. But the parishioners didn't seem to mind. At least they enjoyed their get-togethers there after the 10:00 Spanish Mass. The food was always tasty, homemade by the same group of ladies every Sunday. Carlos was relishing his second bowlful of menudo in the corner with his newfound friends. The first time he met them a month ago, he had told them he had crossed the desert to enter the country and was looking for someone who would hire him without his papers being in order. They sympathized with him and welcomed him into their group. All seemed to be going well that morning until Coach David walked into the room. Being tall and the only gringo, he was very conspicuous.

Carlos groaned to himself, "He's going to ruin everything!" In fact, they had arrived together some hours ago, but David had left him on the edge of town, saying he would wait there for him. Carlos had appreciated the ride, since the other three times he had traveled hours on a dusty bus to get there. Apparently, however, David had grown impatient with waiting and decided to act on his own. He stepped up to the counter and requested a bowl of stew. Next, he moved to a table already full of people and sat down at the end. Carlos' friend, Pedro, nudged his eight-year-old cousin, Juanito, to figure out what the newcomer wanted, so off he went.

Meanwhile, all eyes were on David to see how he liked the "stew." He dipped in his spoon and brought it to his mouth, biting down on what he thought was a chunk of meat—but it squished under his teeth like a lump of fat. Trying to control his features, he asked the woman next to him what he was eating. She told him it was called menudo, knowing full well he would have no clue what that was.

The parishioners were amused. It was rare indeed that people not raised on this dish could eat it without showing disgust.

David pointed to another hunk of faux meat and asked, "And can you tell me what this is?"

The woman smiled innocently and replied, "Cow intestine. Do you like it?"

David suddenly realized that many amused eyes were upon him. Gulping, he replied, "Yeah," and took another spoonful. He knew he would have to eat the entire bowl in order not to offend the cooks, but it was going to be hard. "Hey, I'm looking for the parents of a boy named Santiago Pérez, who was given up for adoption by them about sixteen years ago. Their names are Manuel and Maria Paz. Would you have any idea if they still live here?"

His interlocutor's friendly eyes cooled noticeably. Though her English had seemed fine, she said in Spanish that she didn't understand his question.

Undeterred, David patiently took out a piece of paper and slowly stumbled his way along: "Busco Manuel y Maria Paz Pérez, los padres de Santiago Pérez, un niño que dejaron adoptar..."

She interrupted, answering once more in Spanish that she didn't understand, and then she excused herself and left the table. The other people at the table added that they didn't know the couple either.

Taking a deep breath, David gulped down the rest of his menudo, and then stood up and began to make his way from table to table, asking in bad Spanish whether anyone knew the whereabouts of Santiago's parents.

Juanito reported back excitedly to Pedro. "He's looking for Manuel and Maria Paz, the parents of Santiago Pérez!" The glint in their eyes showed their amusement at David's search.

Pedro commented to Carlos quietly, "He's never going to find them. There's not a single person in the room who will give them away." Carlos' heart jumped. They knew something! But he would have to be careful not to seem too eager to find out.

"Too bad for him." But his laugh and smile transmitted that he identified with them. "Are they or Santiago in the country illegally and this man thinks he's going to catch them just by asking around for them?"

Pedro shook his head. "No, no. It's not that…" Carlos did his best to appear only mildly interested. "It's that Santiago's been dead now for almost seventeen years. He died when he was only six years old."

Carlos tried a question. "What did he die of?"

"Double pneumonia. The problem was that his parents got nervous about the way one of the hospital doctors, who didn't like immigrants, was treating their son. This doctor said there was no hope, so they took him out of the hospital. That same doctor warned that if their son died, he would send the police after them for removing him from the hospital. He said he could put them both into jail for negligence—or send them back across the border."

Coach David was nearing the third row of tables, just one more before he reached Carlos' corner. He hoped David wouldn't arrive before the story was finished.

"Weren't they worried about bringing their child home when he was so sick?"

Pedro replied emphatically, "Of course they were! But then this nice Canadian doctor named Foster realized what was going on at the hospital and told the parents as they were leaving that he would come to their home for free and treat the boy, no questions asked. He tried really hard to save Santiago, giving him free medicine. But Santiago died anyway."

"The poor parents! On top of that, they must have been worried about the threats from the other doctor."

"You got it. But then this same kind doctor, Foster, offered a weird solution. He volunteered to adopt the boy even though he was already dead, saying that in that way he would take the blame if the authorities discovered he had died!"

Carlos' couldn't hide his shock. "What! You can't do that!"

Pedro and Juanito laughed knowingly. It was the perfect encouragement for them to go on with their tale. At this point, Juanito interjected, speaking rapidly. He was proud to have something significant to say.

"It was my big brother who pretended to be Santiago in court. Dr. Foster paid him good money for acting like he wanted to be adopted by him and his wife and for saying he didn't want to stay with Manuel and Maria Paz... who weren't even his parents anyway..."

Carlos made no effort to hide his amazement and amusement. "That's incredible!"

"Yeah, Dr. Foster was a good man! Nobody ever inquired about Santiago, because his death was never officially registered. And now this guy is the third one to come around looking for his parents in the last year!"

Carlos raised his eyebrows. "Are they worried about so much interest?"

The boys smirked, and then Pedro assured him: "C'mon. Do you think anybody is going to give them away? Besides, Pérez is the most popular name around..."

The little boy piped up once more: "I'm Juanito Pérez! There are tons of me!" Pedro ruffled his hair affectionately, while Juanito offered: "Do you want to see Santiago's gravestone?"

Of course he did, but Carlos replied calmly as if he were considering whether he would go or not. "Okay. But it's not too far away, is it?"

They left before David reached their corner of the room.

TWENTY-FOUR

Chance encounters with Liz were few and far between once David's little informant had been decommissioned. There was the odd time they would happen to meet on Sundays, but Liz had studiously avoided attending the 8:30 Mass regularly after their first encounter there—and she changed where they sat each time so that she could leave without even speaking to him when they did happen to coincide.

Come fall, David was happy to be coaching Mikey's volleyball team. It didn't matter that they always lost. He would usually hang around after the games when Liz stayed to practice with her son. Mrs. Luciotti would help Stefano, too. Jackie would join in, as well as some of the other boys on the team and their parents as well. At times it amounted to a friendly family game.

When the Fosters were ready to leave, David always walked Liz to the car. The first time he did this, Jackie and Mikey reached the car along with them and then waited inside while David and Liz chatted pleasantly for a few moments. The next time, Jackie and Mikey didn't happen to come right away, so David got to be alone with Liz for a little longer. From then on, it worked out that they would have a good twenty minutes together before Liz would call for her children to come. He was careful not to "chase" her in any sense of the word; he was happy just to have the opportunity to spend some time with her. Both of them enjoyed these conversations and looked forward to them although neither mentioned this to the other.

When the winter season came along, Jackie's presence on the varsity basketball team provided perfect occasions for casual interchanges between the two, since the varsity boys, whom he coached, generally played their games right after the girls. There was nothing odd about Coach David showing up early for the girls' game and joining the parents in the crowd. In fact, the Luciottis and other parents of the boys' team did just that. It was a pleasant moment for socializing between the adults as they watched, discussed, and cheered for their children.

Ever alert to opportunity, Mikey did his best to capitalize on these occurrences. Although he had been expressly forbidden to scheme with Coach David over meeting up with his mother, it didn't go against his conscience for Mikey to enlist the help of others in his place. Jackie and Mrs. Luciotti proved up to the task. Being a close friend of Liz's by now, it was natural for the two mothers to sit together, and when

Coach David came on the scene Mrs. Luciotti would often invite him to join them. Once he had done so, she soon absented herself for good chunks of time, ostensibly for the purpose of purchasing food from the concession stand. Being warm and likeable, it was easy for her to stop on her way there and back to chat with different people. Thus David and Liz spent precious moments together.

Jackie devised the plan to bring her mother and David together for dinner at the Luciottis. It had to be one of the rare times when the boys played first. During the girls' game, Mikey stealthily reached into his mother's purse to take the car keys without her noticing. Soon afterwards, he left the gym for a short period of time with the excuse of using the restroom, slipping the car keys back into the purse upon his return.

Liz had already accepted an invitation for her and her children to join the Luciottis for dinner at their home after the game, and she had given permission to both Mikey and Jackie to walk there since it was only a few blocks away. They had already left when Liz reached her car. David had accompanied her and was already walking away but stopped to look back when he didn't hear the engine start up. Though she was turning the key in the ignition, there was no response. David offered to check under the hood and immediately spotted the problem: no spark plugs. He smiled to himself, recalling Jackie's surmise that Miss Townsend had faked her car breaking down to be able to spend time with him. He was positive something would happen soon, and so he just tinkered around, pretending to be looking for the problem.

Sure enough, Liz's cell phone rang: it was Mrs. Luciotti wondering why Liz hadn't arrived yet. When she heard that Coach David was there, she asked to speak to him directly and invited him to join them all for dinner. Her husband had a knack with cars and would be sure to fix Liz's in no time after the meal. Beaming, David accepted and conveyed Mrs. Luciotti's message to Liz, who was too well-mannered to object.

On the way there, David gently raised the matter of Jackie's unofficial place on the volleyball team.

"Liz, I've been meaning to ask you if Jackie could be officially registered on the team so that she could play in case they make it to the play-offs."

She frowned and answered softly, "It would be better that she stay off the list for now. She's only a freshman and isn't the most outstanding player anyway."

That was true. However, David had to add the qualifier: "Yet. She's not one of the best players *yet...*"

Liz kept her face and tone free of any emotion, choosing to respond dryly: "Quite right. However, I'm content to cross each bridge as it comes. Who knows what the future holds and where we'll be next year?" David didn't like the way that sounded but held his tongue. "Right now my family needs to stay under the radar." He would have liked to ask her to expand on that statement, but they arrived at the Luciottis, and Liz got out of the car immediately.

Mrs. Luciotti outdid herself on the food. The meal and conversation was agreeable for everyone, though something uncanny happened once dessert was done. One by one, everyone but Liz and David left the room. Mikey and Stefano were the first to run off to work on model airplanes. Jimmie headed back home by bike to work on some project he had going. Mr. Luciotti took Louie with him to go fix Liz's car, and Jackie disappeared into the kitchen to work on some concoction, while Mrs. Luciotti puttered around in there as well.

When everyone was gone but David and Liz, he grinned from ear to ear, commenting playfully, "I'm innocent!" She favored him with a becoming smile. What else could she do? Although she did her best to avoid running into David, she savored any moments they did happen to spend together. Besides, she felt safe with him there in the Luciotti's home, and he was careful to avoid any thorny issues. Thus, they whiled away the time very pleasantly alone together in the living room. It seemed that they had so many things to talk about and that they agreed on a great number of things, and yet they were both quite free to voice their differences energetically but respectfully. Both of them were surprised to discover how late it was when Mr. Luciotti drove up in her car with Louie following behind in his own.

It was Jackie who masterminded the plan to bring the two together again through the Angel for a Day service project hosted in December by the parish for poor children. The event consisted of thirty volunteer high school students, mainly enlisted by Jimmie and his sister, each adopting a needy child for the day. There was time for group games, and then the "angels" helped the children string beads for rosaries; after praying the Rosary as a group, they all trooped over to a movie theater together, followed by lots of pizza. It ended with each of the children receiving a nice gift, which local businesses had donated to their "angels."

Jimmie had originally asked Mr. and Mrs. Luciotti to be the chaperones, and they had agreed; however, at the last minute, Mrs. Luciotti asked Liz to take her place and Mr. Luciotti separately asked David to fill in for him. Neither David nor Liz realized that they were cosponsoring the event until the morning it took place. David blissfully claimed innocence again, and Liz shook her head in amusement. The Luciottis were not going to fool her again, but in the meantime she accepted the chance to enjoy his company for the day, and he made the most of it, rarely straying from her side. During one of the few moments they were apart, Jackie came up to David as he was putting the furniture back.

Obviously bursting with news, she began: "Guess what, Coach?"

He smiled down at this feisty girl. "What?"

She made a face and countered: "Don't you want to guess?"

He answered amiably as he continued to fix the chairs, "No."

She was nonplussed at his lack of enthusiasm. "Of all people, Miss Townsend is engaged!" She thought he would be at least slightly impressed to hear this, but she was to be disappointed.

"So, at last you find out what some of us have known for months!"

Jackie uttered a little shriek of disgust. "So you knew already! Did you know when we spoke about her?" There was an accusing edge in her voice, as if he had wronged her by not informing her.

"We did not speak about her. You spoke about her at me, if I remember correctly."

"But if you knew, then why didn't you just tell me?" She couldn't believe he hadn't shared his knowledge with her.

"It wasn't my business. Something like that is for Miss Townsend to share when she's good and ready."

"But what's wrong with sharing that information? It doesn't hurt anyone. It's good news, isn't it?"

David replied patiently as he set one more chair straight: "Sure… but she's also free to keep things to herself if she so chooses, isn't she?"

That was enough for Jackie. She uttered a disdainful "Men!" and strode off in a huff.

At the end of the day, everyone left in a good mood. The children were happy with the fun they'd had, the gifts they'd received, and their new friends. The volunteers were even happier. Theirs was a deep satisfaction that comes from helping those in need. Liz and David were glad that the day went off without a hitch, but above all that they had spent it in each other's company. Once everyone was gone—except for Mikey, who was dutifully waiting in the car, playing with his Game Boy—David looked over at Liz as they packed up the last of the leftover food items together.

"Would I spoil the day by speaking of my affection for you?"

She gave him a severe look, but answered gently, "Yes. Please don't!"

He sighed deeply, and they finished packing in silence. Then, with a meek "Thank you!" she was gone.

In late February, as the basketball season was drawing to a close, a tall, distinguished gentleman dressed in a suit showed up at Jackie's basketball game. He paid the fee at the door, but then stood still, scanning the stands for Liz. When she noticed him, she turned pale and shuddered, then rose and walked stiffly to meet him.

David had been sitting at her side. On seeing her reaction to the stranger, he also got up and followed behind her at a short distance. The two left the building and spoke in low tones in the parking lot. David watched them, unsure whether to approach or not, but when he heard Liz's voice suddenly rise shrilly, he hastened to her side. Wrapping his arm around her protectively, he addressed the man gruffly: "I don't believe we've met before. I'm Coach Johnston."

The man must have been close to fifty in age. His short black hair, lightly peppered with gray, matched the color of his neatly trimmed beard and mustache. He looked David over before responding coolly. "Dr. Pearson: I'm Jimmie's father."

This was the last thing David expected to hear; Jimmie had always maintained that his father was in heaven. His mind reeled, wondering what manner of man this might be whom Liz would conceal from her son. "I was merely inquiring about my personal rights over my son, which Ms. Foster has steadfastly trodden over for all these years. She's very good at running."

David felt Liz leaning against him for support but when he turned to see her reaction her face was expressionless. Her eyes were fixed on the man, who continued in the same accusing, cold tone. "I was also warning Liz that her life and that of all her children, including my son Jimmie, are in serious danger. She knows the remedy but seems to find the medicine too bitter to her taste. Perhaps you would be better at convincing her to seek real safety and finish with her futile flights."

David looked from one to another. Each of them was trying

to stare the other down. Seconds ticked by. At last the man looked away. "You know where to find me when you're ready, which would be better sooner than too late..." Nodding curtly at David, he walked across the playing field and his retreating figure soon blended into the night.

As soon as he was out of sight, it was as if Liz came to. She quickly extricated herself from his arm and stood for a moment with her eyes closed, breathing in deeply, almost forgetting David's presence. He felt a hot rage washing over him as he experienced the passionate desire to protect her and a powerlessness and frustration at being shut out when it was obvious she needed help. He fired questions at her.

"Liz, what was that all about? What kind of trouble are you in? Does Jimmie realize that his father is alive? Doesn't he have the right to know him?"

Liz's eyes shot open. She replied emphatically, "No!"

He presumed her answer was to his last question. "Why not? Don't father and son have a right to know each other? Or is this man malicious? I'd like to pound him!"

Liz looked away from his eyes. "I can't tell you anything until Jimmie knows his own story. He needs to hear it from me, not this man, or you, or anyone else."

He barked back, "Then tell him!"

She shook her head. "Jimmie needs some more time before he would be ready to hear his whole story."

David objected, not too kindly, "You don't seem to have a lot of time on your hands."

That was enough. Between the meeting with Dr. Pearson and David's angry pressure, Liz felt overwhelmed. Tears burst forth. David relented a little. "I'm sorry. I didn't mean to make things worse for you. I just want to help you, and I feel so helpless to do anything that it drives me crazy!" He put his hands on her shoulders and rubbed them but didn't pull her close as he was longing to do.

"David, I need to tell Jimmie, for his sake. I can't explain why, though I wish I could."

He answered softly, soothingly, without thinking, "Okay. You tell him."

She looked into his eyes pleadingly. "Do you give your word?"

He checked himself. This scene was similar to the first time he met her. "Only if you'll promise to tell him soon."

"Yes. Yes!"

"Then, on that condition, I'm willing to wait a while." He later kicked himself for capitulating so readily. But she was so distraught, so worked up, that he gave his promise without even requiring that she specify when she would tell her son.

Visibly relieved, Liz thanked him sweetly, then warned him, "Dr. Pearson is right about my danger. You would do well to have nothing more to do with me." She turned on her heels and headed back into the gym.

David, however, stood still, full of anguish at his incapacity to do anything to help her. Suddenly he began sprinting across the field after the man. As he reached the street, he heard the sound of a nearby car door shutting lightly. The interior lights of the car had not gone on. Forgetting all caution, David lunged at the passenger door and yanked it open. Sure enough, there was his man—and in the driver's seat sat Hugh. Dr. Pearson gasped slightly and pulled back from the door, while looking to his companion for guidance.

Unperturbed by David's brusque action, Hugh greeted him as cordially as ever, "David. How ya doing? This is a mutual acquaintance of Liz and mine. But it looks like you've already met."

David had no use for any small talk. "What's going on? What are you trying to do to Liz? Aren't you supposed to be on the side of the law?"

Dr. Pearson adjusted his seat to lean further back, in order to distance himself from the exchange between the other two men. Perhaps he intuited David's urge to drive his fist into the man's face.

"Now, David, I can understand that from your point of view it doesn't look too good. But we have powerful reasons for trying to convince Mrs. Foster to cooperate freely with us." Hugh hurried on before David could interrupt. "We've recently heard that a group that has ties with her has been making overtures to some international terrorist rings. Once they find her, we can't guarantee her safety."

David's face registered shock. But after a moment's reflection, he persisted. "If she's aware of that, then why won't she listen to you?"

Hugh chuckled. "You seem to be on pretty good terms with the lady, but haven't you realized that she's headstrong? Have you succeeded in winning over her trust? Because if so, I'd be happy to take some lessons from you! We can't even successfully engage her in a simple conversation." He looked to the man at his side to share in his amusement, but Dr. Pearson didn't smile back. He clearly wasn't comfortable with David looming over his head. "You would be doing her and her children a huge favor if you could convince her to listen to us soon!"

"Why can't you arrest the members of this group?" asked David.

Now Hugh really laughed. "You think my job's easy? Suspicions aren't enough. We need to catch them with their fingers in the pie and have usable evidence to shut them down. And that ain't no piece of cake, let me tell you! Do you know how many times we Feds have arrested bad guys only to have to set them loose again because of some minor slipup on our part? In any case, we've got great hopes of getting somewhere through your friend. They're gonna find her sooner or later—and they're lookin' real hard."

David's blood congealed at the thought. Hugh started the car while David stared at him glumly. "If you can get anywhere with this dame, give us a call. You have our number!"

The door was still wide open. David wasn't holding onto any part of the car, so Hugh slowly inched it forward until Dr. Pearson could freely shut the door. They drove off slowly without putting on the headlights.

TWENTY-FIVE

Jackie stood on the sidelines, considering the scene before her with a meditative eye. It was over nine months since her brother had proposed his preposterous plan to the motley excuse for a team, and now, on the last early Saturday morning practice before their first game, they looked unbeatable. All of them, including Louie, were in top physical condition. Given their new personal motivation and focus, they had succeeded in developing their own abundant natural talent, which was heightened still more by her brother's vector theory. But above all, what made them so outstanding was their unity and teamwork. Little by little, their group studies, volunteer work, regular practices and moments of fun together had forged unbreakable bonds of friendship between them.

Each of them had mastered a short, middle, and long-range kick that would go a very precise distance. Based on the length and timing of each kick, the team next had learned running patterns and elaborate plays to move the ball from one end of the field to the other. That's where Jackie came in. Since her brother couldn't appear to be guiding the show, and since she herself had the genius capacity for mental arithmetic, her job was to stand on the sidelines partway up the field, applying the vector theory and calling out the corresponding number sequences of steps for the forwards to run. She was willing to try, although it was a tall order. They didn't need her all of the time, but she could help out with the more difficult plays.

Mr. West happened to be walking his beagle again that morning, as usual. He seemed to be the only person to regularly observe their early morning presence, though he never greeted them nor seemed to pay them any attention at all. On this day, however, he twisted his head and looked piercingly at Jackie right after she called out a set of numbers for Roberto to follow. She noticed his reaction and went running anxiously to Jimmie.

"Mr. West is watching us again! He just stared right at me!" she whispered nervously.

Jimmie patted her arm in his kind, brotherly way. "Don't sweat it, Jacks. He's not gonna bother us. What does he care that we're out here? He's never said anything before. C'mon. We need you for the next play too."

She wasn't satisfied. "But Jimmie, I promise you that he was watching me suspiciously! He makes me feel so uneasy!" Though she was deliberately speaking quietly to Jimmie alone, Nick overheard. He couldn't resist teasing her.

"Do you think he's planning a secret crime involving you, Jackie? Don't worry! We'll protect you!" Seeing that Josh and Roberto were perking up and heading over to learn what was going on, Jackie gave up and ran back to her place.

"Oh, just forget it!" she exclaimed, trying unsuccessfully to seem indifferent at not being taken seriously.

A very reduced group of fans, including the Luciottis and Liz, showed up for the first game since it was so early in the season. Liz hoped the team would turn out to be of little account as it had the season before. But she was bitterly disappointed. Within minutes, they scored a goal from a corner kick. Jimmie shot the ball from the corner, while six of his teammates scattered in a seemingly disordered fashion. The ball soared over the majority of the players' heads and was met by Nick's head, who tipped it in effortlessly.

Five minutes later, Roberto tore down the sidelines to receive a long pass from Andre. The defense was caught by surprise and rushed back, but Roberto shot the ball into the corner of the goal before they could reach him. Eight minutes after that, Carlos, Jorge, and Miguel took the ball right down the center of the field, kicking the ball between them. Their passes were exact, and they wove in and out so smoothly that they almost seemed like dancing performers. They made it all the way to the goalie, where Carlos tapped the ball in for the third goal.

Liz watched all this with growing dismay. Little did she know that the players, their coach, the Luciottis, and her own children were watching her closely for her reaction. They were hoping she wouldn't mind the victory since Jimmie was playing defense and had barely touched the ball so far. In fact, throughout the rest of the game, he would prove to be the most expendable of all players. No more goals were scored on either side, although the Chargers clearly dominated the game. It was just as well that Liz didn't know this was one of the better teams. She left to bring the car around before it ended.

Soon the whole school was ablaze with news of the steady victories. Just like the first game, the usual scenario was for the team to score three goals early in the first half of the game, and then to lighten up somewhat. Jimmie had convinced his teammates that it wasn't necessary to completely trounce the other teams, reminding them of how much it hurt for them to lose by too much. If the other side happened to score a goal, which was rare, then another goal was "permissible" to maintain the solid lead of three. It was hard to pick out the most outstanding players on the team since they rotated positions and everyone scored goals—except of course, for Jimmie, who always remained on defense.

None of them made any attempt to offer an explanation for their amazing turnaround to their coach. He, in turn, was content merely to take everything in for the time being. In any case, he already knew the source of their success.

David had his chance a month after the first game. He was turning onto the main street when he spotted Jimmie heading home on his bike. Pulling his car alongside Jimmie, he called out: "Let me give you a ride since it's raining."

Jimmie smiled back graciously: "That's okay, Coach, it's only drizzling. I don't mind."

David, however, insisted: "There are some things I'd like to talk about with you, and now is as good a time as any!" Jimmie acquiesced, though not without trepidation. It wasn't hard to guess what

Coach wanted to talk about. In no time, his bike was lashed to the roof of the car and they headed off.

David wasted no time. "I'd just like to know when you're planning to fill me in about how the team suddenly became so outstanding?"

Jimmie smiled. "I wasn't planning on it…" he responded lightly.

"Well, at least you're being honest," conceded David. "But really, don't you think I deserve to know something—since I am your coach, after all?" Jimmie remained silent for a moment, then tried an evasive tactic.

"Coach, what does it really matter as long as we're doing better? I mean, we're not causing harm to anyone or getting into any trouble. In fact, did you notice that none of the players were suspended this year for anything?" He tried to sound chipper. But David was undeterred.

"Certainly. And I know about everyone's grades, too. It's unbelievable. All part of the wonderful but big mystery that I'm hoping you'll help me solve."

The boy took a deep breath, while racking his mind for a way to soften the negative he was to give. "Sorry, Coach, but I've got nothing to tell you."

David was unwilling to let him off so easily.

"Jimmie, I've already had three scouts from good universities call me." Jimmie's face brightened. "Not only are they planning to come out here to see the team, but they're dying to know the secret of my success. What am I supposed to tell them?"

Jimmie readily assured him. "You're more than welcome to take the glory for how well we're doing. You're a great coach."

David gave him a questioning look. "There's no way I'm going to claim any glory! That would be the height of dishonesty."

Jimmie shrugged his shoulders. "Well, tell them what you know. Wouldn't it be sufficient to say something like it seems that the students have chosen to improve their lives? Maybe you could add that our good fellowship has been decisive." The entire time he kept his voice calm and steady. He seemed imperturbable. By now, the car was already a good distance out of town on the lonely road leading to the Foster home. David pulled over and stopped so he could fix his eyes on Jimmie and play his biggest trump card.

"I also know that you and your siblings have been tutoring the team for almost a year now and that you're the one who's taught them the amazing moves every Saturday morning, even though you hide your talent during games. You're always on the defense. Should I say that as well?"

Shock registered on Jimmie's countenance, but only for a moment. He quickly gained control of his features. "I'd rather you didn't for personal reasons," he responded placidly. "But it doesn't even matter that much. The team can make it now without me." An easygoing answer was the last thing David had expected. After all, he was bluffing in order to get Jimmie to open up. He peered at the boy searchingly. Jimmie met his gaze resolutely.

"You mean, you're ready to up and leave just like that, no big deal?"

Jimmie shrugged his shoulders. "We're used to it. We were on the go for eight months before settling here. But don't get me wrong. It's been nice while it lasted. Anyway, it's no surprise that we'll have to move on soon."

"What do you mean?" The tables had turned on David; now he was the one who was shaken up.

"Mom has been warning us that we'll be leaving soon, so your calling attention to my talents wouldn't speed up our departure by much."

At such terrible news, David couldn't hold back a cry of dismay. "No!"

His passenger looked surprised. "But why not? We've been here for much longer than we've ever been anywhere else. I mean, we all like it here and all, but what's the big deal?"

David gazed down the road morosely, pondering whether or not to admit his love for Liz to her son. Kind of awkward, but instinctively he knew he could trust the boy. Jimmie better than anyone else would understand.

"Do you remember how I lost my temper last season because your Mom was driving me crazy and you stuck up for her? Well, now she's driving me crazy in a different kind of way..."

Jimmie's eyes widened as he mouthed the word, "Oh."

"If you pull out of town now, what are the chances of my seeing her again?" Jimmie's expression and shake of the head confirmed David's fears.

Neither spoke for a moment, each lost in his thoughts. The young boy felt compassion for his coach. He grasped without being told how David could have fallen for his mom and how she would have kept him at a distance. Jimmie even felt a twinge of guilt, knowing his mother's diffidence was rooted in her complete dedication to protecting her eldest son from a danger he couldn't fathom because she kept him in the dark about it.

Meanwhile, David was wondering whether there was some way he could dissuade Liz from leaving. But on what grounds and when?

Almost as if he were thinking aloud, he commented, "Do you know how hard it is to get near her? I've been invited for dinner by the family of every player on the team except yours."

Jimmie seized on the idea. If he could help his coach, he would!

"Coach, why didn't you tell me sooner? Please join us tomorrow for dinner at 6:00." He smiled sincerely at David, who blinked and stared back in disbelief. Could it really be as simple as that?

"Do you mean it? Are you able to invite me?"

Jimmie nodded confidently. "I'm the man of the house, aren't I? Trust me on this."

David started the car again and began driving. He felt dazed. Hadn't all of this started because he had been trying to help Jimmie?

David tried to go over in his mind Jimmie's responses to his earlier questions. David hadn't been able to get anywhere with him.

It did occur to him to say, "Amidst all the secrecy which surrounds your family, Jimmie, there is one thing that concerns me about you in particular. I've found out some things about your past that concern me a great deal."

That was enough to trigger Jimmie's emotions. "What? Tell me, please!"

David made a rueful face. "Unfortunately, I went and promised your mother that I would let her tell you." He added lamely, "You know how it is."

Jimmie clenched his teeth and slouched down but said nothing.

"But at least I did so on condition that she tell you soon."

The boy made no effort to dissimulate his eagerness, "When did she promise you?"

"About six weeks ago. I kicked myself afterwards for not specifying what 'soon' meant. But maybe now is the time for you to put your foot down—before you move out of this town. You could let your mom know that you'll ask me to fill you in if she won't."

Jimmie nodded curtly, avoiding the older man's gaze.

Silence reigned the rest of the ride. Each of them commiserated with the other, knowing the source of their pain was in the same woman. When they reached the Foster property, David dropped him off at the lower gate, and Jimmie headed in alone on his bike.

As soon as he was inside the house, he searched for his mother. Popping his head in his brother's room, he addressed the reading figure without so much as a "hello."

"Where's Mom, Mikey?" Mikey noticed a certain tension in his big brother's tone and expression.

He answered affectionately, "Hi, Jimmie! She's in the lab. You wanna try something challenging?" But his last sentence was lost. Jimmie was already descending the stairs two at a time on his way to the barn. He found his mother cleaning up the counter and petri dishes.

"Hi, Mom!"

She gave him a welcoming smile. "You're home earlier than usual."

"Yeah. Coach Johnston gave me a ride home because it's raining."

She smiled again. "That was kind of him!" She went back to cleaning.

Jimmie got up his nerve and blurted out:

"I found out that we're the only home on the team that Coach hasn't visited yet, so I invited him for dinner tomorrow night."

Liz sucked in her breath in surprise. Their eyes locked. Jimmie kept his gaze unbending under her sharp gaze. To his surprise, she gave in without a fight. "Very well."

Delighted by her capitulation, he pressed further: "I want us to treat him like all our other guests, including showing him the lab."

In response, Liz threw out her arms in exasperation and exclaimed, "Certainly not. It's too much of a risk already just to have him here on our property!"

She had been taken aback at Jimmie's invitation to David and had conceded, but this was going too far. Her son was undaunted.

"I share this project with you, and I say Coach Johnston is just as trustworthy, if not more, than all of those other people."

She flashed back: "That's not the point. He's from around here and knows too much about us already. I won't have him in here." Never had her son defied her before. She didn't know what more she could say and do to convince him not to bring David inside. Jimmie didn't budge.

"I'm sorry, Mom, but I'm planning on letting him in." Liz suddenly felt deflated. She relied on her son completely. How could she stop him? Without another word, she left the lab, slamming the door behind her.

Seconds later, Mikey popped his head through his hole in the floor. "Wow, Jimmie. Mom sure was mad!"

A bemused big brother gazed benevolently down at his little brother and chided gently, "You shouldn't have listened in on our conversation, Mikey. That's rude!"

The young boy made an attempt to look contrite. "Sorry, Jimmie. But you made me so curious the way you asked for Mom. Anyway, I'm glad Coach is coming for dinner!" In fact he could barely contain his glee. "Okay, Jimmie, hold out your hands and close your eyes and you will get an extraordinary surprise."

Jimmie reminded himself that Liz had asked him to be a father to Mikey when their dad passed away. He crouched down by the trapdoor, closed his eyes, and obediently extended his arms. He felt cold metal around his wrists at the same time as he heard two snaps. Sure enough, there he was, handcuffed. He patiently sat down Indian-style.

"What's up, Mikey? You're not the type to play cops and robbers."

Mikey looked full of self-importance. "Certainly not! These cuffs have a secret release clasp. You need to beat Jackie, who has the fastest time so far. She got out in six minutes. Mom took ten minutes, but it wasn't fair because she was in the middle of cooking dinner and was distracted. I helped her stir the meat, but it's not the same. Stefano still hasn't figured them out even though I've cuffed him the last two times we've gone to the Luciotti's."

"Shh. Don't talk to me." It took Jimmie three and a half minutes. Mikey cheered triumphantly.

"The boys beat the girls. You did it in almost half of Jackie's time! I knew you'd win! By the way, I fixed the latch on this door so now you can open it from your side. Do you want to learn how to do it?" Chuckling at his brother's enthusiasm, Jimmie bent down and submitted to a demonstration.

TWENTY-SIX

Jackie was waiting for David at the gate below. She jumped into his car unceremoniously, then chatted away excitedly as they pulled around the curve towards her house.

"We all told Mom that you have to be given the full treatment just the same as everyone else!" She sounded proud of the fact, so David concluded this must be something good, at least in her eyes. "And that includes going to the barn! Jimmie's the one who insisted on it. He's never argued with Mom about anything until now. I'm the one who does that… but he did over your getting to see everything!"

David kept his curiosity in check. It seemed he was soon to find out what made the Foster barn extraordinary. "So when the offer comes, no matter how it's put, be sure to agree to go see it or you'll ruin everything."

"All right, Jackie."

He wasn't given the opportunity to say more, as Jackie went on breezily, "Something's up with Mikey: he's been moping around all afternoon! He's never acted that way before. I think something happened at school… Mom would normally have noticed by now, but she's been so busy cooking all day for you and arguing with Jimmie that she hasn't yet. Mom's put on her prettiest dress and perfume. She hasn't used either since Dad died."

David couldn't help smiling at that tidbit: very encouraging.

"Anyway, Mikey's happy you're here even if he doesn't show it too much." Good warning. He would have been surprised if his little buddy was out of sorts.

They pulled up to the front of the house. Jackie jumped out of the car and dashed up the stairs two by two. "Oops! I gotta warn Mom you're here, because she's expecting to hear the buzzer from the gate below…" She vanished into the house, while he waited at the door to be received by her mother. Liz appeared a minute later, looking somewhat flustered but radiantly beautiful. She had on a simple but elegant black-and-white dress.

David struggled to come up with a fitting greeting, settling for an appreciative, "You look great!"

Liz smiled cordially, thanked him for the bouquet of long-stemmed red roses, and motioned him in. As foretold by Jackie, he did get the full treatment: delicious food, pleasant conversation, and then mother and children entertained him at the end of the meal by playing for him. Mikey was the only damper. He hardly spoke during the meal, though it was evident he was delighted to welcome David. Once the music was over, he whispered to his mother that he would like to go to bed early because he wasn't feeling well. A few minutes after he had gone upstairs, Liz excused herself to David.

"If you'll forgive me for a few minutes, I think I should go check on Mikey. His moping worries me since he's not like this usually. I think it would be good for me to check on him before he falls asleep."

"Of course! Take your time. I hope he'll be okay!" Jimmie excused himself too as soon as his mother left the room.

"Please tell Mom I'll be waiting for the both of you in the barn. I need to go set up…" Jackie made a face at David to agree, and he complied.

"Certainly! Thank you." Now just Jackie and David were left together, but then even Jackie stood up to go.

She commented enigmatically, "Coach, Mikey's room is the first one on the right when you go upstairs. The fourth and the tenth steps creak…" Without offering any explanation for abandoning him, she left the room. Though it wouldn't have occurred to him to go upstairs on his own, Jackie's words intrigued him. But what did he stand to gain? What if he offended his hostess in doing so? In the end, he didn't know why he did it, but he found himself going softly up the stairs, carefully skipping the fourth and tenth.

At the top, he could hear Liz and Mikey conversing together in low tones. Peeping into the room, he saw that Mikey was already tucked in his bed, laying on his back, and Liz was sitting by his side, lovingly stroking his forehead. Neither of them noticed David comfortably leaning against the entrance to the room with his arms crossed, watching the tender scene unfold. Liz was gently prompting her son.

"Did anything interesting or different happen at school today?"

Mikey took his time considering. "Well, I guess you could say that." She waited for him to go on. "A number of boys in my class were ridiculing someone during recess because he found no humor in an off-color joke."

Liz kept stroking his forehead. "You mean they made fun of him because he didn't get a dirty joke?"

"Precisely. In vulgar terms they kept proclaiming derisively that he must have a far inferior intelligence."

Liz looked him square in the eye. "Were you that boy?" He nodded slightly. A single tear trickled down his cheek. She wiped it away with her hand.

"Mom, I know I'm deficient at sports, so I can accept that my schoolfellows deride me for that; and I admit that I have shown social ineptitude on more than once occasion, so I can accept disparaging sobriquets in that vein; but to label me as a 'birdbrain' is utterly nonsensical!"

Hot tears now streamed out down his face. Liz took the corner of his bed sheet and wiped them away since she didn't have a Kleenex handy. At this point, David felt in his conscience that he should leave or make his presence known, but he was loathe to do either. He was mesmerized by Liz's soothing words to her son.

"Oh Mikey, I know it hurts to be made fun of, whether there's any truth or not to what others say. But you and I both know that you are definitely not a birdbrain." She smiled down at her son, wishing she could suffer in his place.

"Why are they so mean, Mom?" he asked dejectedly. She bent down and hugged her son hard.

"They don't know what they're doing or saying," she answered. "They don't realize how mean they're being. So we need to forgive them. That's what Jesus did on the cross, right? He was mocked so cruelly by the ones who had him crucified, and his answer was a prayer: 'Father, forgive them, for they know not what they do.' Mikey, people do things to hurt others because they're unhappy on the inside. You've been loved so much by God, your father and mother, and Jimmie and Jackie that you're happy on the inside." She kissed his forehead and sat back up. She had made him feel better in one way, but now he also felt guilty.

"Mom, it would have been better if I had done nothing back, right?"

She looked surprised. "Yes. We should excuse and forgive others right away in our hearts, even if it's not the right moment to forgive them out loud. Is that what you did at school today?" He made a face, and then admitted bravely:

"Not exactly. I tried out on Landon the same moves Jackie did on Josh, with more or less the same results." David didn't know what Jackie had done to Josh, but he approved. He had to hold himself back from congratulating the boy. Liz had to check a smile too.

"Christians are called to act like Christians at every moment, but most especially in trials. Jesus teaches us to turn the other cheek…"

"But, Mom, I didn't hurt him. I just stunned him into a respectful silence."

But she countered, "Landon's not going to learn how to be a Christian by being knocked to the ground, is he?"

Mikey opted for silence. Then he tried the tactic of distracting her from the issue, since he sure didn't want to have to give Landon brownies!

"Mom, I have always trusted in your indications and obeyed you and Dad when it comes to purity. I don't read bad magazines or try to see or find out things on the Internet, so I am not well-informed when it comes to that field of knowledge, while all my classmates are…"

"…And that's good!" Her words cut into his as she rubbed his arm soothingly with her hand. "Jesus promises that the pure of heart will see God. What's the good of your knowing a whole lot about something Our Lord wants you to keep for marriage? And you're not going to be married for many years yet..."

"But you have explained everything I need to know for now, right?" He looked up at her earnestly and she smiled down at him lovingly.

"Right."

He persisted, "Because it seems like the minds and hearts of an astronomical number of people are fixated on the 's' word... To be quite frank, I must admit that I'm very inquisitive over all the fuss!"

Liz replied firmly, "It's better that you focus your attention elsewhere! Let's remember what love is all about, because all these people are fixated on the wrong thing and missing out on the nature of real love."

Mikey waited expectantly for her to go on. So did David.

"Your father and I got married because we loved each other very much. And we loved each other so much that we wanted our love to last forever. We'll be together again in heaven some day... but we wanted a way to perpetuate our love in this life too. So we had you. You come right out of your Dad and Mom's love for each other. Your origin is love: your parents' love and the love of God the Father. On the other hand, so many people get confused because they look out for themselves and forget that love is a gift—and life is a gift that goes with it." She caressed his forehead now. "You, Michael P. Foster, are a wonderful gift of love."

Mikey liked being told that he was a wonderful gift of love, and lay there savoring the idea. But then he thought of his brother Jimmie.

"But Mom... does absolutely every single person have his origin in true love?" Liz answered back thoughtfully and seriously.

"If parents lack true love for each other, which sadly can happen, still a child's origin is from the love of God the Father, which never fails. But it would be better for each child to come from the love of his or her parents as well. That matches the dignity of the human person."

Mikey pushed the question further. He was suddenly on to something. "Did Jackie come from true love, too?"

Liz was about to answer yes, but she realized where he was going: that his next question would be about Jimmie. She stood up before answering, gave him a parting kiss, and replied, "Yes… but now I had better get back to our special guest. I've left him downstairs far too long!"

Mikey had spotted David in the doorway some time ago, but he realized his mother had not. He asked her one last question before she turned away. "Mom, do you think you could ever love anyone again now that Dad's in heaven?"

David coughed discreetly, since that was going too far. He didn't want Liz to be embarrassed, although he would have liked to hear her candid answer. When Liz took in his presence and realized he must have been there some time, she was disconcerted.

"Coach Johnston! Do you make it a habit of eavesdropping on your host's private conversations?" she asked in icy tones.

David sheepishly apologized. "No, not ordinarily. I'm sorry. That was rude of me as your guest! It's just that I got so wrapped up in what you were saying that I forgot I was uninvited… I guess it's partly because I feel so much at home in the company of you both."

Mikey piped up encouragingly, "That's okay, Coach. I don't mind!" as the two adults left his room. Somehow, Liz really didn't mind either, though she kept that to herself. He did seem to fit right in….

TWENTY-SEVEN

David took the stairs ahead of Liz. Halfway down he turned around, put his arm against the wall, and remarked: "That whole scene was beautiful!" He paused to look her in the eyes. "You're beautiful!"

He might have gone further, but she ducked under his arm and hurried down the stairs.

"It's late, Coach Johnston. You should be going now." She wasn't going to get away with dismissing him so easily though.

"Jimmie insisted on showing me something in the barn. Would you mind taking me over there first?" he requested innocently.

She hesitated and then sighed deeply.

"Okay. Let me get something to drink first. Could I offer you anything?" He said no. She returned in a moment with a large glass of ice water and then hurried across the space between the house and the barn. He could hardly keep up. She offered no explanation of the edifice inside the barn, but simply held the door for him to go through.

Once inside, David looked around in wonder. He took in the beakers, test tubes, petri dishes, fancy lab equipment, and rows of cages of rats and mice.

Letting out a soft whistle, he exclaimed, "Whoa! I never would have imagined this! What are you doing in here?" Jimmie motioned him to sit on a tall lab stool at the table. There were a series of pictures and diagrams he had laid out to show him.

"Our purpose is to propagate the use of adult and amniotic stem cells for research instead of human embryonic stem cells, which requires taking the life of human persons, even if they are just in the beginning stages of life."

David found it hard to focus completely on Jimmie's words, but he immediately grasped the import of what he was saying. He nodded for Jimmie to go on.

"There are more than seventy diseases right now that are being successfully treated by adult stem cells, while human embryonic stem cells haven't provided a single cure!"

"But I've seen news on the television of cures through—what do you call them—human embryonic stem cells! The three blind mice..."

Jimmie's demeanor manifested disgust. "They were cured of their blindness, that's true. But they all got brain tumors! It's always the same problem: cancer. And as long as they get tumors along with their so-called cures, it's no real cure at all. But the media likes to cover up that part of the story! Until very recently, they deliberately kept the public from hearing about the advanced successful research that's being done using amniotic stem cells which don't have the problem of tumors!"

Liz had come up to the edge of the table and was watching David, but said nothing.

"Our fight last summer was to make the amniotic stem cells known well enough so that members of the House wouldn't expand federal funding for embryonic stem-cell research. And now we're trying to convince as many groups as possible to replicate the work that's been successful so far. That's what we do here in this lab. We pay doctors and researchers to fly in from around the country, and we teach them procedures for applying amniotic stem cell cures. Our only request in return is that they keep our anonymity so we can maintain our work, unimpeded by opposition. Our goal is to make procedures with amniotic stem cells so standard that even the press can't deny it their worth. We want to direct federal funding towards this kind of research because it doesn't involve experimentation on tiny, helpless human beings!"

David was deeply impressed. He did have one question, however. "But if what you're saying is true, and I don't doubt it, then why would people spend so much money on research that seems so useless?"

Jimmie shook his head. "I wonder about that myself. I've read articles that assert it's because many of the labs secretly wish to do therapeutic cloning—" he began.

"What's that?"

"Well, as I already said, the problem with embryonic stem cell research is cancer—but not if they wait for the baby to develop further in the mother's womb. What they want are the organs themselves from the babies. Now, in therapeutic cloning, you take a woman's egg... and remove its nucleus. Then you take any cell from your body and remove its nucleus and put it in the egg and 'activate' it electrically or chemically to get a new human being with exactly the same genetic code as your own: your clone. Then you let the baby develop until the organs are big enough for you to use. The baby is then aborted, and you transplant the organ you want to your own body..."

David cut him off, appalled. "Stop! That's worse than cannibalism! We would never permit that in the United States!"

Jimmie raised his eyebrows skeptically at his coach.

"No? What about slavery and abortion? They're not too pretty either. But what's to stop them since our country doesn't recognize natural law anymore? We're governed by utilitarian principles. Of course, these people won't present their work for what it is... yet. First they'll develop the procedures quietly and then, when public opinion has been softened..."

David exclaimed, "That can't ever happen!"

Jimmie smiled wanly. "We agree. That's why we're so dedicated to our work, Mom and I. And perhaps that's why Dad lost his life."

As Jimmie spoke, David had experienced a flood of relief. He had steadily grown more exuberant and even jovial. At long last, he knew the supposedly "dark" secret of the Foster family! They were doing something noble and courageous after all. They weren't Mafioso! What's more, they were freely letting him in on their secret. All along he had unconsciously been worried that he might be falling in love with a woman who was mixed up in something underhanded. Now he discovered it was completely to the contrary. Then and there, he wanted to swing Liz around in his arms and hold her close, but he could wait until he was alone with her outside. Controlling the giddiness he felt, David managed to thank Jimmie for his explanation.

"I appreciate your taking me into your trust regarding this project!" He was standing near Jimmie, though he was addressing both

him and Liz. She ignored his words, while Jimmie gave him a friendly smile.

"You're like one of the family, Coach." David tried to see Liz's response to her son's high compliment, but she had deliberately turned
her back, busying herself with the animals in their cages. In fact, she had
been standing apart for some time. He crossed the room now to join
her. As he approached, she began to speak without turning to face him.

"I hope you've enjoyed the evening, Coach Johnston. The children and I certainly did." Her tone was deliberately cool. She called
out to her son offhandedly. "Jimmie, would you please see our guest
out to his car?" David was surprised, but not daunted by her sudden
apparent lack of warmth. He was sure it was only some kind of cover.

"Don't bother, Jimmie. Liz and I have some unfinished business
we still have to take care of in private."

The boy looked from one to the other. Both were sending sharply contrasting nonverbal messages. His mother was imploring him
with her eyes and rigid body, while Coach David was outright glaring. Jimmie deliberately went back to looking through the microscope before beginning his answer.

"Mom, it seems Coach prefers you to see him out. I would too if
I were him… so I think *you* had better do the honors…"

Ever polite, Liz sighed quietly to herself and then turned resolutely to the door with David close behind.

TWENTY-EIGHT

Most of the house was in darkness and there were no floodlights,
so they had to be guided by the light of the moon. Little did they
know that Jackie and Mikey were watching from Jackie's upstairs
corner room. Her lights were off to escape detection, and the two of
them were laying across her bed in silence, each peering steadily out
the window that faced the barn. Jackie spotted them first and whispered excitedly to her younger brother.

"Here they come... and oh, look!" she declared gleefully."He just slipped his arm around Mom's waist! Bet you any money he kisses her when they reach his car!"

Mikey couldn't help but exclaim in disgust, "Aw! Yuck!"

"Shh! They'll hear us. The window's open!" She would have reached out to jab him with her elbow but Mikey had already rolled off the end of the bed onto the floor.

"Tell me when the mush is over!" He was content to let his sister describe what she saw. Jackie grinned at her fellow conspirator.

"What were you expecting? Isn't this what you wanted?" Mikey shrugged his shoulders noncommittally.

"Just because I happen to nourish an ardent desire for them to grow enamored with each other and thus embrace the matrimonial state does not necessarily imply that I need to personally relish all the intermediary steps to that end! Please be so kind as to keep me informed of any further significant developments between said parties."

Jackie smiled benignly, commented "You're crazy," and turned back to her window vigil.

David, in the meantime, had begun to pour out his heart to Liz.

"It never crossed my mind that you were doing something like this. It's incredible!"

She countered emphatically, "This changes nothing in our relationship! Please remember your promise not to chase—"

But he cut in before she could go on. "Yes, it does! Everything is changed. I'm a grown man. I can make choices for myself. I would rather have you close and live in danger than be far from you and safe. Let me love you. That's enough for me."

With these words, he pulled her closer to his side as they walked along. They had almost reached his car. "In fact, there's just one nagging, unanswered question I have left that's keeping me from proposing to you here and now. Everything else makes sense to me. And I bet you've got a simple answer for that one, too." Keeping his right arm around her, he reached confidently to embrace her with his other arm, but Liz struggled to escape his grasp.

"David, please, no!" she protested.

He wouldn't desist, however. Instead, he tried the same line which had been so effective in the gazebo. "Can you tell me that you don't care for me?"

Jackie yelped in surprise when she saw Liz's response to his question. Mikey instantly sprang back to his outlook position.

"Shh! They'll hear you! Remember, the window's open. What happened?"

"Mom just dumped her drink all over Coach!"

It was a large cup, so she drenched him. He let her go. Liz, both calm and contrite, immediately apologized.

"I'm sorry, David! Here, these handkerchiefs are yours. I've been meaning to return them to you..."

He accepted them, but made no attempt to dry himself with them since they were so small. He stood there, struggling to contain his temper.

"It's just that you weren't listening to me. I can't tell you 'yes' with my body right now. That would be a lie, because I have no intention of pursuing any kind of relationship with you."

He still remained silent.

"I've told my own children that you have to be decisive in this area, so how could I act against my better judgment right under their noses? Please try to understand."

She spoke as though she knew her daughter and son were in fact listening to every word she said.

"Go Mom!" declared Jackie proudly. Though she was disappointed there had been no kiss, she was nevertheless impressed at her mother's example.

"That's our Mom!" echoed Mikey. But Jackie hushed him, because David's voice was so quiet they couldn't hear. His pride was hurt more than anything else, and her poise only annoyed him all the more. Without reflecting, he let his anger get the better of him, even while he winced internally at the bitterness of his own tone.

"It's certainly commendable that you're striving so hard to be, as you say, honest. That assures me that you must have a very good reason for why you adopted a dead boy and gave his identity to the boy you call your son. You can understand, of course, that I doubt his parentage based on the fact that normal mothers don't ordinarily go about adopting their own children..."

He would have gone on, but she broke in on his words, stepping closer and signaling urgently for him to be quiet.

"Please! Not so loud! Don't let my children hear you, please!"

Jackie and Mikey turned to each other simultaneously to ask, "Did you hear what he said?" But neither had.

When she realized she was standing so close to David, Liz stepped back in dismay, but then looked back and forth from him to the car hesitatingly.

"Could we speak about this in your car, please?" she pleaded humbly. Her look of fear and distress dissolved David's anger. After all, she was being congruent with what she had always communicated to him. He moved to open the passenger door for her, but she stopped just before entering, looking at him plaintively.

"David, do you promise not to ..."

He finished off her sentence with a chuckle, "Manhandle you? Yes, I promise to behave myself. Besides, now that you're out of ice water you might gouge my eyes out if I try anything." Then he added more seriously: "On the condition that you'll promise not to leave until we mutually agree to end our conversation."

She nodded, smiling ruefully. He knew her too well—she had already thought of making an escape if his questions became too awkward. Once inside the car, David pulled a photo of Santiago

Pérez's gravestone from the glove compartment. He handed it to Liz without any comment, watching closely for her reaction. It was obvious that she recognized it, although she tried to appear unruffled.

"What made you adopt a dead boy and give his identity to your own son?"

She replied flatly, "For his own good. For his own safety. I can't tell you any more. But Jimmie doesn't know yet, and it's best that I be the one to tell him."

He persisted gently. "Why can't you tell me? You trusted me with your other secret."

"My children committed mutiny on me. I didn't invite you here tonight, and I didn't want to show you the lab. It's the only time Jimmie has openly defied me!" Her voice was toneless.

"But you look so beautiful tonight. Wasn't that for me? You cooked all day: Jackie told me. Wasn't that for me?" He omitted the part about the special dress and perfume. "Can you honestly tell me I mean nothing to you?"

She looked away. "I've told you before: I'm weak. I should be running from you."

He pushed further. "Liz, marry me! Let me choose to share your danger with you. I'll take you: secrets and danger and all! If I'm willing to take on your nightmares with you, let me!" It was so hard not to reach out and touch her, but he kept his word.

"I can't marry you."

"Why?"

She sat absolutely still, staring out the front window and saying nothing.

"Okay, if you won't answer, I'm going to guess."

At that, Liz reached for the door, but he reminded her of her promise, so she left her hand there, tapping nervously.

"You might be saying this because there's another man in your life." The jittery fingers stopped their drumming. "But I don't think so. So if it's not love, then it must be duty."

Her hand returned to her lap and lay very still while the telltale blush crept up her neck and across her face. "Now I've heard of single parents worrying that remarrying might not be good for their children, so that could be why. Only I've got a wonderful rapport with all three of your children."

She started fidgeting again with her two hands together. "But perhaps it's not that I would disrupt the family, but that I might cause harm unwittingly. Could my presence in your life and home somehow be dangerous for one of your children?"

Her eyes fixed on him and he knew he had found the reason. "Jimmie..." he said softly... and then "Bingo..." when her eyes filled with tears.

"Please, David, don't dig anymore. I'm not strong enough. You're right: the closer you and I get to each other, the more Jimmie is in danger. He doesn't know. He can't know, please! I would never forgive myself! He might leave for my sake, but he's not safe on his own!" In her anguish, she seized David's right arm with both her hands. Once she realized what she was doing, she let go of him suddenly. His mind clicked along steadily all the while. Then it came to him in a flash.

"You're not even free to tell me why you're not free, are you? Why can't you tell me Jimmie's danger? Is it something to do with the secret project you were involved with years ago?"

She gasped in dismay that he knew so much and avoided his probing gaze. "If you can't tell me, I understand. But it doesn't have to be an obstacle between us."

Liz lay back against her seat, closed her eyes for a moment, and uttered a prayer for strength. When she opened them again, she turned and faced him somberly. "I think I know now how they found me..."

David looked guilty. Hugh had told him as much. She pressed

her point. "You say this doesn't have to be an obstacle, but you're wrong. No matter what I do or don't tell you, it would be exactly that. In my conscience, I could tell you the whole story because nobody can ever be obliged to hide what is evil! However, if I share this secret with you and later 'they' question you, would you deny that I told you? If you admit that I did tell you, then they'll be able to extradite me back to Canada for betraying top-secret information, and who knows what would happen to me then? And if I don't tell you, and some day 'they' show up on your doorstep with seemingly unmistakable evidence against me, could you keep from coming between Jimmie and I?"

She didn't ask if his love would hold out, which was another matter. He stayed quiet, searching inside for an answer that would satisfy them both, but nothing occurred to him. After all, wasn't he interfering when it came to Jimmie? He considered her to be sane in everything except when it came to her eldest son, and there he did think she lacked good judgment. How could he in all honesty promise not ever to interfere when he thought she was mistaken in her dealings with Jimmie, if he was even her son at all?

She waited, watching him sadly. "Let me go now, David." She reached for the door, and he made no move to stop her.

As she turned to get out, he entreated her, "Liz, at least give me some hope that things could work out for us down the road."

Before answering she rolled down the window, stepped out of the car, and then leaned back in. The pain in her eyes was evident. "Hope? How can I offer you any hope when all I can see on the horizon are thick, dark clouds?" They gazed at each other forlornly, neither having the stomach to say anything more, not even good night. Liz reached out and briefly cupped his cheek with her hand, the only sign of tenderness she had ever showed him. Then she retreated into her house without a backward glance.

Once she was inside, David held one of the wet handkerchiefs to his nose, catching the slight scent of her perfume. He felt something on it. Turning on the inside car light he discovered Liz's handiwork.

She had delicately hand-embroidered his initials into the corner of each one.

"It could be worse," he said to himself as he pulled away.

TWENTY-NINE

Mikey thrust open his secret door into the lab. From where he was cleaning up, Jimmie shot him a quizzical look that Mikey didn't know quite how to read, so he took up a defensive stance.

"Jimmie, I wasn't here when you were showing Coach around, I promise, even though I wanted to be."

Older brother walked over to peer down pensively at younger brother. Mikey was in pajamas.

"Good job. I thought you weren't feeling well and that's why you went to bed early. What are you doing still up?"

"I feel better now. You know what? Mom threw a cup of ice-water all over Coach when he tried to embrace her."

Jimmie shook his head. "Now, how do you happen to know that? Were you listening in from somewhere else?"

Given his brother's disapproval, Mikey declined to expand. Instead, he tried changing the topic as he'd done with his mother earlier that evening.

"Don't you want to know why I'm here right now? I've come to give you a tour of my new hideout. Nobody gets to know about it but you and me. I've been waiting for a nighttime opportunity like this because it's eerier."

He moved back from the trapdoor, beckoning for his brother to join him, adding eagerly, "Come this way."

Jimmie felt compelled to go along with the invitation even though it was so late. It was obvious that it meant a lot to Mikey.

"Okay, wait just a minute while I finish up in here. I'm almost done." In a couple of minutes the two brothers climbed out of Mikey's secret barn trapdoor. Shep greeted them joyfully.

"Guess where it is."

Jimmie shrugged his shoulders. "In the trees ,I suppose."

His little brother grunted. "Too elementary. C'mon."

Though he was armed with a flashlight, he chose not to turn it on. They walked in the opposite direction of the house about fifty paces. Jimmie almost stumbled into his old Chevy chassis he'd been planning on fixing up someday.

"Wait a minute." Mikey moved around to the other side of the chassis and pulled a wide thin board from underneath it. He instructed Jimmie: "Okay, now open the back door and go in carefully. Watch the first step."

At first Jimmie felt letdown. "You're kidding! You mean your hideaway is the inside of this car? How secret is that?" Shep pushed through first, as soon as the door was opened and nimbly took the the narrow steps going down. Mikey reached his hand inside and gave a dramatic flick of his flashlight.

Jimmie commented appreciatively, "Hey, it's deep."

"I trained Shep to help me. I'd put the dirt in bags strapped to his sides and he would run into the trees, roll around until he dumped the dirt and then come back for more. It took us forever."

Only when they had reached the bottom did Mikey switch on his flashlight. The dugout was about eight feet deep, directly underneath the chassis. At the bottom, it was five by eight feet, big enough for the three of them. He had lined the muddy walls and ground with large plastic garbage bags. The floor had a blanket and pillows, several large bags of Fritos, a bowl of chocolate bars and other candies, and some fat university chemistry text books.

"What are you doing with these?"

Mikey thought he meant the food. He opened up a bag of chips and held it out to Jimmie.

"Junk food is my admission price for kids at school to attend the Houdini acts I sometimes put on during recess." Jimmie took a seat on the ground and began to munch on the Fritos. His little brother dropped down beside him and did the same. Shep wedged in between the two of them and lay there thumping his tail.

"No, I meant these chemistry textbooks."

Mikey shrugged his shoulders.

"I find inspiration in them for my inventions," he replied enigmatically. He was thinking along another line. "Hey, Jimmie, do you understand women?"

Jimmie cocked his eyebrow at his kid brother.

"Aren't you on the young side to be having trouble with girls?"

"Not me. I mean, why do you think Mom threw water on Coach David tonight?"

Jimmie took some more chips and leaned against the cool wall, pondering the question.

"Mom's been avoiding him, even though she likes him," Mikey added. "That doesn't make sense either!"

"Beats me how they could have grown attached to each other in the first place," mused Jimmie. "Mom isn't exactly the easiest person to get to know."

Mikey burst with pride. "Oh, I can explain that one!"

To his older brother's intense amusement, Mikey divulged everything he'd done up until then to bring the two together. Jimmie gave Mikey a respectful high five at the end.

"Wow! And the funny thing is that it worked!"

"But it's not funny. Mom's freezing him out and yet sad about it at the same time. As soon as she came in tonight, she went to her bedroom and cried. I could hear her sniffing and blowing her nose when I snuck out."

Jimmie frowned. He popped a hard candy in his mouth and

sucked on it. After a while, he admitted ruefully, "I think I know what the problem is."

Mikey perked up. "What?"

"Me!"

Mikey shook his head vehemently, suddenly regretting having shared his story. "No, Jimmie! Why would you have anything to do with whether Mom loves Coach or not?"

"Because Mom's worried about protecting me from some danger we don't know about."

"Mom's worried about all of us, not just you, because of Dad getting killed," Mikey countered. "It has to do with the experiments you and Mom do."

Jimmie shook his head slowly. "That's just it. She doesn't think our lab work is so dangerous. She even admitted to me once that Dad wasn't killed for that reason. Otherwise she would have stopped."

"But why does she have to worry more about you than us?"

"We have different fathers, remember?"

"Yeah. But you told me Mom said your dad was dead too, so what's the problem? How scary can a dead man be... unless he's a ghost."

Jimmie let out a deep breath. "Couldn't tell ya; but I can't wait to find out. I'm just glad I'll know soon. Then Mom's and yours and Jackie's troubles will be over."

Mikey's uneasiness was steadily increasing. "Why?"

"Because I'm going to head off on my own so you won't have to run anymore. You'll be safe as soon as I'm gone. Then Mom can marry Coach, and you won't have to be moving all the time."

Mikey threw his bag of chips aside dejectedly. "Jimmie, I'd rather have you around than a new dad. Mom and Jackie too!"

Jimmie was firm. "I'm not going to be a cause of suffering for you all anymore. I can't stand it. Anyway, I'm almost eighteen. Lots of kids leave home at that age. Besides, I've already worked out what I'm going to do. I bet you'll like the idea."

He made a mental note to follow up on his plan the next day.

"What are you going to do?"

His big brother wasn't sure he was ready to trust Mikey with that information. He preferred to make sure everything was confirmed first. While he was thinking what to reply, his eyes fell on the chemistry books once more.

"What kind of invention have you been working on lately that finds inspiration in a chemistry text book?" he wondered aloud.

The answer was matter-of-fact. "Smoke bombs."

Jimmie sputtered, "Smoke bombs!"

"No need for concern. They'll be quite innocuous. But they could serve us well in the case of an unforeseen attack. We have the advantage since we know the lay of the land. They'll provide a marvelous cover."

Fear and a parent-like anger washed over the older brother at the stupidity of Mikey messing around with explosive chemicals.

"Listen to me," he belted out energetically. "You can do escape artist stunts and build as many secret hideaways as you want, but you're not allowed to play around with chemicals."

Mikey was stung by his brother's words. "Who said anything about 'play'? I mean business." He added enthusiastically, "I know exactly what I'm doing and I've almost perfected—"

"Forget it! No more working on smoke bombs or anything else in the explosive line."

Mikey bit his lip in distress, staring back mutely at Jimmie. He felt terribly let down by his big brother. Up until now, he'd been able to share all of his secrets with Jimmie alone. But here he was dishing out orders as if he were his father, and not very nicely at that.

Before he could respond, they heard their mother's voice anxiously calling into the darkness from the front door of the house:

"Jimmie! Mikey! Where are you? Jimmie, Mikey: come now!"

Smoke bombs forgotten, the two boys looked at each other in mock trepidation. "We're in for it now!"

Mikey snapped off the flashlight. Scrambling out of the hideaway, they raced to the house, Shep in the lead.

THIRTY

On the way back from their home visits in the area, Father Matt understood why Jimmie had requested they make them together.

"I think I need another of your highly selective talks, Padre."

The priest raised his eyebrows questioningly. "Perhaps I could manage that, but self-complacency isn't the theme, is it?"

"No. Letting go."

Father Matt's lips puckered and his brow furrowed.

"Oh." He waited for the boy to go on.

"I'm certain now that if I leave home and this town, Mom, Jackie, and Mikey will be safe. They won't have to be on the run anymore."

"What brought this on?" his mentor asked gently.

Jimmie answered matter-of-factly, without any trace of bitterness in his voice, "Mom's been warning us that we'll have to move on any day now. When I mentioned that to Coach, he practically broke down. That's when it dawned on me that there's something between them. Mom's just keeping her distance because she doesn't feel safe enough to settle down... as long as I'm around, anyway."

"How do you know *you're* the cause of your frequent family migrations?"

Jimmie crossed his arms, looking off into the distance. "A bunch of hunches that all add up to the same thing. I'll know for sure soon, though, because this time I'm going to insist that I'm not leaving until Mom tells me about my father. Then, once I've found out, I'll let her know I've made plans to go elsewhere."

Father Matt kept his tone even.

"You sound like you've got it all worked out. Where are you going?"

Jimmie glanced sideways at the priest.

"That's where you come in, Padre."

The priest held up a hand in warning.

"Don't immerse me in your family troubles!"

"No need for my help," Jimmie countered. "You dove in long ago all by yourself! Might I remind you that it was your self-complacency talk that got me started in the first place?"

Father Matt looked sheepishly at the boy.

"Ah, now I get the connection. Thanks for making it clear for me. By the way, you've done wonders with your fellow players. I knew you had it in you."

Jimmie was quick to press his point. "You see. You got me into this fix. Don't you think it's only right you lend me a hand to get out?"

The answer was noncommittal. "Where are you thinking of going, and what do you want to do?"

Jimmie's face brightened up. "Mexico or Brazil. I want to do missionary work like my parents did when I was small."

"Why?"

"If I'm buried in some deep jungle, I'll be safe from the bogey man who's after me. More importantly, I'll be doing the only thing that makes me happy: helping people." His eyes grew radiant. "The only time I ever really enjoy myself is when I'm accompanying you, or working with the people in the parish. It's like a good kind of drug, you know; it gives you a high when you realize you can make a difference for others." He hurried on, "Don't worry, I'll remember not to be satisfied with the mere humanitarian side. And while I'm there, I can contemplate what else I want to do with my life."

"Wouldn't it be better to ask God what he wants of you? Our Lord has a special plan for each person's life. But you've got to ask him humbly to take a look at those blueprints. Your happiness lies in fulfilling God's holy plan for your life."

Jimmie's eyes glinted mischievously. "I thought you told me it's not effective to preach to adolescents."

Father Matt grinned back.

"Begging your pardon. It's just that the last time I tried, I was inordinately successful." After a minute, he added in a more serious tone: "A piece of advice for when it comes time to talking to your mother about leaving. Don't tell her. Ask her, or at least word it that way. She's going to take it hard, so as the loving, grateful son that you are, you need to soften the blow."

THIRTY-ONE

Mrs. Luciotti considered the younger woman at her side as they watched the Chargers score the first goal of the game. Despite the many wins, the former had observed the latter grow more and more ill at ease as the season progressed. It's not that Liz said anything. It was more her body language and her silence when the Chargers would score or make some phenomenal play. Mrs. Luciotti had thought that Liz would be fine as long as Jimmie didn't stand out, and he didn't at all. In fact, he was the biggest benchwarmer of late. She couldn't fathom Liz's cause for concern. But the older woman wasn't about to pry. She didn't think Liz would divulge anything anyway.

Just as the half-time break was about to end, Mrs. Rorke bustled up, evidently teeming with some tidbit of news. She excitedly waved a piece of paper under Liz's nose as she huffed and puffed from the exertion of marching out to the soccer field from her office.

As soon as she got her breath back, she gushed, "Oh, Mrs. Foster,

I thought you should be the first to know about how our small town has been put on the map!" Here she lowered her voice and added significantly: "Though I can't help thinking that you might not be quite as excited as the rest of us." The good woman flipped the paper about triumphantly, impervious to Liz's apprehensive gaze.

"I'm not sure what you're referring to, Mrs. Rorke..." responded Liz hesitantly, while holding out her hand for the paper. As the newsbearer had no intention of turning it over so easily, she ignored the gesture and took care to keep her prize beyond Liz's grasp.

"Of course you don't! This article is hot off the press! I have a good friend, you see, who works for the *Texan Times*, and look at the benefits I reap! I'm sure I must be the first in town to have seen this article."

Mrs. Luciotti wondered how this woman could be so oblivious to the effect these words had on Liz, for her friend had visibly paled.

Mrs. Rorke blustered on blissfully: "I was just thrilled. Then it occurred to me to print it and hustle it out here immediately so you could be the next one to find out. After all, you're her mother!" She paused to beam complacently at the recipient of her kind favor. "Our small town will soon be buzzing in wonder at your talented daughter. She'll certainly be the pride of our entire school community!"

Mrs. Luciotti could stand it no longer. She tried to be nice, but her words came out more as an impatient order than a polite request: "Show us the paper, please!"

Mrs. Rorke blinked in surprise at the hint of sharpness in Mrs. Luciotti's tone. Was she that jealous at someone else's child winning recognition? Limiting herself to a "Humph!" and a cold look at Mrs. Luciotti, she surrendered the article. To say the least, Mrs. Rorke was disappointed by Liz's reaction. She had been given the chance to steel herself for the worst amidst all the paper waving. Once the offending document was in her hand, she only gave it a cursory glance.

Maintaining her composure, she commented dryly to the expectant woman, "Mr. Jackson assured me that the teachers of your school would be willing to protect our identity from being made known publically. I'm disappointed."

Mrs. Rorke never felt quite comfortable around people like Liz, people who didn't seem to possess sufficient feelings. So hard to read! But that wasn't going to hold her back from speaking her mind, and she did so while taking little breaths that permitted her to run her sentences together in such a way that it was impossible to get a word in edgewise.

"That's partly why I thought you should be the first person to know what's going public. Now, I have my guess as to who the anonymous teacher is, but it's not for me to say! Of course, you can rest assured that Mr. Jackson will get to the bottom of this. He always does! But if you ask my opinion—though some may say it's admirable that you wish to keep your daughter's talents hidden—I'm sure you can appreciate all the benefits that will come to your family and our town through this article. It's always important to remember the common good when raising a family."

While Mrs. Rorke droned on, Mrs. Luciotti burned with curiosity to know the contents of the article. Finally, she cut short the other's monologue, observing blandly, "It doesn't seem that Mrs. Foster sees it the same way as you, Mrs. Rorke."

Now the good woman really felt out of sorts. Wasn't she doing Mrs. Foster a favor by hurrying out here to share the big news with her? And not only did she lack fitting gratitude, but this other intrusive woman was meddling in their conversation! She, at least, would be the magnanimous one and withdraw politely rather than respond in kind.

"Well, Mrs. Foster, I'm certainly sorry if my good deed for the day has been taken the wrong way. I'll think twice next time it occurs to me to share a bit of good news with you. Good day."

A polite nod to Mrs. Foster, a cold glare at Mrs. Luciotti, and Mrs. Rorke turned to huff her way back to the school building. Liz crossed her arms tightly, leaned her head down, and squeezed her eyes shut. She remained that way for a while.

At last, Liz remarked despondently to her friend, "I hate to leave this town! It was so good for all three of my children! They've been happy here... and so have I, despite my grief and worries."

This was a rare show of emotion coming from Liz. It made Mrs. Luciotti's gasp, particularly because she had been in on the soccer team plot from the beginning.

"It can't be as bad as that, can it?" Liz didn't reply in words. Only turning her gaze on her friend was enough: her eyes were full of sadness. Mrs. Luciotti struggled to comprehend but didn't succeed. She wondered if she should own up to her deception, but didn't have the courage.

Instead, it occurred to her to ask, "How soon are you thinking of leaving?"

Liz reached down to pick up her bag and then stood up. "As soon as we can: within a couple of days. A week would be pushing it..." She waved her hands to get the attention of Mikey, who was sitting contentedly beside David on the player's bench. As soon as he saw her, he excused himself from Coach David and started cutting around the field to come to her.

Many protests welled up in Mrs. Luciotti's heart. It was so terrible to think that the Fosters would suddenly disappear. She loved the whole family dearly. Ordinarily, she would never be so forthright; however, her biggest concern simply came bubbling out of her.

"But Liz... what about you and David? Are you going to tell him you're leaving? You would make such a good couple!"

At the mention of David's name Liz grimaced, although she got a hold of herself right away. "I was beginning to hope... but not now," she answered bitterly. "Not after what he's just done. He at least knew how much I needed my family to stay low-key!"

Mrs. Luciotti held out her hand for the article. "Let me read it." Liz handed the paper to her.

Mikey came up just then. Liz said to him, "Something's come up. We need to go home now."

With a soft "good-bye" to Mrs. Luciotti, she headed for the car. The boy knew better than to argue with his mom when she used that tone of voice and had that particular determined look in her eye. He turned and waved somberly to Coach David, then gravely trailed behind his mother.

David's eyes followed their retreating figures. He wondered what had happened and whether he should chase after them to find out what was going on, but he controlled the urge and remained on the bench.

As soon as she could after the game, Mrs. Luciotti pulled David aside to show him the news article and inform him that the Fosters were leaving town. He pored over the offending piece. It was about Jackie, the "hidden wonder of Fort Davis." Apparently, some teacher had discovered that she was secretly a genius and fantastic sports hero rolled into one. She was the mastermind behind the brilliant success of the soccer team, and she was single-handedly tutoring those same players, and they were all achieving extremely high grades. Furthermore, she was ready to beat up any player who didn't toe the line, as the teacher himself had witnessed during school hours.

David exclaimed in disgust, "Mr. West! Now why did he have to go and do this?"

Mrs. Luciotti waved both her hands back and forth in front of her. "Of course! It was Mr. West! But Liz thinks you're the teacher who shared this information."

David's clenched fists and murderous glare were not lost on Mrs. Luciotti. She hoped that he wouldn't happen to run into the guilty party anytime soon.

After a long pause, he asked despondently, "How soon are they leaving?

"A week at the most."

"Thanks for letting me know."

Picking up the net of balls, he ambled off, lost in thought.

THIRTY-TWO

Lily's heart skipped a beat when she saw who was entering her parents' restaurant. After helping her gain back her self-respect at school, Jimmie was her number one hero in life. Sure, he only wanted to be friends with her, but that was better than for most other girls, and besides, she could still dream…

He had chosen the perfect time, since the breakfast rush was over and it was still too early for lunch; she would be able to lavish her attention on him.

Bouncing up to his table, she greeted him warmly. "Hi y'all!"

He looked her up and down appreciatively and smiled back.

"Hey, good-looking! Do I know you?"

Uncomfortably surprised at the way he was leering at her, she replied petulantly, "Jimmie! You don't mean to say you forgot my name, do you?"

He frowned in confusion, but then spotting her name tag answered gallantly, "Lily! Of course I would never forget the name of a girl as gorgeous as you!" Following the humiliating episode with Josh, Lily had dropped her extra weight. With her new straight hair, cut according to the latest style, and her contact lenses, she was now very attractive. "But could you please remind me how we've met? I've got a crushing headache that's keeping me from thinking straight."

"Jimmie! Are you poking fun at me?" she demanded incredulously. Seeing her lower lip trembling and her eyes welling up, the boy's furrow once more wrinkled in concentration.

Then, suddenly, light dawned across his face and he pronounced assuredly to himself, "Jay!"

Springing to his feet, he laid his hand gently on the girl's arm and steered her to the seat across from him, all the while apologizing profusely. "I'm so sorry for upsetting you. Please don't be angry with me. Let me explain what's happened to me, please." She waited expectantly. "Look, you're going to find this really hard to believe, but I've got this gut feeling I can trust you. I think you'd be willing to help me, because I'm in big trouble."

Her eyes grew big, tears forgotten.

"Jimmie, of course you can trust me. I would do anything for you. We're friends, remember?"

He took her hand and gripped it, as if for strength. Lily started. He had never taken her hand before. She had wished he would; yet everything about today was so odd, so unlike him. Still, she decided not to retract her hand for the time being.

"I'm just going to tell you straight, 'cause I don't know any other way: I've got a bad case of global amnesia."

As she had no idea what that meant, Lily first exclaimed, "Oh, I'm so sorry, Jimmie!" Then she added sheepishly, "But what does that mean, exactly?"

The boy was in his element now. "It means I forget absolutely everything about myself, my family, my friends, my name, my address. I normally even forget that I have this condition... but I bet your sweet face has triggered my memory to remember that." He caressed her hand.

"That's absolutely terrible!"

He nodded, massaging his temples with one hand while keeping a tight hold of her hand with the other.

"I'll say! And the worst thing is, I'm supposed to be wearing my GPS system so that I can be found easily... but I must have forgotten that too. So now I'm really gonna catch it from Mom!"

"I wish I could get you home!" Lily answered wistfully.

He jumped at the idea as if it hadn't occurred to him.

"Of course! That would work. Will you show me how to get home?"

Her heart melted all the more under his beseeching gaze. How she wished she could have done what he was asking.

"Jimmie, your mom doesn't let anyone near your house. I'm not even sure exactly where it is. Nobody in town has ever been there..." Her voiced trailed off for a moment. "Well, Jackie did tell me that Coach Johnston went there for dinner... but I honestly don't know of anyone else."

He sat up in his chair. "Lily, you've gotta take me to Coach Johnston's house. He would help me, wouldn't he?" Lily nodded her assent, ran into the back of the restaurant to call out to her parents that she would be back soon, and they left the restaurant together. As they began to pass by the house behind the restaurant, Lily said apologetically:

"Do you mind waiting for me while I change out of my waitress shirt?" At the door to her home, she reached under the big flowerpot on the left and pulled out the house key. "I'll be right back."

The boy poked his head in the door and scoped out the house while she was out of sight. She was back in a minute looking fresher in a frilly blouse. He whistled appreciatively. Flustered, she began to walk down the street but stopped to see why he didn't move. He nursed his brow with both hands, his face wracked in pain.

"My global amnesia makes me dizzy. Could you please help me to walk?"

Coming back, she held out her arm for him to take. Instead, he slipped his arm around her shoulder leaning on her slightly. Lily wasn't comfortable with how closely he was holding her, but she didn't want to protest since it was Jimmie, whom she had always trusted. They walked along the sidewalk that way for awhile. At one point, he stopped and turned to her. He looked dreamily into her eyes.

"Your perfume is heavenly, just like you." Lily didn't reply. Everything about him was so odd, so unlike Jimmie.

"Lily, do you have a boyfriend?"

She gazed up at him in shock. "No, Jimmie. You know I decided like you..." She began, ready to launch into the beautiful explanation he had offered her for why he wasn't going to date during high school, but he cut her off eagerly.

"Wonderful. I knew it!" That sounded more like it, until he continued: "I knew it because I wouldn't be able to go out with any girl but you!" Lily stopped dead in her tracks in astonishment. "I'm sure my global amnesia must have been set off by my unrequited love for you!"

Her mouth fell open in a big, silly smile. She could hardly believe her ears. But everyone knew that Jimmie never lied. Her mind raced. Hadn't she dreamed of Jimmie telling her just such a thing? And now he was...

Suddenly she caught herself and cut off her train of thought decisively. Something just wasn't right. For his part, he easily read the hope and delight in her eyes. He took advantage of her stillness to reach his other arm around her and would have succeeded in embracing her if she hadn't ducked down and away from him at the last instant. This was too much for her. It was too confusing, too sudden.

"Jimmie, stop! You've got to get better before we do anything else." She meant it and broke out into a brisk walk. He followed behind with a triumphant gleam in his eyes.

"Okay. Just let me know when I can come and see you soon. I'm longing to get to know you better." This made her quicken her pace all the more, though with a dazed smile on her face. "Tell me, is there a day soon that I could come and see you? After all, you are my cure." Lily still wasn't able to process this new turn of events.

She answered without thinking, "If you want to take me out, you need my dad's permission again."

"Well, how about if I just come over to your house... when your parents aren't home... so we could be together, just you and me?"

Lily looked at him askance. "Jimmie, what's gotten into you? I'm not sure if I want to be your girlfriend if you're going to act this way!"

He answered contritely, "Sorry! I don't know what's gotten into me either. Must be the global amnesia. So when do I need to come by to meet your father before taking you out?"

"Any night but Friday. Mom and Dad work late in the restaurant."

He smiled to himself.

With an inner sigh of relief, she came to a halt. "This is Coach Johnston's house." He tried reaching for her again, but she stepped away from him. "Jimmie, you've got to get better first!" she said firmly. He smiled back appreciatively.

"This just makes me love you all the more. Thanks, Lily." With a wink he turned toward the house, while Lily headed back to the restaurant, her mind and heart reeling. Looking back and seeing him at the door, she pulled out her cell phone and called Jackie. It was a good thing her friend answered right away. Lily didn't even take time to greet her.

"Jackie! What's up with your brother? he's acting really strange right now!" There was a pause on the other end.

"What do you mean 'right now,' Lily? He looks okay to me," she said, sounding puzzled.

Lily demanded, "What do you mean?"

Jackie laughed at her friend's nervousness.

"Well, he's playing chess with Mikey, and he's winning, so no major catastrophes right now." Then it hit Lily. Her pulse raced.

One last check, "Do you mind my asking where y'all are right now?"

"In our living room." That confirmed Lily's theory. No wonder the boy had acted so uncharacteristically: he wasn't Jimmie at all. "Were you expecting us to be?"

"Yeah, yeah..." Lily felt the need to think before sharing her news. It was too strange. She wondered why nobody in the family had ever mentioned Jimmie had a twin brother. They must know he was in town, but why did he pretend to be Jimmie? Hard to tell with the Fosters. She needed a while to process it. Meanwhile, Jackie was waiting on the line.

"Is there anything else, Lily? Are you okay?"

"No. I mean, yes! I mean no to your first question and yes to the second. I'll talk to you later, okay?"

On her way back to the restaurant Lily mused over what had just happened. She decided she would first tell Jackie about it and ask for an explanation. They would have to get together soon if it was going to happen. But she would wait until she had calmed down before calling Jackie again.

THIRTY-THREE

David suspiciously eyed the Jimmie-look-alike lounging back on the couch. Thinking an adult might not buy the global amnesia story, he had tried claiming he had a big hangover. He planned on begging for a ride home.

"Since when have you taken up drinking?" came the retort. The boy quickly realized he wasn't going to get anywhere following that line. Before trying another tactic, he needed to sum up this man's character. David grew impatient with the silence. "Jimmie, what's going on?" The fatherly, anxious concern provided the necessary clue.

"It's no good: I can't hide it any longer. Coach, there's something kinda far-fetched that I have to tell you, but it's the truth." David sat down across from him, relaxing somewhat.

"Try me. I'm used to your family quirks."

The boy inhaled deeply, then blurted out, "I'm not Jimmie. I'm his twin named Anthony, but I go by the nickname 'Gamma'!" David's jaw dropped open. The Fosters never ceased to surprise him. Yet he doubted whether Jimmie were trying to pull a fast one on him for some reason. Not much sense in discussing the point when there was an easy way of proving it, so he reached for his cell phone.

"Gamma" guessed what he was about to do and added urgently: "Please don't tell my mom I've come or I'll never meet Jimmie! She's hidden him from me my entire life!" David wondered at this new bit of information. Very strange indeed, a twin coming on the scene from nowhere.

When Jimmie answered, David asked whether he would be coming to practice on Friday, then hung up, gazing at Gamma disconcertedly.

"It's quite a shock to meet you! I didn't know you existed." he admitted.

"You don't know how long I've looked for Mom and Jimmie!" responded the boy plaintively. "All I've ever dreamed about is getting to meet them both, even if neither want anything to do with me after that!"

"But what happened?"

The boy shrugged his shoulders. "Who knows? Dad says Mom ran out on me and him when I was only one, taking Jimmie along with her." When he observed the compassion in David's eyes, he added, "Do you know what it means to have your father gradually become an alcoholic because of what your mom did to him, and to know that your own mom couldn't care less about you? Do you know what that means for a guy? Maybe Jimmie doesn't drink, but is there any wonder I do?"

David wasn't sure how to process this new information. He knew Liz had been avoiding Jimmie's father. But why? This kid didn't seem to know. It would have been heartless to have abandoned one of her twins. But this didn't make sense given her over-protectiveness where Jimmie was concerned.

"I'm sorry," was the only thing he could think of saying.

"Will you help me?"

David felt for him, but wasn't sure how much he could trust his story. "What kind of help do you want?"

"Help me set up a meeting with Jimmie. I just want to spend a little while with him. After all, he's my brother!"

If he had expected an immediate promise of support, Gamma was disappointed. It was now David who fell quiet for an uncomfortable period of time. He was trying to fit this kid's story with his impression of Liz, and they didn't match. The Liz he knew did go off the deep end when it came to concealing her eldest son's identity, but it didn't seem to him that this was for selfish motives. Her three children had noble characters, like she did. So how could she have run out on the father of the twins and one of her boys? Something didn't gel. Perhaps she would have liked to leave with two but didn't feel she could handle them both.

"Well?" asked Gamma peevishly. "Are you going to help me or not?"

David tried to put it gently. "I guess it depends on what you mean by help. One thing is sure. I'm not going to do anything behind Liz's back. If you want my help on that condition, I'd be glad to…"

The boy shot to his feet. "No! You'll only mess everything up by telling her I'm here. I've worked so hard to find Jimmie and now you threaten to ruin everything!"

The older man held to his decision. "I don't believe I'm threatening you with anything! I'm simply letting you know what kind of help you can expect from me."

Gam sneered, "Okay, I get it. Then do me the favor of not 'helping' me at all! I'm gonna see if I can meet Jimmie on my own somehow. Thanks anyway." He thrust out his hand to David, who stood and shook it.

David, however, still had many more questions he would have liked to put to the boy. "Wait! You're welcome to stay for dinner." The boy muttered back something incoherent and left without a further word.

From his front window David watched the boy saunter down the street. There never was a shortage of surprises when it came to the Fosters!

He thought for a moment and then pushed Liz's number on his

cell phone. She deserved the chance to explain how she came to be separated from one of her sons. He wasn't about to pass judgment until she had a chance to speak for herself.

He got a message informing him that the number he had dialed was no longer in service and that he should check the number and try again. He thought about jumping into his car and driving to see Liz that minute, yet he hesitated. Deep down, he wasn't absolutely sure if Liz was entirely upright in regards to Jimmie. Now his secret twin showed up, tilting the scales against her. He would hate to be the one who came between Jimmie and his brother. Perhaps their father had somehow seriously wronged Liz, but if she had left him so long ago the son wasn't at fault. Why should he have to suffer?

David balked at the idea of confronting Liz head on. After all, Jimmie was the sore point between them. It would be unfortunate to clash with her in what could very well be their last meeting. He would be seeing Jimmie in two days for soccer practice and could send a note home through him to Liz. That way, she could peacefully decide whether or not to answer his questions.

THIRTY-FOUR

At the end of soccer practice, David pulled Jimmie aside. "Has your mom told you yet the information about your past that I've found out about you?

Jimmie informed him dispassionately, "No, but she knows I'm not leaving until I find out. Carlos promised to take me in if Mom decides to leave without me. She's pretty upset, but I'm not going to give in. I don't want to run anymore until I know what I'm running from."

David clapped the boy on the shoulder, while looking him in the eye compassionately. Things were obviously very tense at home.

"Uh, your mom's cell phone number changed, and I don't have her new number..." David said, in hopes that Jimmie would volunteer her new number; however, he didn't bite. "Okay. So I wrote her this letter. Could you please give it to her as soon as possible? There's something important she ought to know."

They began to walk away from each other, when David called out: "Jimmie!" He turned back expectantly. "Be careful!"

Jimmie looked at him blankly, unsure where his coach was coming from, so David added: "Just be careful, especially if you hear stories that go contrary to what you know about your mother. Has she ever lied to you?"

The boy shrugged his shoulders. "Not as far as I know... It's more like some answers are hard to come by."

As Jimmie reached the sidewalk and was about to mount his bike, someone stepped out from between the cars and greeted him. He turned around and observed a boy his height removing a fake moustache and beard. To his utter amazement, he saw the spitting image of himself! But before he could cry out, the boy motioned for him not to make noise or call attention to himself.

"Is there somewhere private we could go to talk?" asked his twin. Jimmie nodded, still dumbfounded.

"We're on the edge of town already. We just need to walk a little farther and we'll be out in the country." They walked together in silence until they were out of sight of any possible prying eyes, and then the boy opened his arms to embrace Jimmie.

"My twin! My brother, at last! I'm so happy to meet you!"

Jimmie stood frozen, letting himself be hugged but too shocked to respond in kind.

"Who are you?" he stammered.

The boy answered cheerfully: "My closest friends call me by my nickname, Alf; and since we're twins I guess you fall into that category. C'mon, let's sit down and talk."

They plopped down on the edge of the road. Alf reached over and shook Jimmie affectionately by the arm.

"Do you know how hard it's been to track you down? So far Mom's been the winner at hide-and-seek. I can't tell you what it's been like for Dad and me! But now that we've met, everything's going to be okay." At the sound of the word "Dad," Jimmie's heart leapt. Hadn't Mom specifically told him that his dad was in heaven? Questions poured out in a rapid stream:

"You know my father, I mean, our father? When did he die? What was he like? What did he die of?"

The other boy grinned and again shook Jimmie's arm enthusiastically. "And I've got a pile of questions for you about Mom too! Let's see who goes first. Anyway, who told you Dad died? He's still alive, and he'll be ecstatic to meet you!" Alf launched into the same short story David had heard about their father becoming an alcoholic after Liz took off with Jimmie.

Jimmie tried to pay full attention, but he began to seethe more and more at being lied to by his mother about the one thing he really cared about in life: meeting his father. His father was alive and he could meet him: how incredibly wonderful! At the same time, his mother's lie burrowed deep into his heart and sowed a burning resentment he'd never experienced before. What a betrayal from the person he had trusted the most! His father could have died, and he might never have had the chance to know him. And to top things off, she had never once mentioned that he had a twin brother. Alf was too little to have wronged her at the time she abandoned him. So how could she have neglected him by avoiding him all these years? And didn't he, Jimmie, at least have the right to know of his brother's existence?

At that moment, Coach David's warning cut through his stormy thoughts. David had said to remember that his mother had never lied to him. Jimmie dismissed the thought impatiently. Who knew what other lies she had spun to keep him away from the rest of his natural family?

Meanwhile, Alf noticed that he had lost Jimmie's attention, and punched him playfully.

"What? Don't tell me you're already bored with me?"

Jimmie snapped himself out of his reveries to smile back reassuringly. "No, no! Of course not! Are you kidding? This is the greatest day of my life, getting to meet you, my twin, and hearing I still have the chance to meet Dad!"

Alf guessed by these words that Jimmie was chafing from having been told his father was dead. "I don't know which of the two of us was worse off: you being lied to that our dad was dead, or me knowing that my own mother had abandoned me as a baby and not getting the chance to be near my twin either."

At these words, Jimmie unsuccessfully fought back bitter tears. Alf looked away and kept chatting about all the things they had to do to catch up with each other. When Jimmie was calm, he proposed, "I don't know if you're going to think the idea is too crazy, but I bet Mom's not going to approve of our being together. How about we just disappear for awhile so we can at least spend one quality day together, no matter what else happens!"

Jimmie responded fiercely, "Nobody is going to separate us now that we've met! I'll move out if I have to! Mom's not keeping me from Dad any longer."

Alf smiled gratefully. "Glad to hear it. Thanks! It's good to feel loved at least by you. But couldn't we go away for just a day in any case, before all hell breaks loose? Wouldn't it be good to get to know each other before we throw ourselves into a crazy battle that's not our fault anyway?"

Jimmie thought about it. He was so angry with his mother right then that he really didn't care if she worried about him. She wasn't going to go calling the police in any case. Yet… he was loath to deliberately cause her pain. Alf was watching him closely, trying to guess his thoughts.

"Look, if you don't want to make Mom worry too much, how about we leave a message for Coach to give to her saying we're just going to be together for a day and then we'll come home together?"

Jimmie brightened up. "I could ask him to deliver it to her in person. He would like that! I'll leave the code for him to get through the gate so he can make it as far as the house." He set to writing the note. Before they headed off together for Coach's house, Alf pulled out some blue shorts and a t-shirt that were exactly the same as his own.

"Here, I bought these for you in case you were interested in dressing like the twins that we are." Laughing at the idea, Jimmie ducked down into the trench on the side of the road and changed his clothes, leaving the ones he had been wearing on the ground.

"And how about if *you* wear the disguise and I see if I can pass myself off as you?" Again, Jimmie readily agreed to the plan.

When they reached Coach's house, his car wasn't there, so they left the note on his doorstep. Alf then proposed that they go to his trailer to spend the night. Off they went, like two pals who hadn't seen each other in a long time and had a lot of catching up to do.

THIRTY-FIVE

Mrs. Luciotti could hardly believe her ears when Liz invited her for tea Friday afternoon and told her to bring Stefano. She knew what a privilege it was to be invited into the Foster home, given that so far only Coach Johnston had made it past the big gate. When she arrived, she saw packing boxes everywhere taped up and ready to go; she wondered to herself if that was why she had been invited—they were leaving within days anyway, and all the secrets had already been packed away.

The two women were sipping their tea peacefully in the dining room when the buzzer from the gate sounded. Mrs. Luciotti could hear Coach Johnston announcing that he had brought Jimmie home since he was too sick to come home on his own. Liz opened the gate electronically, and then, visibly pale, she excused herself to Mrs. Luciotti so that she could go outside to wait. Mrs. Luciotti followed after her, as well as the two boys who had heard the buzzer sound. It wasn't often that someone rang at the Foster gate, and Mikey wanted to be in on the action.

As soon as Liz wrenched open the passenger door, Shep growled warningly at the boy within the way he did for any stranger that came to the house for the first time. Mikey pulled the dog back from the car, urging him to hush.

"Shep, be quiet! Can't you tell it's Jimmie?" Liz made her typical gesture of brushing her hand through his sweaty hair. Then she herself almost collapsed. In fact, she would have if Mrs. Luciotti had not supported her for a moment. Everyone assumed it was because she was shocked by Jimmie's poor condition, for he lay back half-unconscious, trembling and feverish. David offered to drive him directly to the hospital.

"I would have liked to have taken him right away, but I know it's your judgment call," he remarked respectfully.

It took a moment for Liz to focus her panic-stricken eyes on David.

"No!" she exclaimed, then repeated the word more calmly. "No. I know exactly what he needs. He doesn't have to go to the hospital. Please just help me bring him upstairs to his room."

With Coach David doing the bulk of the work and Stefano and Mrs. Luciotti pushing and pulling as well, they got him upstairs. Mikey had to restrain the dog until the group had gotten indoors. Liz followed behind in a daze, barely able to drag herself up after them. Once he was in bed, Liz asked Mrs. Luciotti to start preparing him some tea while she saw Coach Johnston to the door. He was pleasantly surprised when she got into the car so she could speak with him. Her company was precious to him even if it were only for a few precious moments.

"What happened?" she asked coolly as soon as both doors were shut. "Are you cooperating willingly with this charade?"

David blinked in surprise at her questions and accusing tone. Before he could respond, she demanded, "Where's my son?"

David bristled inwardly at her treatment, though he strove to respond peacefully.

"Jimmie appeared at my door looking like that and leaning on his twin." Liz pursed her lips and glared. "So I drove him here immediately, knowing you would want to decide what to do."

Her eyes narrowed.

"Is that the first time you met Jimmie's look-alike?" she inquired with the same coldness. That did it! After all, who was *she* to be grilling *him*, when he was the one who had some tough questions for her?

"As a matter of fact, no," he snapped, glaring fiercely at her. "I met him two days ago when he appeared on my doorstep pretending to be Jimmie. When I got suspicious, he admitted he was Jimmie's twin and requested that I help him meet up with Jimmie behind your back. I just so happened to reply that I wouldn't do that to you." Liz had the grace to look down. "As soon as he departed, I tried calling you to let you know, but what do you know: your phone number had changed and I don't happen to be privy to your new number."

Her eyes, full of contrition, met his once more. She realized she had wrongly judged him and was ready to apologize.

"Today at practice I gave Jimmie a letter for you informing you that his twin was in town. I had even contemplated driving out here to let you know in person, but frankly I wasn't up to being rebuffed by you once more, which seems to be the common pattern between us. It's a hard thing for a guy to take, particularly when he's so well-intentioned! And by the way, if you're wondering who furnished the information for the article about Jackie, Mr. West is your man, not me!"

She looked away again, attempting a soft reply. "Oh."

Her response wasn't enough for David now that he was all wound up. "'Oh?' That's all you can say? Couldn't you at least thank me for bringing you your son out of respect for your wishes and against my own better judgment? If I had followed my gut instinct, he'd be at the hospital right now. Wouldn't common decency dictate that you thank me?"

She countered in an even tone, "I suppose yes, if you had brought me my son, but you didn't!"

"What?" David was completely taken aback. It hadn't occurred to him that the twins would try a stunt like switching places. He'd been taken in by them. Suddenly he didn't feel like an offended hero anymore.

"The boy upstairs isn't Jimmie! I'm sorry for suspecting that you were complicit; at least I know now that you weren't." David gazed at her dumbfounded, as she softened her voice still more: "In any case, thank you for your good intentions… You didn't mean to be a Trojan Horse."

He shook his head. Never at a loss for long, he objected weakly: "But… how do you know? He's wearing the same clothes as Jimmie wore to practice, isn't he?" She reached over and tapped the top of his skull on the left, near the front just barely under his hairline.

"Jimmie has a tattoo right here so Henry and I could have a way to instantly recognize him. The boy upstairs doesn't have the mark. I checked for it because Shep was growling at him as if he were a stranger."

It was David's turn now to answer back with a soft "Oh." He couldn't fathom the import of the exchange of identities, but he knew it didn't bode well. They were quiet for a moment. Liz leaned back in the seat and closed her eyes as if willing herself elsewhere. Though he knew it might not help matters David ventured to raise the question that had been bothering him. He tried a tactful approach by voicing his concern as an observation:

"The twin says you abandoned his dad and him when he was only one, which devastated the father so much that he turned into an alcoholic." Liz fixed her eyes intently on him. "What's your side of the story?" This last sentence was put gently, coaxingly.

She looked away and replied obtusely, "Why do you ask?"

David half-frowned and sighed deeply. "Because, despite the evidence, namely, the sudden appearance of Jimmie's twin, and your frantic effort to remain undiscovered, I can't bring myself to accept his story. I know there's got to be more to it. I don't believe you would do something like that."

To his delight, David saw the coldness melting from her eyes. He read gratitude there, and wonder.

"How can you be so kind in your judgments when you witness me acting suspiciously at every turn?"

He answered affectionately, "Yeah, you have done some fishy things. But I've realized that you're not going out of your way to deceive anyone. You're just darn good at avoiding nosy questions."

His loyal belief in her broke her. Without another word, she lay her head against his chest and began weeping. At first, David was taken aback, but he was delighted to wrap his arms around this enigmatic woman and comfort her. Somehow he managed to reach for his embroidered handkerchiefs and hand them all to her.

After some time, she asked him, "How could you possibly believe in me when I'm so uncooperative?"

David stroked her back soothingly. He went for a lighthearted response. "It's not you that convinces me as much as your kids. In fact, I still think you're slightly off your rocker." He heard her laugh softly, though she also kept sniffling. "But there's something so special about each one of them—they're full of goodness and real happiness. You can't fake that, and kids can only be happy when they're loved unconditionally. Abandoning one of your own children doesn't match the way you treat all of the others."

The tears gradually stopped, but she remained in his arms, resting quietly against his chest.

David's mind raced. Here was the woman he loved in his arms and open to him. However, he needed to keep hold of himself. This clearly wasn't the moment for romance. She was in need. Not only that, but the boy who must be Jimmie had asked if he could wait at

Coach's house. Who knows if he would still be there when David got back home? Plus, there was a strange kid in her house that had to be dealt with. How could he help her—or better put, in what way would she let him help her?

She was so stubborn, so proud, so solitary, so very vulnerable. Most likely, she would sit up any second and be back to her business-as-usual manner. *How can I help her?* he asked himself again. *What does she need?* One thing was sure, she wasn't about to offer any explanation for how she had come to be separated from Jimmie's twin, and she evidently wasn't in any hurry to see her long lost son. But why? How could such a loving mother be so offhanded in tending to her own son whom she hadn't seen in years, even if she hadn't cruelly abandoned him? He knew a big piece of the puzzle lay here. Why was she afraid of someone to whom she had given life?

"Liz, why are you afraid of your own son, whom you haven't seen since he was a baby?" No answer and no emotion. He insisted: "Did you somehow wrong him and so now you're afraid of his revenge?"

After a long pause, she managed to whisper back, "Yes."

His heart beat faster: this was the first time she had ever answered one of his probing questions. He wondered if he could go any further on that same track. "Are you sure that he means to do you harm?"

"No."

In a flash, David guessed the heart of her problem. She was a prisoner of her past. "Liz, if I'm not mistaken, you're sorry for whatever you did, aren't you?"

She nodded into his chest.

"Have you turned to God with your sorrow?"

Another nod.

"No doubt he's forgiven you. But have you accepted his forgiveness?"

"I went to confession…"

"But have you accepted his forgiveness?"

No answer this time. Keeping one arm around her shoulder, he used the other to gently pull her away from himself. Then, using his free hand, he tenderly brushed the tears from her face.

"Do you have any idea how lovable you are to your Creator? Do you know how lovable you are to me, no matter what mistakes you made in the past?"

More tears silently fell. Eyes full of deep sadness held his own. He pushed on, "Isn't it about time for reconciliation? How can you teach your children about the unconditional love of Jesus Christ and his mercy if you don't accept his absolute forgiveness? He hasn't been chasing you down through the years to take revenge on you, has he? Isn't it about time that you faced your fears? You can only do that if you permit yourself to be forgiven by our Lord."

Liz managed a smile, then leaned back against his chest and breathed a soft thank you.

The front door opened. Mrs. Luciotti ventured down the stairs towards the car. She was torn between interrupting the two and Jimmie's needs.

"Liz?" she called out tentatively. Liz didn't stir in his arms. "Liz, Jimmie is asking for you. He doesn't want the tea I brought him. He wants his mother to bring him some hot chocolate. I made it already, but don't you think it would be better if you brought it to him?"

Liz sighed again. David signaled that all was well and answered: "She's coming in a moment." Mrs. Luciotti retreated back into the house, puzzled at Liz's seeming neglect. It didn't match with her typical doting concern for her children, particularly Jimmie!

Liz rested in David's arms a while longer.

"I wish I could just stay right here..."

In response, he held her more tightly and kissed the top of her head tenderly.

"Well, I'm sure not sending you away!"

THIRTY-SIX

Mikey most reluctantly followed the two Luciottis out the front door. He never would have expected that his mother would ask Mrs. Luciotti to take him in for the night. It was completely unlike her, especially now, when she was so nervous and they were about ready to leave town for good. To top it off, she had called Jackie and given her permission to sleep over at Lily's house that night too and was sending her overnight things with Mrs. Luciotti! It didn't take a genius to realize something big was up. He had pleaded with his mother to let him stay and help with Jimmie, but she had insisted that he leave right away with the Luciottis. He knew his mother well enough to realize she wasn't going to bend, but as he shut the front door, it occurred to him that Mrs. Luciotti might not be aware of that fact.

Setting his backpack down, he called out that he was going to try just one more time to get his mother's permission to stay. Mrs. Luciotti nodded understandingly as she got into the car. A minute later Mikey danced triumphantly through the doorway.

"It's okay! I get to stay home after all!" He added a little tug on her heartstrings to dispel any doubt she might have. "Mrs. Luciotti, I'm so glad I get to help because Mom is scared stiff and Jimmie is so ill! I'm going to be a big help for them both!"

That made sense to her. She thought to herself that she would also want Stefano around if Louie were to become dangerously ill. Mrs. Foster was so hard to fathom.

"That's good, Mikey! I'm glad you're staying, especially because Jackie's not here!" He smiled and waved energetically as they pulled off. Stefano deliberately looked away, thinking dourly to himself that he had just lost his last opportunity to have Mikey's help assembling his "Mission Impossible" model airplane.

Once the car was completely out of sight, Mikey scooped up his backpack and headed over to his barn hideout to stash away the evidence that he was still at home. Then he snuck upstairs carefully, avoiding the fourth and tenth steps. He permitted himself only the quickest of peeks into his brother's bedroom, where Liz was perched on the edge of the bed, and Jimmie was propped up on two big pillows, sipping away at his hot chocolate. Next, Mikey lay down inside his sister's room, which was right next door. When his mother came out of the room, he only had to push himself back a little and roll behind the door of the room to escape notice. Pleased with the arrangement, he settled down and concentrated on what was happening in the next room.

Neither was talking for the moment. His mother merely watched while the fake Jimmie silently savored his hot drink. He wasn't trembling anymore. Liz reached out to put her hand on his forehead and cheeks, and he smiled sweetly, leaning his face against her cool hand. At last, Liz asked him outright:

"What's your name?" The boy looked aghast at her but said nothing. She softly repeated her question as she caressed his cheeks with the back of her hand: "What's your name?"

He ventured a hoarse whisper, "What do you mean? I'm Jimmie!"

She shook her head gently and smiled back, asserting kindly but firmly: "No, you're not. What's your name?"

He made a face, set down the chocolate roughly and lamented in a childish fashion: "Everything's ruined! And I was enjoying my hot chocolate! You can't imagine how much I've been dreaming of this moment all my life!"

Liz picked up the cup and set it back in his hands. "Who says everything is ruined? Drink your chocolate! Tell me what you've been looking forward to, and perhaps I can still help you with it."

The boy blinked in surprise, then relaxed back into the pillows and brought the cup to his lips. He didn't look at her nor speak for a while, but Liz knew now that he would.

She wanted to grab him and demand that he tell her where Jimmie was, but she sensed that would only be counterproductive. Besides, after speaking with David, she was glad to have the chance to speak with him. At last she was facing her fears. When he had drained the drink, he eyed it sorrowfully, so she picked up the pot and poured him some more. She never would have put hot chocolate into her teapot, but she was glad that Mrs. Luciotti had done so.

As he took the cup from her, he asked, "Why are you being nice to me?"

Liz replied evenly, "You're my son too, aren't you?"

He frowned but nodded.

"Throughout all these years, I've thought about you and loved you. And to tell you the truth, I've also feared you." He gulped. He hadn't expected to hear such things from her. "After all, I've done you great harm, haven't I?" His eyes welled up as he nodded again. "Well, I'm sorry I hurt you! I've regretted it all my life. If I could have undone the wrong or somehow been able to help you, I would have."

That is what she had been longing to say, but she never imagined she would get the opportunity. How much she had feared this moment, but David had helped her to be courageous.

He answered accusingly: "Do you mind telling me how much you got paid for each egg? I've often wondered what price my own mother set in selling my possibility of existence to a group of cold-hearted scientists."

Liz's stomach twisted within her. But she leapt at the chance to explain herself.

It took her a minute to get a hold of herself, and then she answered calmly, "I didn't sell my eggs. I was only seventeen and didn't know any better. Henry, my boyfriend, and Dr. Pearson both convinced me that the project was a noble one that would help humanity. I no longer think so, but at the time I actually felt honored to be chosen to take part in the experiment." The boy grunted though he didn't interrupt her. "I mistakenly thought it would be something good and that all of you would be superior human beings. I believed Dr. Pearson that I was actually doing you a favor."

The boy jerked himself up to a sitting position, scowling fiercely.

"A favor!" he spat out. "Since when is it doing a favor to a child to abandon him to be raised like a lab mouse?"

For the second time that day, Liz's façade of composure broke down completely. She wept. He was absolutely right. She profoundly regretted what she had done. He sat there watching her, trying to discern if her tears were sincere.

When she could speak again, she gripped his arm with both her hands. "It wasn't! It wasn't! Of course it wasn't! I haven't been able to live with myself all these years, imagining what you all must have gone through and knowing I was absolutely helpless to undo the wrong I had done to you, my own children. I'm so sorry! I wish I could have been the one to pay for what I did, and not you." His look of reproach softened as she went on. "I wish I could have rescued you and raised you as my beloved children, but I couldn't see the way! I'm so, so sorry."

Despite himself, the boy found himself inclined to believe her. Perhaps that was because he had never quite been able to think of his mother not caring about him, although the others ridiculed him for it. However, doubts still nagged at his heart. At least when he asked his next question, the bitterness was gone from his voice. He simply wanted to understand what she had done and why.

"But then why have you been running and hiding from us all these years?"

She used the last clean handkerchief that David had loaned her to wipe her eyes before answering.

"Do you know what was supposed to be done with Jimmie?"

He nodded. "We found the control sheets. You were down to have a partial birth abortion of 'J.'" The boy made a face of disgust. "They were planning to chop up and freeze his body parts for our future needs, particularly those of us who were raised in the lab. They wanted his organs as well developed as possible." He added with repulsion: "How could you agree to carry your own child to term and then permit him to be killed while you were giving birth? How could you possibly think that would be a good thing to do?"

Her whole face and body registered her own repugnance at the idea. "The problem was I hadn't thought at all about what I was doing. I had been orphaned the year before and had nobody wise whom I admired to counsel me, so I just went along with the entire plan. I guess I was focused on providing for your future needs." He rolled his eyes.

In recalling the next part of her story, Liz closed her eyes, smiling at the memory. "But from the instant I became pregnant, my world was turned upside down. I felt different and began to wonder what was going on inside of me. At first, I wanted to know what was happening, so I began devouring books about life in the womb. Very soon, when I saw pictures of what a tiny baby looks like inside her mother, I knew I loved my child and that I would prefer to die rather than let any harm come to him."

She opened her eyes again and smiled at him. The boy was leaning back against his pillow again, listening attentively. He gave her the faintest of smiles and a questioning look for her to continue.

"Henry, my boyfriend, was one of the doctors working on the project. In fact, he was the one who had originally gotten me involved. My love for my baby included a conversion of my heart regarding the goodness and beauty of life; this happened to me at the same time as it did to Henry. In fact, he had already starting to feel uncomfortable about the whole project.

"And once we had begun truly loving life, we both felt a hunger to know the Creator of life better. Henry started bringing me books about prayer and faith, and we both grew spiritually together as well. Early on, I confided to him that not only must my son be permitted to live, but that I must be the one to raise him. Henry assured me that they would never let me out of the hospital with our baby alive. They would possibly pretend to agree... but then see to it that I 'accidentally' lost my child. There had been a couple of other strange occurrences involving other women in the project who had second thoughts once they were already pregnant.

"All of us mothers had been 'invited' to stay at the hospital throughout our pregnancies, ostensibly so that they could monitor us and offer us the best care. Only once I was there did I find out that I would never be permitted to leave as long as I was pregnant with a top-secret baby. Henry was the one who came up with the plan for the both of us to fake my miscarriage and then leave for the United States. He had to wait longer, but when he joined me in Texas, we were married right away. Everything we have done has been for the sake of giving Jimmie the opportunity to grow up in a normal way... or at least as normal as a 'super-boy' can be."

The boy's response reflected the loneliness he had experienced growing up. "So Jimmie got all of your love, and we got none of it. My egg was fertilized in a petri dish. My birth mother was a rubber sack in a laboratory and my dad was a splicing of genes from fifteen different geniuses, both men and women. I missed out on having real parents! What's more important in life than that?"

Liz knew instinctively how to respond. She reached out her hand and caressed his cheek. "Jimmie didn't get all of my love. I loved you, too. Hardly an hour went by that I didn't think of you and pray for you and offer my sufferings to our Lord for you. I loved you too, and I love you still. God is your Father, and he has loved you with an unconditional love from all eternity, and he wants to bring you home to him in heaven. Human beings may mess up God's holy plan of having children born into a loving family, but he still personally loves each person who comes into existence. You have been loved and you *are* loved."

The boy closed his eyes and screwed up all of his facial features in an effort to process interiorly all that she said. She kept still in the meantime, longing to bring up the whereabouts of Jimmie but sensing that showing concern for him right now wouldn't be wise.

At last, he looked up at her with confusion in his eyes. "If what you're saying is true, it changes everything," he said.

Liz began praying earnestly for help: for grace for herself to be loving and prudent, and for grace for him to decide to go the right way. She could see there was something frail about his psychology, that he was very young for his age. Dr. Pearson had warned her that they had gotten together and intended to do her harm. Perhaps this boy might end up helping her somehow. She told herself that she needed to be very patient. She hesitated, but then she ventured to ask: "What do you mean by everything is changed?"

He looked away, not answering.

She tried again: "Would it be good or bad if things are changed now?"

He laughed wryly. "Good for you... probably bad for me."

That gave her courage to push a bit more: "Were you or any of the others intending to harm me or Jimmie?" The boy looked away again, keeping silent. Liz's heart began to race. She waited a while, and then repeated softly, "Do you mean to do me harm?"

He shook his head decisively. "Not now," he replied frankly. She smiled gratefully down at the boy and squeezed his hand. He smiled back. Inwardly Liz relaxed somewhat, but the question remained open about the others.

She ventured another question. "But would the others hurt us?"

He hesitated, then appeared to be thinking out loud: "The ones that matter are Alf and Delta." He threw in as an aside, "I'm Beta, by the way. We're the three lab mice. The others were raised in families and didn't have contact with us until we came up with our plan. It was my idea to establish our brotherhood, but then Alf took charge, like he always does. He changed the whole idea, and Delta sided with him like he always does."

His eyes narrowed at the thought and his voice had hardened. She nodded to encourage him to keep going though she didn't fully understand what he meant.

"To top it off, they cut me out of their planning when I protested." These words were soaked in bitterness, as well the ones that followed: "They've always left me out!" Liz rubbed his arm compassionately, hoping that he would come back to the point. But he didn't. "Do you know what loneliness is?" he asked her. She nodded, thinking back on the past months since her husband died. "Can you possibly imagine what it is to grow up in a lab without a mother or father, and to be slighted by your brothers?" He was starting to get worked up, but Liz had no idea what to do or say. "Do you know that the nurses had strict orders not to get attached to any of us? They were closely watched so that they wouldn't make the big 'mistake' of showing us affection!" Liz stopped rubbing his arm and just sat very still, keeping her eyes on his. "Do you know what it is to be sick, and to lay in bed in fear that you were dying, with absolutely nobody to offer you a single word of comfort?" He added as an afterthought: "It was then that I dreamed of having a mother who would sit by my bedside taking care of me." He broke into sobs then, great, heaving, heart-wrenching sobs.

Liz was overcome with tears. She moved closer to him, leaned his head upon her shoulders and embraced him, rubbing his back soothingly and saying gently all the while, "Let it out! Let it out! I know that it hurts! I know that you suffered. I'm so sorry. I would have gladly given my life to keep you from that fate, but I couldn't think of how I could save you or reach you. I'm truly sorry. I'm so sorry!"

Gradually he calmed down and stopped crying. When he was done, he leaned back again on the pillow and wiped his face and nose on the sheet. Then he picked up his train of thought again.

"To be initiated to the brotherhood, you have to promise to take the side of your fellow brothers and stay united around the head. Alf is the head, at least for now. When he does something for you, then you have to do something for him. He got me here to be with you. That's the only thing I've ever wanted: just to meet you." He added, smiling shyly: "And it was worth it."

She smiled back kindly.

"But he said I could only be here for a couple of hours. Then I have to go. I think Alf and Delta are planning to do something after that, but I don't know... they don't let me in on their plans, and I'm not sure I could stop them." He wiped his face and nose on the sheets once more. "I wish I could just stay right here."

Liz hugged him again and kissed the top of his head tenderly. "No one is sending you away."

THIRTY-SEVEN

David was a man of action. He had left Liz alone with Jimmie's twin only because he hoped he would find the real Jimmie when he got home. He would give the kid a piece of his mind for causing his mother so much grief and then return him safely to her as soon as possible. There was no reason to mention this to Liz in advance, since he didn't want to get her hopes up. He simply wanted to act. In any case, Liz had given him her new cell phone number so he could call her right away with the news that he'd found Jimmie. In the meantime, it might do her good to have some time alone with her long lost son. At least she had seemed ready for the encounter when she left his car. So he breathed a sigh of relief when he found Jimmie lounging on his couch with half a pack of empty beer bottles.

He snapped at the boy: "What the heck has got into you? Since when do you help yourself to my beer?"

Unperturbed, the boy stretched his arms languidly and yawned. "Sorry, Coach. Didn't think you'd mind. How's Jimmie?"

David ignored the question and began pacing up and down the room lost in thought. He couldn't understand how such a great kid could change so drastically in a short period of time. Had he fallen into drugs? How could this be Jimmie? Then again, perhaps Liz had made a mistake in checking the other boy's hair line. Maybe she did have Jimmie after all. He wondered if he should confront this boy outright.

"Coach, what's up? You gonna tell me how Jimmie's doing?"

David eyed the boy warily. "Perhaps you could tell me the answer to that question better than I can."

The boy made a face. He sat up straighter in his chair, watching David warily. "Coach, you're acting real weird. Why won't you tell me how Jimmie's doing?"

David decided. He would first check the boy's scalp for himself to ensure he had the real Jimmie. But should he do this by the frontal approach or the oblique method? Deciding for the latter, David walked behind the couch where the boy was sitting. Once he was directly behind him he lunged suddenly to put the boy in a headlock. The kid squealed in outrage and struggled to get loose.

"What are you doing?" The older man wasn't about to waste his breath on this haughty kid. Holding him more or less steady with his right arm, David attempted to brush his left hand through the boy's hairline where the tattoo was supposed to be. But the boy roughly shoved David's arm up and stepped gingerly away from him.

"C'mon Coach, what's got into you?" he demanded angrily.

Still no explanations. David instead kicked off a chasing, wrestling, boxing, and throwing match.

It was fifteen minutes before David had him cornered behind a table. The boy was boxed in, but there was no possibility of reaching his hair. So he flipped open his cell phone and called Liz. The boy guessed what he was about and warned.

"I wouldn't call her if I were you." David ignored him.

"Liz, how's it going with the boy?"

She answered dolefully, "He's gone already and didn't tell me anything about Jimmie."

"Well, I've either got Jimmie or Jimmie's twin. If the boy you had there really is his twin then this must be Jimmie, but I think you must have made a mistake. Mine sure hasn't been acting like him."

Liz exclaimed in horror, "What are you saying?"

He explained proudly, "I didn't want to tell you in case the twin wasn't here when I got back, but he had asked to wait here for me, and sure enough he was still…"

Liz cut him off before he could go on. "David! Get away from him! Run for your life! I was so much in shock that it didn't occur to me that they would take any interest in you!"

That was puzzling. "Liz, what do you…"

She desperately interrupted him again: "Jimmie's a clone. There are lots of them, and they mean trouble. I'll never forgive myself if you're hurt."

David looked at the boy in astonishment and saw a revolver pointed directly at him.

"Hang up."

David hung up slowly.

"Put your hands up and slowly take three steps back." David did as he was ordered.

The boy pushed the table out of the way and directed David to kneel in the corner where he himself had just been standing.

"Put your wrists behind your back." David did so. Once hand-cuffs had been snapped on his wrists his face was shoved harshly into the corner.

"Don't move!" The boy pulled out his cell phone and pushed a button.

"I've got him in the corner. Turns out he didn't know after all, but he just found out." A very brief pause. "Right." The cell phone went back to its pocket.

David couldn't see the boy open his backpack, take out a needle, and prepare it, so it was a good thing that the kid felt he had to speak about what he was about to do, or his plan might have worked.

"I'm going to give you something to make you feel sleepy."

"What do you want with Liz?" David hoped to get the boy talking.

He sneered, "So *now* you want to talk. You should have done that when you walked through the door. Too late now."

A cold sweat came over David. This boy sounded menacing. There was no telling what he might do.

"Don't turn around!" A swift kick stopped David from looking over his shoulder at the boy. "You should be proud to know you're probably the first person Liz has ever told that she's the mother of a clone. Personally, we prefer to keep a low profile. The less people who know, the better."

As he stepped towards David with the prepared syringe in his hand, Hugh and two policemen burst through the door, pointing guns at the boy and ordering him to put up his hands as he had done with David only minutes before. He had set down his gun and so was unarmed. In no time, the boy was led away by the police.

David was sat on the couch nursing his wrists. Hugh eased back in his easy chair to get more comfortable. He was in a very good mood.

"Sorry to let the kid get so far, but it's best to catch them red-handed: makes prosecuting them a whole lot easier, let me tell you! 'Specially because they're still minors. Good thing we decided to wire your place, huh? Doesn't always pan out, but you weren't taking my advice about not getting too involved with the little lady. Can't say I didn't warn ya. Thought you might land up in hot water, and boy, I was right, huh? And don't think that was just any sleeping potion Kappa was going to give you: you would have had a real long sleep, if you know what I mean."

David listened in a daze, not sure if he could believe what had just happened.

"Jimmie's a clone?"

Hugh signaled for him to be quiet, even though they were alone in the room. Then he stood up, pulled a small bug from the side of the big armchair in the room, turned it off, and winked at David. He stared back dumbfounded. All this was too much for him to fathom. He let Hugh run on.

"Now, you've gotta keep that one under your cap, understand? Liz shouldn't have been the one to tell you. Top secret, you know; but for her sake we'll just turn a blind eye on that one. That's good news for you, anyway: it shows that she does care about you after all, because she knows the punishment she could receive for revealing state secrets. She could be extradited for that!" He added to himself for good measure, "Yeah, we'll just keep that under our caps. Of course, I would have done the same if I were her! Yup, I can go to sleep tonight knowing I've done a good day's work, rescuing a faithful citizen like you." He patted himself on the shoulder. As if that chapter were closed, he moved on. "Boy, I sure could use a cup of coffee. How about you?"

Still feeling somewhat disoriented, David moved to the kitchen to put on a pot of coffee. Halfway there, he spun around.

"That means the boy who was with Liz is also a clone. She's in danger! We've got to help her." He made as if to dash out the door, but Hugh held out his arm to stop him.

"Hold on now. We gotta fill you in on a few more details before you do anything else. As a matter of fact, for your own safety you're under a kind of house arrest."

"What?" David frowned in confusion.

Hugh motioned him to calm down. "The coffee, remember? It's good to go over these matters with a nice, hot cup of coffee. You got any gourmet flavors to choose from? Any Danishes?"

David swallowed back his rising impatience, then went back to the kitchen to brew some coffee. Neither spoke until they were seated at the table, coffee and Danishes in hand.

Hugh commented with deep satisfaction, "Now that's my kind of Danish. Looks homemade to me."

He looked questioningly at David to confirm his opinion, but David didn't bite. Instead, he went right to the point.

"If Liz's house is not a safe place to be, then what's Liz doing there?"

I know how ya feel, believe me I do," Hugh answered compassionately. "Liz is very aware that we need to catch these guys redhanded, or they'll be out of prison in no time. You have no idea how dangerous some of them are, so we've just got to catch them in the act like we did with Kappa and you."

David suddenly got it. He flushed in anger. "You know they're dangerous, yet you're using Liz as a decoy!"

Hugh smiled. "You're a bright one, you are. But it's not as pre-
carious as you think: one of the clones is a secret agent who's been
filling us in all along. Don't think I would tell that juicy detail to just
anyone, by the way."

He smiled at David, who glared back stonily at him. Hugh tried
offering some more information to assuage his concern. "We know
where they're hiding out. We know what they're up to. Everything's
well under control. Besides, Liz offered herself as long as her two
youngest kids are kept out of it all, and we're happy to oblige on that
point. They're out of the way, sleeping at their friends' houses. In the
meantime, we watch and wait. You'll want to be hanging around with
me anyway. That way I can keep an eye out for you, and you'll know
what's going on."

David frowned. "I don't like it!"

Hugh laughed tolerantly. "Do you think I do? Now, I do like this
coffee. What's the brand?"

THIRTY-EIGHT

"Now that I've told you all about Mom, Jackie, and Mikey, I'm
can't wait to learn from you about Dad and your life growing up with
him. All my life, my only dream has been to meet him and know
about him. And I want to know how you found us too."

Alf had been so eager to know about Jimmie and his family that
he had tacitly accepted to "go first," but he too was longing to know
everything about his newfound brother. They had been sitting for
hours at the dining table in Alf's roomy RV. Alf had excused himself
to take a phone call and was just coming back into the trailer.

"Sure thing!" he replied cheerfully, as he walked by Jimmie into
the kitchenette. "But first we need to celebrate our family reunion
with some rum and Coke."

Jimmie heard the fridge open, a bottle cap go ricocheting, and
the fizzing sound of a bottle of soda. As he sat waiting, an awful

thought came into his head. His mother had striven all his life to protect him from some grave danger. When he first met Alf he had lost all faith in his mother and trusted completely in his twin. Now, after hours of talking, he realized Alf had told him nothing, whereas he had confided many personal details about his family. It occurred to him that his mother might have some legitimate reason for her actions and fears. But what? Alf hadn't acted suspiciously so far, except not divulging anything about himself. Jimmie concluded that he at least better be on his guard for anything unusual.

Alf returned with two large plastic cups of bubbling drinks. "Let's toast our newfound brotherhood!" Jimmie tapped his cup against Alf's, wondering to himself if he should bother explaining that he preferred not to drink alcohol. He had to keep from choking on his first sip since it was so strong. Rather then putting a damper on the fraternal gesture, Jimmie asked if there were anything to go with the drink as he was feeling somewhat hungry. As soon as Alf disappeared into the kitchenette, he surreptitiously stole his way to the bathroom and poured his drink down the sink. When Alf came back in armed with nacho chips, peanuts, and hot tamale candies, Jimmie pretended to be drinking so that Alf wouldn't see that his cup was already empty.

"Hot tamale candies! My favorite! Don't tell me you like them too?"

Alf grinned. "They say twins experience the same tastes even when separated from birth. Here's proof of it."

Jimmie made sure to keep his drink tipped toward himself as he munched on the food and periodically brought the cup to his mouth, pretending as if he were drinking. He had been playing this trick for over a year with his teammates, so he had it down. In the meantime, Alf began describing how hard it had been for him growing up with an alcoholic father. His life up until now had been colorless and empty. After a while, he stood up and offered to refill Jimmie's drink. From that vantage point, he saw that it was empty and went for more.

Jimmie called after him, "Hey, go easy on the rum, please. That first cup's hitting me real hard!" In fact, he did feel woozy, which was strange because he had drunk so little. Alf came back and stood looking over him with a concerned face.

"Hey, you're not looking too good, bro. Don't tell me you can't handle a little of the good stuff?"

Then he crossed his arms and leaned against the wall watching attentively. The alert look in Alf's eyes and his question caught Jimmie by surprise. It was as if he were expecting something to happen. But what? After all, Jimmie only felt slightly bad. Was he really thinking Jimmie couldn't take the alcohol? Almost against his will, his mind unexpectedly began whirring in the direction he preferred to avoid. If Alf were expecting him to feel worse, he had to have some reason for it. He thought of his potent drink. Hadn't he recently heard his soccer buddies warning his sister to pour her own drinks at a party and not take her eyes off it?

What if Alf put something in my drink? Jimmie asked himself. He wanted to dismiss the idea, peering at Alf plaintively, as if to say: "Don't betray me, brother." His stomach quailed inside when Alf seemed to smirk back. Was Jimmie just imagining something negative in that sideways smile and narrowed eyes? He hoped so, but figured just in case he would find out by trying out some playacting. He half-closed his eyes and began reeling back and forth. Alf, all solicitude, was instantly at his side, taking him by the arm and suggesting:

"Hey, if you're not feeling well, you're welcome to lie down for a while. What's mine is yours."

So Alf really must have put something in his drink! Jimmie nodded and acted like he was attempting in vain to move, so Alf put his arm around his back, pulled him to his feet and half-carried him to the bed. Once Jimmie was lying down, he closed his eyes and tried to breathe deeply as if he were sleeping. Alf was apparently satisfied by Jimmie's pretense, because in no time he abandoned the trailer and drove off in the car that was parked beside it. Jimmie lay there stunned.

He chided himself. What had he got himself into? He knew nothing about Alf, but he had confided in him, telling him about his brother and sister, the lab, his mom and dad. Who knows if the little Alf had told him in return was even true? Jimmie's earliest memories included his mother's fear of being discovered by someone apparently very bad, and yet he had exercised such a lack of caution with Alf. Annoyed with himself for his naiveté and full of remorse for not trusting his mother, he got to his feet and searched for his backpack to get out his cell phone. The backpack was there, but his phone was gone. Next, he went outside and looked up the road Alf had just taken. They had biked around the back of the lake on the other side of town and taken a dirt road to get to this isolated spot. It was odd that Alf had driven off in the opposite direction of town: further back through the lonely woods. *What could be back there?* he wondered.

The most intelligent thing to do was to head back into town, only he didn't want to be surprised by Alf coming suddenly from behind in his car. As he stood there trying to decide what to do, he heard a car coming from the direction Alf had taken, so he jumped into the underbrush to hide himself. He breathed a sigh of relief when Alf drove right past his RV and continued towards town.

Once the car was out of sight, Jimmie's conscience bellowed at him to get out of there as quickly as he could, but he felt an overwhelming impulse to investigate what was in the other direction. Alf must have had some good reason for going that way. Hopping on his bike, he headed down the road as quietly as he could. There, around the next bend, was another, even bigger RV. He could hear raucous laughter coming from it. *Okay,* he told himself, *now I really ought to fly...* But then the thought that had been niggling at his mind came upon him full force. What if his father was in that RV? It was possible, wasn't it? Alf had told him that his father was nearby and that they would meet soon. What if that part of his story were true? Sure it's not wise to trust someone who drugs you, but at least they were brothers. Perhaps he would have an explanation for what he did. If he ran now, he might never meet his father. He couldn't bear the thought of possibly being so close, yet never finding out for sure.

Dreamlike, he found himself abandoning his bike and slowly

tiptoeing toward the RV. He would just peek through the window and see who was there and then be off.

THIRTY-NINE

Just as Jimmie was about to slip around the back of the RV, he heard the sound of stomping feet and froze. Too late to take cover! Two boys came crashing out the door, the one behind evidently chasing the other who was clutching a big bag of Fritos and laughing hilariously. They both stopped dead in their tracks when they spotted Jimmie, while his own blood curdled within him. They looked exactly like him. The one who had burst out first berated him angrily.

"What are you doing sneaking up on us, Alf?" But the other whacked him on the head for his stupidity, then greeted Jimmie affectionately:

"Jay! Our long lost brother! It's about time we meet!" Jimmie looked from one to the other trying to fathom what this meant. Normally he was a quick thinker, but he was completely floored by what he was seeing: two more lookalikes. He hoped that meant he was a quadruplet. The one who had just spoken nodded understandingly: "Yeah, it's a shock, eh? It's not every day you meet so many 'twins.'"

Jimmie's mouth opened and closed. The boy held out his hand, smiling warmly. "I'm Beta, and this is Gamma. We decided to give ourselves new names using the Greek alphabet in honor of the fact that we were brought into existence as numbers... or letters, if you please. Alpha, the one who thought he drugged you, is our chief for now. Congratulations, by the way. It's not often that someone gets the better of him. Believe me, we're not going to let him forget about it!"

He elbowed Gamma in the side knowingly, who grinned oafishly. "There's three more 'twins' inside: would you like to meet them too?"

Jimmie's mind reeled, then seemed to freeze. His chest felt as if a terrible weight were crushing all of his air. It wasn't possible for him to

reflect about whether it was wise or not to enter their RV. He just followed Beta in, walking like a zombie, with Gamma taking up the rear.

Once inside, Beta reached past Jimmie to snatch the Frito bag
from Gamma's hand, then turned and put them into the outstretched
hands of one of the two 'twins' seated at the table. The boy took them
eagerly, smiling his thanks in return. Beta introduced him: "This is
Pi. As you can see, he likes to eat, and some of the others like to give
him a hard time about it."

Pi was noticeably chubbier than the others, but the resemblance
was still unmistakable. As he opened the bag, he smiled up through
blurry eyes at Jimmie, and in a half-slurred voice he said: "Welcome
to the club. Here's to our brotherhood! Want a little rum and Coke
to toast properly?"

Jimmie shook his head. Beta snickered at the offer.

"And this is Lambda."

The boy greeted him with a genuine smile, though his eyes were
dull.

"It's a pleasure to meet ya. Always a pleasure to meet, how did
you put it? A fellow twin. Ha ha ha. That was a good one!"

His speech was slow, not very intelligent sounding, like someone
who had been smoking marijuana for a long time. Beta clapped Jimmie on the back.

"Sit down and join us. We've been dying to see you for ourselves."

It was a round table with a single seat built into the wall. Jimmie
slid in with Gamma and Beta following suit, effectively blocking the
way out. Jimmie was boxed in, though this didn't register with him
until later.

In a louder voice, Beta called out towards the back of the trailer,
"Delta, you wanna come and meet Jay?" When there was no answer,
he shrugged his shoulders apologetically. "He can be kind of surly at
times, but I'm sure he'll come out to meet you soon."

Gamma was the most cheerful and outgoing of them all. He explained glibly, "Let me give you a quick rundown on us because you look kind of out of it. Alpha, Beta, and Delta are what we call the lab mice, since they were raised in a lab mostly. There were six of them in all, while the rest of us grew up in normal families, clueless that we were super-clones. We were the control group. But if you ask me, we're outta control."

Jimmie repeated the word dumbly: "We're super-clones?" The others laughed. Gamma nodded as he patted Jimmie's arm consolingly.

"You got it. You know what our recipe is?" Here he assumed a mock salesman-like pitch: "Blimey lad, we've 'ad genes clipped from the very best of 'em we 'ave: blistery shiny geniuses, top-notch athletes, beauty queens and kings, if that's the way ya wanta put it. Top 'o the line representatives of the 'omo sapien species."

As he was speaking, Delta came out of the back room. Beta, who had deliberately sat at the edge of the seat, turned when he heard the door open. He saw Delta smugly shutting his cell phone. The two locked eyes for a moment. Delta smirked, while Beta frowned back suspiciously. Neither spoke to the other. Delta pocketed the phone, then crossed his arms and leaned against the wall by their table.

Jimmie missed the interchange because he was facing the front of the RV. He was drowning interiorly as the reality of his origins washed over him.

"Wait a minute. If we're a conglomeration of genes from a whole bunch of people…"

"Fifteen to be exact," Beta interjected.

Jimmie gulped before asking, "…Then who are our parents?"

They peered at him curiously.

"He sounds just like you, Beta," Lambda observed.

That brought on raucous laughter from the rest of them, except for Beta. Jimmie gazed around, bewildered. Gamma waved his arm in the air as if he were a student in a classroom.

"Oh, oh, oh! Pick me! I want to take a shot at it. Tell me though, if you prefer a metaphysical, political, biological, sociological, or judicial answer. I'm adaptable. Frankly speaking though, I'm personally inclined to the practical side. I want to know if a clone can have relations with one of his mother gene and egg contributors or not? Seems to me you can. Otherwise, it wouldn't be fair. Too many chicks out of the running!"

While everyone else guffawed, Beta slugged Gamma hard. "Shut up!"

That only made the rest laugh harder. Jimmie was appalled. His stomach churned with revulsion at Gamma's quip and at the realization that as a clone he didn't have a proper father at all. At least his mother had given birth to him. That was motherhood in some degree. Despite the craziness of his setting, her answer sprang into his mind like a single ray of light in a pitch-dark room:

"Your father is in heaven." The wisdom of her insistence on making him wait until he was ready went home to his heart. It was a terrible blow to discover he had no human father, yet knowing that God was his Father above all infused his heart with courage.

Beta, meanwhile, had been peppering Gamma with blows until the laughter subsided. Obviously flustered, Beta looked around menacingly.

"We were at the lab mice part," prompted Lambda helpfully.

Beta took up the story: "Lancaster and Tyler committed suicide within weeks of each other two years ago, so the government called off the whole experiment. They thought they would get bad press. We were an embarrassment for them. So Dr. Pearson, the head doctor, shut down the lab. He took the four of us who were left into his home and acted like he wanted to be a father to us."

Despite his aloofness, Delta spat out bitterly: "But he was faking—the only thing he's really good at. He couldn't care less about us. He wanted us dead so he could move on in his scientific work to something more gratifying."

Beta nodded agreement, adding, "He started promoting 'quality euthanasia.'"

"You know what that is?" Lambda interjected.

Jimmie shook his head. He didn't have the heart to speak. At least he was glad they were so freely offering him information about their past—and his.

"It's euthanasia by a doctor's decision that his patient is no longer living a 'quality' life," cut in Beta. "Do you know how many people would be eligible for it?"

There was no need for Jimmie to answer since Delta explained, his voice dripping with scorn, "Everyone on the face of the planet if Dr. Pearson, good ole Dad, gets what he wants: for the doctor to get the power of decision."

"We realized his intentions to do us in too late," continued Beta. "He had given Silvano a muscle-enhancing drug. Silvano soon grew depressed. Dr. Pearson next had him hospitalized. When we visited him, he told us Dr. P had recommended voluntary euthanasia. We told Silvano to wait, that we'd do an analysis on the drug he'd been given. Delta checked on it right away, and sure enough, it causes depression. But when we returned to the hospital, Silvano had already been euthanized. We knew we were next on the list, so Alf devised a master plan for us to escape together, including those who hadn't even been told they were clones. We didn't even know they existed until I hacked into the government's computer files on our project."

Jimmie's head throbbed with pain. He felt for a minute that he might black out.

Beta went on, "But we knew he would come after us all. It seems he'll only be able to get over his failure with us once we're out of the way."

"That's where the brotherhood comes in," Lamba declared somberly.

All this time, Pi had sat quietly as if in a stupor, but he perked up at the mention of the brotherhood.

"Here's to the brotherhood!" he slurred cheerfully.

Lambda punched him affectionately. Meanwhile, Jimmie's keen mind began to kick in again. One thing was clear: he wanted them to tell him as much as they could. So he nodded attentively at Beta and spoke at last to prompt them to go on with their story.

"So you've all banded together to keep safe from our evil creator."

They grinned and Beta responded warmly, "Now you're getting the idea. Only we're not on the defensive exactly. Alf's conceived a whole plan for us. We're not just a group: we're a true brotherhood."

Pi nodded his heavy head while dipping his cup ceremoniously and affirming, "Here's to the brotherhood!"

Beta ignored him. "Alf brought each of us into the brotherhood with a promise: he'll grant each of our biggest desires, and once he's done, then together we grant his, which is for us to combine all of our talents to do something really great together."

"You just said the second and third stages, but you skipped the first," added Lambda. "To join our clan, first you have to play dead."

Jimmie looked confused, so Beta explained: "As soon as Dr. Pearson euthanized Silvano, our 'lab mouse' brother, we set our plan into motion. We treated his body with a special chemical to keep him from decomposing at the normal rate. Then we kept 'recycling' Silvano's body to stage the deaths of myself, Delta, Gamma, Kappa, Lambda, and Pi. Each time, the local doctor would confirm we were dead, and then the body would mysteriously disappear, and another of us would die."

Jimmie's eyebrows raised in wonder at their story.

"According to the system, we're all dead, except for Alf, who's wanted for questioning." Beta, Delta, and Lambda peered at Jimmie to see his reaction.

He mumbled respectfully, "That's incredible! But I'm not sure I get it. What's the good of playing dead?"

"You don't get it?" Delta answered scornfully. "We're out of the system. Nobody's trying to catch us, kill us, or order us around. And we can set up the perfect alibis for Alf when he needs it."

Jimmie eyed the five look-alikes meditatively, then asked nonchalantly, "So, what is it that each of you wants that Alf is granting you?"

Beta bumped Pi with his elbow as he replied, "Pi just wants to eat and drink good food. He's the easiest one."

All eyes turned on Pi. Realizing he was the center of attention, he made a wry face.

"But Alf's had me on a diet since I joined!" he said woefully. "I've already lost fifty pounds, but Alf says I have to lose fifteen more before he'll grant my wish! It's not fair! Why do I have to lose weight to eat and drink to my heart's desire?"

They chuckled compassionately as he poured himself some more rum. He drank it back in one go, then lay his head down on the table.

Lambda went next. "I'm an easy one, too! I just want drugs. But ever since I joined, Alf has been weaning me off of drugs slowly instead of giving me what I want. I've tried escaping a couple times, but Alf keeps finding me and bringing me back…"

Beta explained, "Alf says we all need to be in serious training right now, and then slowly we'll get what we really want."

Gamma and Lambda rolled their eyes. To avoid further negative comments, Beta hurriedly moved on. "Then there's Kappa. The only thing he cares about is money. He was already a millionaire when we lab mice connected with him. Gamma, Pi, and Lambda were just wasting their time when we found them…" Gamma and Lambda rolled their eyes again as Beta kept talking. "…but Kappa was using his smarts big-time. He's already the head of a computer programming firm. Or he was, anyway. Alf promised him many more millions in exchange for investing his cash and life into the brotherhood. Alf's worried about him too, because he sent him on his initiation mission to bring him into the tightest circle of the brotherhood, but he didn't return."

Jimmie probed: "What kind of mission was that?"

The answer was dissatisfying. "Oh, we don't know. It's the inner circle that calls all the shots, and so far only Alf and Delta, my two best friends, are there."

Jimmie detected distinct resentment in Beta's voice. Delta didn't respond to the jab. His face remained cold and unreadable. Jimmie guessed Beta was hurt at being the lone "lab mouse," not part of the inner core of clones. "All we know is that Pi has been allowed to eat and drink heartily again since then. He was Kappa's chauffeur and arrived back without Kappa in a big fluster. But he gave the lowdown to Alf alone. The rest of us don't know what's going on, or at least I don't." He looked pointedly at Delta, whose face remain stony.

Gamma exclaimed peevishly: "Don't forget about me! I like the best thing of all: women. Lots of 'em. Funny thing is, I don't need help from anyone to attract them. We're fine specimens of manliness, we are. Problem is, Alf keeps trying to make me wait until later." With a self-satisfied air, he let on, "But I won't wait. Wherever we go, I find a way to sneak off and make some lady friends, or lots of them. I even share sometimes, don't I, boys?" He proudly looked to the others for acknowledgment. Lambda and Delta leered as they nodded agreement. "Only now Alfy boy has warned me that I better not sneak away again or I'm out of the brotherhood. It's a tough decision, I'll tell ya."

Jimmie had kept his face expressionless up until that point. At this, he had to fight not to betray the repugnance he felt at Gamma's words. In a hurry to move on, he asked, "What about you, Beta? What are you looking for?"

Delta spoke up derisively, "Beta 'just' wants a daddy and a mommy. That's all... even though clones ain't got no parents!"

Delta avoided Beta's glaring eyes. Instead he reached over, grabbed the bottle of rum and took a big swig out of it. "You've had enough, Pi." The chubby clone lifted his head momentarily, then plopped his head down once more.

"And Delta won't say what he wants most, so it can't be anything good," Beta countered accusingly.

"To each his own," Delta sneered.

The sound of a fast-approaching car broke off the discussion. All eyes were upon Jimmie to catch his reaction. He realized then that he was trapped between his fellow clones. There was no choice but to come face-to-face with Alf again.

FORTY

As soon as Alf stepped into the motor home, he addressed himself apologetically to Jimmie without so much as greeting the others.

"Jimmie! Good to see you safe and sound! I was worried about you! Sorry about earlier on. I've got some explaining to do." He joined them at the table. The other clones tensed up almost imperceptibly. They were intimidated by their leader. Delta remained standing apart, watching Jimmie warily.

"It's like this. I guess I'm not the best at handling emergencies. One of our brotherhood, Kappa, had just disappeared and I freaked out. I needed to see at once if there was anything I could do to help him. But I couldn't abandon you either, even though you weren't ready to meet the 'family.' So I hit on the best solution that occurred to me in that sticky situation—probably not the best. I only intended to let you sleep for a while and planned on returning before you awoke. Didn't go too smoothly though, huh?"

Jimmie kept his voice steady and free of resentment, "There's also the matter of passing yourself off as my twin and telling me my father was alive."

The other clones snickered, as Alf assumed a pained look.

"I didn't mean to offend you. But I can explain that one quite simply. You see, it's not an easy thing to find out you're a clone—at least for the rest of us it wasn't. One of these guys even asked me if he was human or not."

Knowing eyes turned to Lambda, who sheepishly shrugged his shoulders. More snickers.

"I wanted the two of us to get to know each other first—you know, build up a relationship—before breaking the news to you. Make the blow softer that way."

Jimmie wasn't satisfied, though he kept a poker face.

"The others have been telling me about what you've promised to grant each of them. What do *you* want in return?"

Gamma brightened up. "Hey now, bloke, that's a right good question! Personally, I haven't asked it in a while, but I'd like to hear the answer to that one too."

"Me too," piped up Lambda. Alf gave them a withering look. He directed his response to Jimmie.

"Have they explained to you that the brotherhood involves stages?"

"Yes. He knows that he would have to die first," observed Delta sardonically.

Alf shot Delta a warning glance. Beta's eyes flickered from one to the other, trying to read the message that passed between the two. He then pointedly interjected:

"Jimmie knows that he would have to fake his death first."

With an impatient wave of the hand, Alf silenced both Beta and Delta. "I asked because the brotherhood proceeds in steps, as does your knowledge of its inner workings. Once you arrive at the third stage, you'll obtain full insight."

Gamma hunched his shoulders, flexed his muscles, and jutted out his jaw as he declared in a pseudo-grave southern accent, "In other words, boy, he ain't gonna tell ya nothin' 'bout what he's fixin' on doing wid us here lackees. But ya shore are welcome to join the crowd. Why, we folks are jist one big, happy family."

Beta and Lambda laughed, but Delta curled his lip in disgust and ordered threateningly, "Gamma, shut up!"

Alf left off, glaring at Gamma. "Why don't you tell me what you would like? Maybe there's something I could offer you."

Jimmie didn't hesitate to answer. "All I ever wanted in life was to know my father. I don't think you can help me with that one. Oddly enough, my mother has."

Delta spat on the ground. "Your momma! Sweet! Do you know what the woman you call your mother had planned to do with you? You were supposed to be spare parts for us lab mice."

Gamma stretched out to pat his arm soothingly. "'Fraid ole sour-puss has got that one right. You were supposed to be a partial birth abortion so your organs would be as developed and therefore as useful as possible for us designer babes." He puckered up his face in distaste before adding, "Ew!"

Jimmie stared back in disgust.

"Only she had a change of heart. So she eloped with Henry Foster, Dr. Pearson's assistant, and had you instead. People can be sorry for the wrong they do and try to make up for it." Beta began his words enthusiastically, but in the end he just sounded defensive.

"You know, Jimmie, your mom did such a good job of disguising your existence that we didn't even know about you," Alf added matter-of-factly. "You were registered as a miscarriage. In fact, we came here looking for your mom, our egg mother, so Beta's wish could be granted."

Beta nodded, then said somberly, "I've longed to meet her the way you wanted to know about your dad. She's the closest person to a parent for all of us." He added ruefully: "And now that Alf gave me what I wanted I have to do what he says."

Alf looked askance at him.

"No need to sound so dour about it. It's all for the brotherhood, you know." Beta looked down without replying. Alf clapped his hands together, turning his attention back to Jimmie.

"So Jimmie, the crux of it all is that we'd love to have you join the brotherhood. We belong together: just take a look around you." Each of the clones tried to put on a welcoming smile, except for Delta, who coldly looked away. "What do you say?"

Jimmie turned up his palms in a gesture of indecision. "This is all kind of overwhelming for me right now," he replied apologetically. "I guess I do know what I want: I want to dedicate my time to helping people, to doing good, to making this world a better place to live in. Is that what your brotherhood aims at?"

Impressed by his declaration, the clones fell silent for a moment.

Then Gamma burst out appreciatively in a faux French accent, "Ooh la la! Zees boy, he is so very gut! I must say zat I 'ave never zought of life zat way before. But of course, I 'ave been a ray of light for all zee lovely women I 'ave graced my presence with."

Jimmie insisted with Alf, "What are you working for?"

Gamma exclaimed, "Why zis boy is makin' me sink about zee very motives of my life; and I am sinking zat I do not sink enough about zis!"

Gamma's remark brought on a quick reaction from Alf. "Gentlemen, would you kindly leave the trailer now so that Jimmie and I can discuss this matter alone for a minute?" He worded it politely, though it was clearly an order. "You can leave Pi there." He was snoring lightly, head still down on the table. As Alf got up to permit those on his side to leave, he nodded significantly to Delta, who gave one quick nod in return. Beta, Gamma, and Lambda complained about having to go, but they did.

Once they were gone Alf took up the question in a persuasive, urgent tone.

"Jimmie, you've got a lot of talent to bring to the brotherhood. Some of the others still need a lot of work, but you're good to go. We could really use someone like you. Now, I don't ordinarily go so much in depth with the rookies of our group, but you're worth it. The bottom line is that the brotherhood is for the sake of the brotherhood."

Jimmie looked disappointed as Alf went on quickly and passionately: "You don't get it! We got a bum deal in life; practically treated like slaves growing up in the lab, and then having to flee for our lives so as not to be put to sleep like dogs, because the same government that brought us into existence then decided the quality of our lives was too low for a human being. But that's just their excuse to do away with us. We're an embarrassment for them, a nuisance, that's all." Jimmie sat perfectly still, hardly daring to blink. "So we're banding together to protect ourselves and to make something of ourselves. You can't imagine the potential we have for greatness, for wealth and power once we focus our energies and talents on achieving something. Then people will reconsider the quality of our lives."

Jimmie cautiously asked: "Will you do what's good and right?"

Alf smiled condescendingly: "Of course. Everything we do is directed towards what is good... for us. But why ask that kind of question? The governments we'll be dealing with follow the same rules as we do, only they're more powerful than us."

Jimmie wondered if he should bother trying to answer Alf. He guessed that it would be useless. Nevertheless, he sat up straight, sucked in his breath and launched into his response.

"I think I've learned to understand brotherhood in a different kinda way, in a Christian way, where you're concerned about others and look after them. Where you try to help each other to be better people. I really care about my mom and Jackie and Mikey and my soccer buddies and the people in my parish and the community." Jimmie glanced at Alf for an instant, then rushed on:

"To tell you the truth, I doubt that your kind of brotherhood brings happiness."

Alf shook his head in disappointment at Jimmie. "What a shame for all that talent of yours to go to waste!" He rose. "I'll have some of the boys give you a ride home."

Jimmie remained seated, not wishing the conversation to end so abruptly. He offered meekly: "Alf, any of you are welcome to join my family. I'm sure you would be welcomed! Once someone gets a taste of Christian brotherhood, they'll only want more."

"It's bad enough for us to lose you. Please keep your sentimental religious drivel to yourself." With a curt nod of dismissal, Alf threw open the door to the trailer and bid his fellow clones to attach Jimmie's bike to the car.

FORTY-ONE

Beta offered his passenger a box of hot tamale candies.

"Alf told me to give these to you. He said you like them."

Jimmie waved them away. "No, thanks. I've lost my appetite." That was the cue for Lambda to reach his hand forward eagerly.

"I'll have them!"

Gamma caught Beta's eyes through the rear view mirror, then congratulated Jimmie: "Wise choice! We were wondering what we were going to do if you said yes. That was plan 'A.'"

In answer to Jimmie's questioning look, Beta explained: "Alf had Delta lace these candies with LSD. That's why Lambda's so excited to eat them."

Jimmie turned to stare wide-eyed at Lambda, who had poured them all in his mouth by then and was chewing away placidly. "The minute you appeared at our trailer, Delta called Alf to tell him you had shown up. Alf gave him the orders to pass on to us. We were supposed to drug you with the candies, then tie you up and bring you back. Or if you refused to eat them, plan 'B' was to overpower you and do the same as in plan 'A.' But the three of us had the chance to come up with our own plan 'C' instead, which is more satisfying for all interested parties, including yourself."

Jimmie looked from one clone to the other, not knowing what to think or say. Gamma cheerfully took up the explanation.

"So Lambda-boy gets the stuff he craves so bad. And Beta's gonna drop me off in town for my hot date. I was wondering how I was gonna make it. Then good ole Beta's gonna bring you home. You're too nice a fellow to treat badly. The two of us will work out our explanation for how we failed on our way back. You'll pick me up in an hour or so, right, Bet?" Beta nodded. "Too bad I'll have to rush my girl. She won't like it. But that's life in the fast lane."

When they passed through town, Gamma called out: "Here's good. I'll find my way. See you soon."

With Gamma gone, Jimmie ventured a suggestion. "You know, Beta, there's also a plan 'D.' Seems you feel you owe Alf something big for merely letting you meet our mother. But you don't have to settle for one brief moment. We would be happy to welcome you into the family, you and Lambda both. I would have made the offer to Gamma too, but I wasn't thinking fast enough. Alf had warned me not to contaminate you with my offer."

Beta answered slowly, reflectively. "I don't think either of them would be much interested. Maybe I would be, only..." He hesitated, looking glumly at his passenger. "I'm not always this upfront, but I to tell you the truth, I don't know if I could stand being the oddball, the least one loved in a close-knit family. I think it would drive me crazy!"

Jimmie looked back compassionately. "Real love isn't something measured the way you're thinking. Real love accepts others unconditionally. You would be happy with us."

"I dunno," Beta mumbled, almost inaudibly.

Beta parked just outside the gate, explaining that he preferred to leave the car on the outside so that he wouldn't have to disturb anyone when it came time to leave. Jimmie had invited them both to meet the entire family, so they trudged up the road together, Lambda leaning on Beta. Oddly enough their approach to the house was quiet—no dog came out to greet them.

As they drew near Jimmie's home, Beta asked Jimmie if he would help him to support Lambda, while he got something out of his backpack. It didn't occur to Jimmie to ask why the other had brought the backpack in the first place, nor what he needed at that moment. Beta stopped, while Jimmie, completely unsuspecting, continued on with Lambda.

Beta snuck up behind him and dealt him a single, carefully placed blow to the head; Jimmie instantly crumpled to the ground, unconscious. Beta immediately stripped him of his outer clothes. Then he coaxed the clothes off of Lambda as well. Next, he dressed Jimmie in Lambda's clothes. Lambda donned Jimmie's clothes without a protest, though he needed help with each step: first the shirt was pulled over his head, then one arm was directed through and then the other.

When the exchange was done, Beta took rope from his backpack to bind and gag Jimmie. He considered Lambda for a moment, worrying whether he could leave him, but the other clone was completely out of it. Beta dragged Jimmie into the lab and deposited him behind the lab table in the back corner. Afterwards, he returned for Lambda, who hadn't budged. After hoisting him back to his feet, Beta led him into the lab as well and sat him down in the chair that he'd set in the middle of the room. Pulling more rope out of his backpack, he bound Lambda's torso and legs to the chair and gagged him as well. Once he was satisfied with the both of them, he headed over to the house to greet his mother.

FORTY-TWO

Hugh and David sat in Hugh's car on a dark street, sipping their take-out coffees from the Dreamery Creamery and munching on doughnuts. When David's cell phone rang, he checked to see who it was first, then looked questioningly at Hugh.

"It's Jackie." Hugh motioned impatiently for him to take the call. "Answer it! Answer it!"

"Coach!" Jackie's voice was so high-pitched it was almost unrecognizable. "I've tried calling Mom, Jimmie, and even Mikey, but nobody answers and I'm freaking out! We need help now! I didn't know who else to call, except maybe the police."

Hugh could easily hear what she said. "What's up?"

"You're not going to believe me, but Lily and I are sitting on

Jimmie's twin here in Lily's house! He attacked Lily—it was hor-rible! You've got to come help us right away. He's real mad, and I'm afraid we can't hold him down much longer. He won't stop saying bad words!"

The tires screeched as Hugh pulled out. "We'll be there in a minute. Hold on," David said reassuringly. Meanwhile, Hugh was already on the phone to call in the troops.

"...No noise, mind you! No sirens. Whatever you do, don't call attention to yourselves. Park up the street and make your way down in twos. We've got to do this quietly!"

On the way over, Hugh had a few moments to fill David in on what he needed to do. "I already told you that Liz agreed to cooper-ate with us as long as Jackie and Mikey are safe. I'm sure it's Gamma who's thrown a wrench into the plan, by the way. He's a sly one. Our inside man didn't know this was coming. Now, I need you to help calm the girls down and persuade Jackie to stay at Lily's for the night. We'll keep an unmarked car watching the house to make sure noth-ing else happens. The head clone doesn't know Gamma's there either, so we have the advantage here if we play our cards right."

The agents who had been radioed by Hugh got there first. Gam-ma let himself be taken away quietly. When David reached the door, Jackie and Lily both flew into his arms. Hugh discretely herded them back into the house where they would be free of their neighbors' prying eyes. The minute they were seated in the living room, with the draperies carefully closed by Hugh, the two giddy and exhila-rated girls launched into their story. David and Hugh looked back and forth from one girl to another like they were watching a tennis match.

"This has been the most horrible experience of my life: a guy masquerading as my brother attacks my best friend with me in the next room."

She grimaced while Lily added in excitedly, "Coach! He let him-self in with the key we keep hidden underneath the flowerpot. He saw me take it out the other day. I had accidentally told him Mom and Dad would be out for the night, and I would have been alone if Jackie hadn't been here. He was on me in a minute. I screamed and tried to run away from him, but he laughed in this horrid way."

She shuddered at the thought and Jackie took her turn: "When I heard her scream, I rushed in here and saw this guy grabbing Lily. Good thing I only saw his back or I might not have reacted as quickly as I did if I had thought he was my brother. Lily hadn't mentioned to me that she had met Jimmie's twin before."

Lily explained, "I was going to tell her tonight, but he arrived before I could. I just didn't know what to think about him because he was such a pig the other day. So I was waiting to tell Jackie in person. But anyway, all of sudden there's Jackie flying through the air at his side. Only he saw her coming at the last instant. He let go of me to swipe her legs and step out of the way, so Jackie just flew by us both." She giggled. "It's funny to remember how you looked as you went by, Jackie!" The two of them tittered uncontrollably. "Sorry. Then I ran." Lily was consumed again in giggles. Jackie took the opportunity to give Coach an order.

"Don't you dare mention this to Mikey! He'll never let me forget! It would have been a good move if he hadn't intercepted me. Anyway, he turned to chase after Lily, but I was somehow able to grab his feet with my hands and he tumbled down. Then he came at me; we were both on the ground and he took hold of me. I don't know what he was planning to do…"

She made a face at the memory, while Lily cut in to give the grand finale: "We'll never know, because I came up behind him and hit him over the head with Mom's favorite clay vase. It shattered on his head…"

Jackie finished her sentence: "…and knocked him out. I'm going to tell Mom that we ought to invest in a bunch of clay vases so I can give up Tai Kwon Do."

Lily loyally objected, "No way, Jackie! I'm going to start taking lessons with you! We would have been in big trouble if you hadn't known what to do in the first place. And you reacted so quickly. He had already covered my mouth so I couldn't scream anymore! And

Coach, you should have seen how fast Jackie tied him up. It was like she was a rodeo expert or something." The two friends giggled and hugged each other melodramatically.

Hugh nodded at David to make his pitch. "Well, you two girls can sleep well tonight knowing that he's behind bars."

Jackie replied soberly, "There's something funny going on! I can tell. Mom always freaks out if the slightest thing happens, and yet it was her idea for me to stay here in the first place! I've never slept over at anyone's house before in my life. Go figure! Plus, she doesn't answer her phone! Nobody does."

Lily hugged her again. "I'm glad you'll stay here with me! I want help explaining to my parents when they get home, and I'm afraid to be by myself in the meantime! Besides, you're leaving in two days, so this is our last chance together."

David nodded in agreement. "Lily's right on every count. And your mom would have the good sense to know you're safe here as long as that nasty kid is in the hands of the police. You had better stay and keep your friend company."

Jackie made a face, but shrugged her shoulders in agreement. Hugh cleared his throat and flashed his FBI badge at both of them.

"There's no need to worry at all, girls. I'm going to leave an unmarked car in front of your house all night, just in case. We're mighty glad we finally caught this fellow. But I'm going to have to ask you to keep his capture to yourselves for now... that is, until we let you know it's okay to talk about it."

Jackie rolled her eyes. "Secrets, secrets, secrets! My family is immersed in secrets!"

Lily asked timidly, "How do I explain the broken vase?"

FORTY-THREE

With only the light of the moon, Jackie pedaled furiously through the back hills in the direction of her house. She had tried

232 Ask Me No Questions

calling her mother again, and each of her brothers... but still none
of them had answered. That was too much for her. Somehow she
had convinced Lily that she had to get home that night; she was sure
her mother needed her. It had been a piece of cake to get around the
marked car... she had to cross the backyards of the neighbors until
she reached the street, and then she was off.

The approach of a car could be heard in the distance. There was
nowhere to hide because of the sheer drop on one side and a cliff on
the other, so she dismounted, pushed herself against the rock wall
and kept still, with the dim hope that whoever was driving wouldn't
notice her. As the car drew near, it slowed down. Panic welled up
inside of her. Should she drop the bike and try somehow to scram-
ble down the cliff? As the car pulled up, a familiar voice greeted her
warmly from the back of the car.

"Jacks! What are you doing out here so late? Get in, and we'll
pick up the bike tomorrow."

Relief flooded over her at hearing her special nickname. "Jimmie!
It's you! I'm so glad to see you!" She left the bike leaning against the
cliff and hopped quickly into the backseat. "I can't wait to tell you
what's been going on!"

As soon as she shut the door the two boys in the front turned
and leered at her. The driver was an exact look alike of Jimmie and
the other was a chubby runner-up. The smirk on the face of the
one in the back told her he wasn't Jimmie either. She screamed and
reached for the car door, but the boy in the front covered the lock
with his hand, as the car jumped into motion. The boy beside her
wrenched her arms behind her back and held them there in a vice
grip.

"Who are you?" she gasped.

The driver snickered. "Don't tell us you can't recognize your
brothers when you meet them, sis! You're hurting our feelings!"

In her confusion and fright, Jackie naively asked: "So you're
quintuplets?"

All three boys glowered at her as they repeated accusingly, "Quintuplets?"

Alf, who was sitting in the back with her, demanded, "Where did you encounter the other one?" She had enough presence of mind to see by their angry interest that they didn't know what one of their kind had been up to. It was apparent to her that she shouldn't give away that he'd been arrested. Alf twisted her arm impatiently. "Speak!"

Jackie let out a cry of pain, then conceded, "He attacked me."

Another rough twist of the arm. "Where?

"In town." She added before he could question her further, "He jumped out at me when I was approaching my friend's house and scared me. I surprised him with a judo move and then got on my bike and started pedaling away from him as fast as I could."

"Did you tell anyone?"

"I tried to, but Mom and Jimmie didn't answer their cell phones, so I was going home now to tell Mom." These last words were accompanied by unfeigned tears. The three visibly relaxed. She hadn't called the police. Alf stopped hurting her arm, though he still kept a tight enough hold on her.

Jackie didn't attempt to ask any more questions, and the three Jimmie look-alikes didn't bother to speak with her, so they finished the rest of the short ride in a grim silence.

At the gate, the boy in the front passenger seat jumped out to punch in the code. Observing her surprise, Alf explained. "Your brother kindly gave us the magic number in his letter to Coach."

Jackie shrank away from him, consumed by fear. When they pulled up to the house, Liz and Beta came out to the porch right away. She stood there waiting in the light while Beta came forward to greet them.

"All set: exactly as you ordered. But what's she doing here?"

Alf snapped back, "Where's Gamma?"

Beta noted the sharpness of the question. It sounded more like an accusation. His eyes flitted quickly from Alf to Delta, who was glaring fiercely; to Pi, who looked distressed; to the girl, who raised her eyebrows in curiosity despite her sense of dread at what was happening. Beta concluded in an instant they had somehow found out about Gamma.

"He talked us into letting him off in town. Lambda and I thought we could handle the task, and we did."

Delta snarled in disgust, "You idiot! You want him to get caught? It'll ruin everything!" Turning to Alf, he continued: "Told you he'd mess it up!"

"Get Lambda and go find him now! Call me as soon as you do!" Alf ordered gruffly.

Beta's narrowed eyes warily switched back and forth from Alf to Delta. Delta jerked his head. "You heard him," he barked. "What are you waiting for? Go!"

But Beta's crossed his arms mulishly. "I don't want you to hurt them... That wasn't part of the deal."

At that, Delta approached Beta, gesturing threateningly. "You already got what you wanted. You got to meet your mommy. Now clear out."

The two would have come to blows if Alf hadn't shouted, "Shut up, Delta! Leave him alone. He's going." Then he turned to Beta and said in a deliberately reasonable tone, "I'm the one who calls the shots, remember? You'll understand everything later. But for now, find Gamma as quickly as possible."

Alf then pointedly said to Pi, "See that the two of them get on their way now, and then join us in the house."

Beta sighed deeply as he nodded his head slightly in submission.

"You probably saw that our car's parked down by the gate. See you in a while."

Alf's face relaxed. Jackie had been silently taking all of this in.

Now she screamed out to her mother desperately. "Mom, run! Call the police! We're surrounded by Jimmie freaks!"

Instead of showing annoyance or worry, the clones joined together in laughing at her. Liz remained frozen where she was. She wasn't about to call the police as long as she didn't know where Jimmie was, and Jackie's presence only convinced her all the more not to call for help. The clones had already guessed that.

As they disappeared into the house. Beta clapped Pi on the back companionably. "Thanks for the warning look, dude."

Pi smiled back awkwardly. "Didn't know what to do to help you."

"Don't worry. Your face said it all." They both chuckled. "Look, you'll understand. Lambda's already sprawled on the back seat of the car. He was more interested in going on a trip than Jay. I took care of him on my own. You want to see him?"

Pi responded dubiously, "I guess so."

A quick peek through the lab door was sufficient for Pi.

"Do you want to walk me down to the car? I'm hoping you'll help make sure they don't do anything bad to Mom and Jimmie and Jackie…"

Pi evidently felt the same. He seemed nervous about getting to the house as soon as possible. "It's fine. I trust you. See you soon."

Beta began walking down the road towards the front gate, while Pi headed for the house. The moment Pi went inside, Beta sprinted back towards the barn.

Alf called out to Pi as he came through the door. "Pi, help me tie our little sister to this chair." Once her hands were tied and the rope was already partially wrapped around her legs, Alf ordered Pi to finish up on his own and then stand guard outside the barn. He had spotted Mikey's handcuffs on the floor and picked them up. Snapping one of the handcuffs around Liz's wrists, he indicated that she should go along with them.

Pi meanwhile knelt by the chair and began tightening the rope.

He didn't hear Mikey come up from behind and was felled instantly by the blow with a clay pot. It shattered upon contact with his skull.

"That does it! I'm never taking Tai Kwon Do again! Mikey, am I ever glad to see you! At least I know you're not a clone!" They smiled joyfully at each other, then set to work.

"It's a good thing I know how to do this so fast," Jackie remarked companionably as they tied up the clone.

Mikey couldn't resist boasting. "All part of the plan! C'mon, hurry up! We've got to get to the barn to save Mom!"

Pi came to as they were finishing up the last knot. When he realized what they were doing, he swore, then declared urgently: "You've got it all wrong! I'm on your side! I want to help you. You need me!"

Jackie looked down her nose at him. "Couldn't you at least try to say something more original?"

The boy rocked back and forth in his chair anxiously while Mikey dashed for the kitchen. "I'll get a rag for you know what..." he called out over his shoulder.

Pi went still and squeezed his eyes shut in deep concentration for a moment. Then he tried speaking again in a forced conciliatory tone. "You don't understand! But that's okay. You can leave me tied up if you want. I just need you to reach into my pocket and dial a phone number. The FBI is waiting for my call to move in. Believe me: your lives depend on it. We have to help your mom and brother now!"

Mikey caught some of his words as he ran back into the room. Brother and sister raised their eyebrows at each other. Jackie's voice dripped with sarcasm.

"Thanks for the big tip!" Then she grabbed his head while Mikey stuffed the rag in his mouth. They only had a thin rope to tie it and did so quickly.

"This isn't gonna hold for long," lamented Jackie.

But Mikey insisted that they go. "C'mon, we don't have time. Mom needs our help!"

When they got outside, Mikey told Jackie to wait a moment as he rushed around the back of the house. He emerged a few seconds later with Shep tightly in his grip, and they ran together towards the barn.

"I tied him up and muzzled him to keep him safe until we needed him..." he explained.

Despite the urgent situation, Jackie's curiosity got the better of her: "I thought Shep was supposed to keep *us* safe..."

Between puffs, Mikey was proud to fill her in. "Naturally. But don't you remember what happened to the dog in the movie *The Bourne Identity?* The assassin killed him first thing."

As they approached the front of the barn, they heard running footsteps. Mikey whispered urgently for them to pull away from the building instead of what seemed more natural: to go up against its walls. In any case, the moon had gone behind a cloud, giving them the cover of darkness.

FORTY-FOUR

Jimmie felt a throbbing pain in the back of his head. When he tried to move, he discovered that his hands and feet were tied. Groping through his memory, he recalled helping Lambda to walk, then groaned as he realized what must have happened. To add to his shock, Beta shook him warningly as soon as he stirred. His voice quivered nervously as he spoke.

"Don't make any noise, or I'll have to knock you out again. It's for your own good. Alf and Delta are coming any moment, and we're both dead if they discover us here. I promised your mom I would do my best to help you, and that's what I'm doing in the way I know how. You've got to trust me. I've hidden you here so you can witness what happens without being involved. And you're tied up and gagged to ensure you cooperate with me."

Beta was hunched down on all fours beside him, both of them hidden from view. With the approach of footsteps, Beta urgently warned Jimmie once more. "Shhh. Not a sound. Our lives depend on it!"

Jimmie strained to grasp his predicament but couldn't succeed in understanding the other's boy's words and warning.

"Jimmie!" Liz gasped when she saw the boy she assumed to be her son trussed up on a chair. The boy stared back vacantly without stirring. She tried to go to him, but Alf yanked her back by the cuffed hand, then snapped the free handcuff around the bar of the long lab table closest to the door.

"Prepare the barn quickly," he said to Delta.

Once Delta had left the room, Alf commented to Liz conversationally, "It's a pity you've indoctrinated our brother so badly with your silly, backwards moralism. He's useless to us now. I had hopes he would join us, that is, as soon as I discovered his existence. He would have been so valuable."

Liz chose her words carefully, speaking softly, pleadingly. "Is there anything I could say or do to protect him? He's done nothing wrong. I would give my life for him and all of my possessions!"

Alf remained aloof. "I'm afraid the arrangements have already been made. You see, you're only useful to me insofar as you're of interest to my boys. And through you, I get two for the price of one. Beta's been satisfied, and now it's Delta's turn. But he drives a hard bargain. Believe me, I would have preferred it otherwise too." He gazed at her sympathetically.

"I must say, you hid Jay's existence very well. It's just too bad for you that you neglected to warn him about his siblings... I'd love to know why. He told me everything, thinking I was his long lost twin." He chuckled at the memory, even turning to Liz to share his mirth.

Liz clenched her fist and bit her lip but made no reply. Her mind went back to her wrists. These handcuffs were Mikey's—the trick ones he had tried out on the entire family, including her. But what made them open? It was so long ago that she didn't remember. She turned her arms around studying them carefully while trying to dis-simulate her purpose.

Delta came back into the lab and nodded curtly at Alf as if to say he'd finished his task. Alf replied to the other's unspoken question.

"Get on with it then. Just remember, we don't have much time."

Delta opened the pouch strapped to his waist. He extracted a sy-ringe needle and a small vial. Liz observed the needle, then went back to the handcuffs, still trying desperately to figure out their secret. Delta unscrewed the vial, sucked up the contents with the syringe, and carefully pushed the air bubbles out of it. Then he laughed and shrugged his shoulders.

"Don't know why I'm bothering about the air in the needle…" Stationing himself right next to the Lambda, he looked over at Liz to make sure she was paying attention.

"This is for your sake, not his. I need to see you suffer. It's part of the punishment I need to ensure you receive."

Liz pulled desperately at the cuff realizing what was about to happen. She had no doubt the injection would be lethal.

"Please don't hurt him. He's innocent, like you. He's done noth-ing wrong."

Jimmie's head was pounding. He didn't grasp what was going on, why his mother was pleading for his life when they apparent-ly couldn't see him. And if he dared to move the slightest, he was pushed down forcefully, because Beta knew full well what was going on. It was imperative for his plan that Alf and Delta not realize they had Lambda instead of Jimmie in front of them.

Delta continued: "It's important for me that you understand what I'm doing. The only thing I want in life is to mete out justice to those who brought me into the world the way they did." He paused, waiting for his words to sink in.

Liz pleaded, "I didn't know what I was doing. They told me it was for the sake of progress. I was sorry immediately afterwards.

Forgive me! But where's the justice in taking an innocent person's life? And he's your brother. Spare him, I beg you. Do whatever you want to me instead."

Delta went on with his discourse as if she hadn't spoken. "When you surrendered your eggs so freely to start off your homo sapiens experiment, you condemned me and my brothers to a nightmare infancy, a childhood of loneliness, and an ever-darkening horizon of meaninglessness. What's life when you're a mere number?"

Alf was standing back, keeping himself out of the picture, but he couldn't resist a sardonic interjection, "He's got a good point, you know. You really are asking for trouble when you start manufacturing kiddies. A person without any bonds of loyalty is a danger indeed. He'll either sell out to the highest bidder, or consume his energies in forming a society of like-minded individuals."

Liz sank down on her knees, crying out in anguish, "I'm sorry. I freely admit to making a bad choice. It was so wrong of me, but I was only a young girl and didn't know any better. I didn't think it through, and I regretted it almost right away... as soon as I was pregnant with Jimmie. I was too late to help any of you except Jimmie. But I've thought about you. I've cared about you. I've prayed for you. Please do whatever you want to me; just don't punish my son for my mistake. What harm has he done?"

"The clock's ticking," Alf snapped at Delta. "Do it! We can't afford to stay here long."

Delta brought the needle to Lambda's arm. "You don't get it. This is the best punishment for you, to witness the demise of your beloved son. Now you'll truly regret what you've done." He added significantly: "Your husband got a similar treatment before his unfortunate crash; he knew why he was about to die, and it killed him to hear we were coming after you next."

At those words, Jimmie grunted in shock. Then things happened fast.

"Who's there?" Alf demanded.

Beta had to decide quickly what to do. He dealt Jimmie another knockout blow (he had kept his arm poised just for that purpose), while exclaiming loudly to cover the sound, "Don't do it!" He jumped to his feet and faced the three people in the room. "That's Lambda you're about to kill. Jimmie is already miles away from here, nice and safe!"

Delta pulled the empty syringe from Lambda's arm and threw it at Beta in unspoken rage, while Alf stepped over to inspect the victim. Pushing up the right sleeve of his shirt he and Delta both saw Lambda's distinctive "mother" tattoo. They glared furiously at Beta for his trick and stepped towards him menacingly. Beta had already stepped around the table to keep them away from Jimmie's hiding spot. Then he jumped up behind the long lab table on the side of the animal cages, grabbed a beaker, and dashed the bottom against the corner of the table. He waved the broken jar warningly.

Meanwhile, Liz had discovered the trick to releasing the hand-cuffs and slipped them off. She inched silently towards the door. The others turned to look at the sound of the handle turning. Liz bolted, with Delta pounding after her. Beta grabbed the top animal cage, which was at the height of his head and hurled it at Alf along with the broken beaker, and then took off after Delta. Alf would have run too, but he heard a moan coming from behind the back table. On seeing Jimmie laying there, he smiled triumphantly.

"Miles away, are you?"

FORTY-FIVE

Liz didn't notice her two youngest children outside the barn. She was running too hard towards the house, intent both on rescuing her daughter and escaping from the clones. Neither Jackie nor Mikey called out to her because they were focused on stopping her assailants. Shep growled fiercely, pulling to get loose from Mikey, but he held on tightly until they reached the barn door. Then he commanded the dog: "Lilliput!"

Shep sprang into action. Like a good shepherd dog, he didn't attack the boys head on. By snarls and snapping, he herded the runners towards the side of the barn. Liz heard Shep and hoped he would slow down the clones, but she didn't waste time turning around to find out.

Delta and Beta were still running full tilt, even while veering away from Shep, when they were caught in Mikey's trap. To their surprise, each of them was ensnared in many fine strings, with the speed of their propulsion binding them more tightly. The more they struggled, the more the strings entwined them, to the point that each of them was soon suspended from the side of the barn in a cocoon-like mass.

Despite the desperation of the circumstances, Mikey permitted himself to prance around victoriously for a few seconds. He chortled gleefully, clasping his hands in the air triumphantly.

"It worked! It worked! I really am a genius!"

Jackie, awe-struck, gaped first at the cocoons and then at her brother.

"You don't mean to tell me that *you* did this?" She added solemnly, "I will never again in my life call you a freak! But how are we supposed to know whether one of them is Jimmie?"

Mikey stood still, and they fixed their attention on the two dangling boys. Both were uttering terrible profanities, so the two children drew the same conclusion simultaneously: neither of them could be Jimmie. Mikey ordered Shep to stay on guard over his prisoners.

Grabbing his sister's arm, he exclaimed, "C'mon, maybe Jimmie's in the barn! We have to help him."

Jackie protested, "We can't just run in, though. There might be another one of them around!"

Mikey dashed off, saying, "I know what we can do. Follow me!"

He led the way around to the back of the barn, carefully skirting the remaining Lilliput strings. Jackie blinked in shock when Mikey stopped at the wall of the barn, some distance from the back door, and pulled open a small secret door. He got down on his hands and knees and scrambled in, signaling for her to follow. As Jackie crawled through the opening, Mikey handed her a lighted miner's cap, like the one he had already put on.

She said accusingly, "You little sneak! Now I know where you were that day in the barn when I was trying to talk privately with Jimmie!" But Mikey shushed her urgently, warning her with a gesture that they might be heard. He crept deeper towards his secret lab entrance, with Jackie close behind. Mikey had the presence of mind to scoop up the book *To Kill a Mockingbird*, which still lay open on the floor where he had left it months ago. He surreptitiously slid it under his shirt. Jackie had always accused him of stealing it from her, and up until then he had claimed innocence. It would be better to avoid any sibling discord at this fragile moment. From their new spot, they could easily hear what was being said inside the lab.

Alf had just begun a far-out pitch to Jimmie after having removed his gag and slapping him back into consciousness.

"Things have changed somewhat, so I can give you one more chance. Any minute, Delta and Pi will report to me that your mother and Beta have been dealt with. I can't stave off your mother's demise. Sorry about that, but you have to understand it's my exchange with Delta for his full cooperation."

Mikey and Jackie looked at each other wide-eyed, then gave each other a silent high five. Jimmie gazed groggily back at Alf, trying to take in what he was saying. He felt that it was useless to protest.

"The modification is that your death is no longer necessary. It was part of the plan to punish your mother... but I suspect she has already gone. So you can live if you choose to join us. In return, I can offer you money, women, power, you name it. After all, you have just as much right to belong to our brotherhood as we do. You're one of us."

Mikey and Jackie stared at each other in horror, while Jimmie on the floor just above them tried shaking his head to rid himself of the stupor that still clogged his mind. One thought came to him only.

He expressed it with great confidence and dignity.

"Mom was right all along. Our Father is in heaven!"

Alf's eyes shrank to mere slits. "What?" he demanded impatiently.

Mikey mumbled to himself, "If only I'd been able to finish making my smoke bombs, we could have rescued Jimmie already."

Jackie asked him what he said, but he hushed her.

Though Jimmie was in dire straits, he felt calm and sure of himself. He went on, "We're not limited to a brotherhood of clones. Even if some individuals have erred and gypped us out of normal parents and a happy family life, nobody can take away our heavenly Father. He is our true creator, and his love is infinite..."

Alf disgustedly cut him off, "You fool! You could be somebody by joining us, but instead you've sealed your own fate! And you've nobody but yourself to blame for your wasted life. I wash my hands of you." He pulled the gag back in place, stating coldly, "We'll put this back on just to make sure nobody hears you cry for help."

Next, Alf looked impatiently toward the door, then flipped open his cell phone and tried calling first Delta and then Pi. No answer. Something was up. They should have finished with Liz and Beta by then... Before opening the door, he turned back.

"Bon voyage! Say hello to your heavenly Father for me—or to nothingness. Whichever comes first!"

He peeped cautiously out and listened. He could hear a dog growling, as well as Beta and Delta accusing each other angrily from their cocoons. He slowly worked his way to the back door of the barn, carefully choosing each step.

FORTY-SIX

Liz flew through the front door of the house and locked it behind her. She hadn't considered where the other clone was. Her only thought had been to get to her daughter. But instead of finding Jackie, there he was in her place, tied to the chair, which was laying on the floor. He had succeeded in pulling his gag off using the fireplace andiron.

"Where's my daughter?" she demanded tensely. Instead of answering her question, Pi called out:

"Southampton!" That was the code word he was supposed to use to identify himself to Liz as the undercover agent. "Cut me loose!"

Relieved to know that he was on her side, she turned momentarily to peer nervously out the front window into the dark, wondering how successful Shep had been at deterring the clones.

"Why are you tied up? Where's my daughter?"

Pi grunted impatiently. "You've got to listen to me! It's urgent for you to call Hugh so they'll move in. Take my cell phone from my waist and push 'send.'" He added, "Ma'am, this is urgent! Hurry!" when she didn't move as fast he wished.

Liz wanted help more than he did. Two of her children were missing and could already be in the clutches of the clones. As she grabbed Pi's phone and pushed the button, she repeated her question anxiously: "Please, I beg you: where's Jackie?"

Pi visibly relaxed when he saw her hit the send key. Reinforcement would be there any minute. Despite his embarrassment, he described what had happened.

"I was tying up Jackie. The next thing I knew, she and your son had tied me to the same chair. Mikey must have knocked me out."

Liz gasped to hear that Mikey was around as well.

"Mikey! Where is he?" She called out loud, "Mikey, Jackie—are you here?" Pi resumed his explanation once she turned her attention back to him. Neither of her children had responded.

"After tying me up, I heard them talking about going to save you in the barn. They took off towards... Hey, wait—let me go first! I can help you!" If his hands were free, Pi would have hit something in anger at himself for not predicting her reaction. She left him laying there on the floor, still tied up, while she headed for the back door with the intention of sneaking around the side of the house in search of her children. Pi yelled again in vain: "Please, just let me go! I can help you!"

When she reached the barn, Liz peered up at the boys in the cocoons. Shep was growling at the both of them, so she concluded that neither of them could be Jimmie.

"Mom, it's me, Beta! I hid Jimmie behind the table inside the lab. Alf hasn't come out yet. I'm worried he may have discovered Jimmie." He left out the part about Jimmie being tied up. "And Jackie and Mikey ran around to the back entrance of the barn to try to help their brother. They thought he might be inside." As he spoke, five unmarked police cars careened into sight and screeched to a halt outside the barn. Heavily armed men poured out.

It was at that very moment that Alf reached the back of the barn. He heard the cars pulling up and knew he had little time to get away. With a smirk, he threw a lighted match into the barn. *That'll get their attention,* he thought, as he rushed away into the darkness. He had already thoroughly studied the map of the area and had three backup escape plans in case something went wrong. Unbeknownst to anyone, including his fellow clones, he had stashed a moped bike up in the hills precisely for a moment like this. He would reach it and be gone from the area in no time.

The entire inside of the barn burst into flames, thanks to the straw that Delta had scattered and soaked in gasoline. Liz screamed in horror at the sight of the high flames blocking the way to the lab. She would have attempted to run through the fire if two of the men hadn't caught her and held her back. Frantically, furiously, she fought to escape from their grasp.

"My children are in there! We have to get them out! Let me go!" David appeared at her side and tried to calm her down, but in her frenzy she didn't recognize him. Hugh bid Dr. Pearson to sedate her. Once the shot took effect, David carried her limp body into the house.

Meanwhile, Mikey and Jackie had burst into the lab as soon as they heard Alf go out the door.

"Is he alive?" asked Jackie tremulously. Mikey took a hold of his brother's arms and started pulling.

"Of course! Look at his chest. Hurry! Help me get him out of here in case he comes back." It was short work for the two of them to lower his body through the opening. Mikey carefully shut the trap door behind them before they dragged Jimmie towards his special entranceway. They had just reached it when thy heard the cars arriving.

"That'll be the FBI," guessed Jackie out loud. At that, Mikey looked expectantly towards his sister, who explained tersely: "One of the clones attacked Lily while I was at her house. The FBI showed up with Coach David. It's gotta be them."

After easing open his secret door a few inches Mikey peeped out. He was just on time to witness Alf throwing the match into the barn. They heard the burst of flames and watched his hastily retreating figure.

Once he was gone from sight, Jackie exclaimed: "Let's get out of here before we get burned alive!" To her surprise, Mikey hushed her to be quiet. He kept the door barely open and signaled for his sister to move closer so she could see out too. Seconds later they watched a bunch of men running towards the woods, obviously in search of Alf. Mikey waited until they didn't hear anymore footsteps before pulling Jimmie into the open air.

"C'mon. We've got to get him to safety."

Jackie's estimation of her younger brother had shot up exponentially in the last half hour, so she asked with remarkable docility, "What do you mean? Isn't he safe here? Shouldn't we untie him?" Jimmie nodded his head emphatically in agreement and grunted. However, Mikey was too agitated to explain his reasoning.

Ignoring his brother's signals, he whispered urgently, "Help me and once we're there I'll elucidate on the matter!"

Jackie gave in. They succeeded in dragging him unseen to Mikey's hideout under the car chassis. Once they were safely inside, sitting in the dark at Mikey's insistence, they both hugged their brother and whispered their joy at being reunited. But when Jackie went to set her brother free, Mikey detained her hand. In his heightened excitement, he forgot to use his usual formal language with his sister.

"This is like *To Kill a Mockingbird*, only Jimmie is Boo. Don't you see how convenient it would be for him if everyone thinks he died in the fire?"

Jackie didn't get it, but her newfound respect for her little brother made her ask him meekly to explain more. He went on, "Mom's been passing him off as dead for all these years, and people have left us alone. So if everyone thinks he burned to death in the fire, then maybe he can live in peace and we can go back to normal."

Jackie sighed: "We'll never be a normal family!" Then tenderly: "Can't we at least let him go?" Jimmie wiggled and thumped his agreement. But Mikey was adamant.

"No! You know Jimmie! He'll insist on racing out there and trying to do something heroic." Jimmie grunted in protest, but the gag held firm. "He's got to stay hidden anyway, so he may as well be tied up for good measure. Now, for our part, we've got to run together to the forest so the FBI agents can discover us there cowering in fear. Then we need to weep and carry on woefully when they break the terrible news to us that our beloved brother has been killed. I'm sure Mom would highly approve of my idea."

Jackie felt for Jimmie's forehead, planted a kiss there, and gave him a big hug. "See you soon! Behave!"

Mikey added apologetically, "Sorry! But you really are better off dead right now!"

Then they abandoned him and scuttled off to the woods. A short while later, a kindly agent found them whimpering under a bush.

Mikey permitted the man to take his hand as he snuffled uncontrollably, while Jackie, stammering incoherently, latched with all her might onto the man's free arm. They were led into the house and brought into the kitchen.

David was summoned from Liz's room, where he had been keeping vigil over her. She was still deep in sleep. Hugh met him at the bottom of the stairs.

"What are Jackie and Mikey doing here? I thought they were supposed to be safe in town!"

Hugh shook his head. He kept his voice low. "Couldn't tell you. Seems the clones picked Jackie up as she was biking home, and Mikey knocked Pi out as he was tying her up. He's not too proud of the fact, by the way, so I wouldn't mention it to him. They were found together just now, hiding in the forest. Went to enter through the back of the barn to help their brother but saw Alf coming out. Poor kids! They witnessed Alf set the place on fire and then they took off in a dither, worried that Alf had seen them. They're both crying in the kitchen, demanding to know if their brother got out safely. We think you should be the one to break the news to them. Their mother's in no shape to do it. Beta's confirmed that Jimmie was tied up inside." He mopped his forehead. "Didn't stand a chance in that fire! Horrible way to die!"

David's heart sank. He had stayed by Liz's side, so this was the first he'd heard of Jimmie's death. "It will break Liz's heart!"

"And their siblings! Get a load of that wailing. Let's go! They need you."

David followed in a daze. He wondered how he could comfort Liz's children when he too felt devastated.

The agent who had found them was standing off to the side keeping a respectful silence. Jackie and Mikey sat at the table with their heads down in their arms. Mikey sniffed quietly, while Jackie sobbed noisily. She picked up her head to grab a Kleenex and blow her nose, then plopped it back down again. Her back was to the door so she didn't see that David had entered the kitchen. Hugh cleared his throat.

"Uh, Jackie, Mikey, we've brought you someone." No response from either of them. "It's your Coach. He wants to talk to you." David made a face of helplessness at him. Hugh returned an encouraging smile. To the children he added: "All of us agents are going to clear out of the house for now and leave you alone for some family privacy. We'll be outside if you need us for anything." With a reassuring wink at David, Hugh and the other agent retired from the room.

Jackie fell silent, but neither she nor Mikey moved until they heard the front door slam. At once their heads shot up, all smiles, to give each other an exultant high five. David's baffled expression made them chortle with glee. He had no idea what to do with them, so he waited until they were calm enough to explain themselves. They launched eagerly into their story, while David sat in rapt attention. When they were done, he stretched out his hand to congratulate Mikey.

"Flawless, Mikey! You had all of us fooled!"

Hugh's voice came from the other side of the door. "Correction. You had the majority of us fooled, but not this old dog!" The children's mouths gaped in disbelief as Hugh sauntered through the door. "It's hard to pull the wool over Uncle Hughie's eyes, so don't feel too bad."

FORTY-SEVEN

Late into the night, the moon was briefly freed of its billowy covers, affording enough illumination to view the late night scene at the Foster homestead. Near the blackened, smoldering skeleton of the barn were the same five unmarked police cars, which hours before had parked so haphazardly outside the barn. At this moment, they were neatly lined up in a row, their engines purring. Orders had been given to leave in intervals to avoid attracting undo attention.

Jackie had gladly relieved Coach David of his coveted vigil by Liz's bed. Very little could have made him stir from her side. However, Hugh McClury had proved up to the task. He had warned David that there would be big trouble if Mikey helped Jimmie to sneak away. So there was David, ostensibly conversing in the fresh night air with Dr. Pearson, Hugh, and Pi, while all the time his main focus was to keep his charge within sight For his part, the small boy was intent on bidding farewell.

Mikey peered into the back seat of car number one. There, in between two large men, sat Delta. In response to a tap on the back pane, the FBI agent rolled down the window.

"Sir, may I please say something to Delta?"

The man nodded kindly. "You'll have to be quick. We're just about to pull away."

On hearing the request, Delta glowered, keeping his eyes forward. Mikey's stomach churned within him, but he stood firm.

"Delta, I know my mother would say this to you if she were awake. I willingly stand in her stead since I echo her sentiments." The face remained stony, eyes ahead. Mikey continued resolutely. "I want you to know that we forgive you."

Despite himself, Delta was shocked into looking for one brief instant at the small boy. In that short glimpse, he read sincere forgiveness and sorrow. For his part, Mikey witnessed a very hurt soul unveil a longing to believe the other and to be free of the mire in which it wallowed. Delta faced forward again as the car pulled away. It seemed to Mikey that the boy sat up straighter in his seat.

On to car number two. The window was already rolled down.

"Sir, may I please say something to Beta?"

After receiving the go-ahead, Mikey stuck his hand past the agent towards the clone.

"Good-bye, Beta. Thank you for trying to help Jimmie."

Mikey based his words on what he'd heard from Pi, who had listened to Beta's side of the story. His version explained why they had found Jimmie tied up. Beta shook it awkwardly, not only because his hand was cuffed to the man beside him, but because he was touched by the warmth of the gesture.

"I'm sorry it wasn't enough to save him. I wish I had died in his place!"

The boy was not prepared for Mikey's solemn answer: "Perhaps God called him home to heaven because he was ready. If Mom were awake, I'm sure she would repeat her invitation to you to join our family. Welcome."

He smiled his best. Beta had to look away and gulp to keep tears from escaping. He wasn't able to reply before the car pulled away.

As he approached car number three, Mikey overheard Pi's lively words: "So it turns out that Jimmie and I were using the same trick of pouring out our drink when nobody was looking. You know they say identical twins think alike. Perhaps there's something to that." All four men fell into an awkward silence at the approach of Mikey. Their cheerfulness didn't match his terrible loss. Hugh finished their conversation by giving a hearty handshake to Pi.

"Stupendous work. We'll be expecting you to report to H.Q. first thing Monday morning. You can start your formal training right away." He chuckled heartily. "You've done it the other way around—baptism by fire—so it'll be a piece of cake for you." Once Coach David and Dr. Pearson had said their brief good-byes, Mikey stepped forward and offered his hand to Pi as well.

"I'm sorry we tied you up and refused to listen to you. Thank you for trying to save my brother."

Tears flowed down his cheek unchecked. Pi ignored the hand and gave him a big hug instead. "I'm sorry we couldn't save him. He was a good guy!"

As Pi's car pulled away Dr. Pearson commented to Hugh, "Just as a polite reminder, the mandate from my government is to ensure that all of the clones are returned to Canada."

Hugh very courteously put his foot down. He wagged his finger back and forth. "Oh no! Not Pi! We're not parting with that boy. Sorry. He cooperated with us from the very beginning and has done nothing wrong. Besides, he's an American citizen now, so that would be an export."

His interlocutor maintained his customary composure, though his hastiness in answering suggested he felt the matter strongly. "He belongs to us."

Hugh's eyes glinted. "Sorry, but in the United States a person is not a piece of property. We had to go through a civil war to learn that one."

The two of them had worked closely together for the past months, so they knew each other well. Dr. Pearson knew that arguing wouldn't get him anywhere. He nodded and returned the smile.

"I see. Well, thank you for everything. I trust that you'll be contacting me as soon as you pick up Alpha's trail."

"Of course! Hopefully sooner than later, though don't hold your breath too long. But what am I doing telling that to you—you're the mastermind who knows them inside and out."

With a polite nod at Coach David (the two had never hit it off), Dr. Pearson turned towards his car. Mikey was waiting there for him. He looked up at the man through his tear-stained face.

"Sir, there's something I wish to inquire of you if I may, please."

Behind Dr. Pearson's back, David and Hugh raised their eyebrows at each other, wondering what Mikey would say. The man smiled condescendingly, disarmed by the boy's earnest, formal manner. "Of course."

"Sir, although I'm young, I'm a fellow scientist. If I have understood correctly, the purpose of science is for human progress."

The senior scientist nodded his head "Yes, that's elementary."

"If someone came along, purporting to make new and improved homes, and then proceeded to produce a jack hammer to tear up the concrete foundation already laid, I think it would be a travesty not to first ask what the person intends to use instead."

Dr. Pearson frowned slightly but waited for Mikey to go on. "Now, if the person said he was replacing the concrete with sand, the homeowners would do well to send the charlatan away."

Dr. Pearson blinked at the boy before patting him on the shoulder. "I would guess that you're in shock from your terrible loss today." He addressed David who had moved behind Mikey. "I recommend that he gets a good amount of sleep. Perhaps I should leave you a sedative for him and his sister if you—"

Mikey cut in respectfully before Dr. Pearson could finish his sentence. "Sir, I may not have the entire picture of the reproductive process, but I know the most important aspect. I have this deep security right inside here." He thumped his chest where the heart is located. "I'm at home with myself because I know I came from love. I'm fully aware that's not a scientific concept, but I assure you that nevertheless it's real. Furthermore, there's no improving on that. I wouldn't trade it for all the brain or all the brawn in the world. It seems elementary to me that you're depriving a person of that basic foundation as soon as you start trying to concoct them in a petri dish. I assure you, that is no progress at all but mere manipulation! Jimmie deserved better!" These words were accompanied by a steady stream of tears.

At this point, David placed his hands on the boy's shoulders. "Dr. Pearson, it's very late. You've got a long drive ahead of you. We shouldn't hold you up any longer."

Surprised at the interruption, Mikey twisted his neck to gaze questioningly up at Coach, who merely patted him on the shoulder. Dr. Pearson promptly accepted the suggestion.

"Thank you. It's true, we have a long drive ahead of us. The sooner all of us can get some rest the better. He added with a rueful smile for Mikey, "Perhaps this isn't the best moment for such a profound conversation."

He froze when he saw Liz coming out of the house leaning on Jackie.

FORTY-EIGHT

The entire group waited uneasily for Liz to draw near. Her appearance was as neat as ever, though her anguish-filled eyes were sunken with giant rings underneath them and her face was ashen. Her grip on her daughter's arm was vice-like.

She addressed herself to Dr. Pearson. "Where are my children?"

Evidently uncomfortable, he gestured towards Jackie and Mikey. She repeated the question imperiously, her voice rising in pitch: "Where are my children?"

He didn't know how to reply. At last he ventured in a consoling tone, "Mrs. Foster, I'm sorry about the untimely death of Jimmie. It was most unfortunate."

She retorted accusingly, "And I'm sorry about the fate of all my children! Where are they now?" The men were at a loss as to what to say or do. Jackie and Mikey deliberately didn't look at each other. They both stood erect and very still. Hugh and David exchanged wondering glances. They too stayed put.

"What will become of them? You deceived me! I was so young. You told me that I was helping humankind to progress."

Mikey made a move as if he were about to add something, but David shook his shoulder gently to catch his eye, then signaled for him to keep silent.

Liz raged on, "What a sickening lie! And my children have had to pay the price of your gross manipulation!"

Dr. Pearson maintained a cool, respectful tone. "Elizabeth, you're overwrought, which is very understandable given your terrible loss. I expect that later you'll see our experiment is not to blame for today's occurrences. In fact, I wouldn't even deem it to be a failure, as your words imply. The government merely called it off for political reasons. Society isn't yet ready for what science has to offer. You will one day be proud of the important role you played..."

Her voice tersely cut off his words. "I will always regret treating tiny, helpless human persons like objects! But I thank God for the years of life God granted to Jimmie and his poor brothers. And I want you to know that I'm going to take a special interest in them. I'm going to visit them and care for them as much as I'm able."

For an instant, Dr. Pearson looked troubled. Quickly he reassumed his professionally detached air. "I wouldn't recommend that, Elizabeth. They're dangerous. You wouldn't be able to do anything for them. The low quality of their lives doesn't merit your wasting your time."

Liz bristled even more. "Are you trying to discourage me so you can have a free hand to euthanize the rest of them?"

He looked askance at her yet kept his voice calm. "You would have made a superb scientist if you hadn't let your religious sentiment darken your intellect."

David had been growing irate with the man. At hearing this last sentence, he sent a warning look to tell Hugh he'd had enough. Hugh urgently gestured back for David to keep out of it.

Oblivious of the silent interchange, Liz retorted hotly, "You hypocrite! It's you who foists your atheistic beliefs on those who have reason on their side so you can have a free hand to play God with the lives of the most defenseless human persons! As for the rest of my living clone children, I warn you: I think you'll care more than me now about their existence going public. Stay away from them. Don't do them any more harm, or the world will hear about it!"

Before he could respond, she turned her back on him and headed back to the house, still leaning heavily on her daughter's arm.

When car number four was safely out of sight, Hugh reached through his window to turn off his car. "Way to go, Mikey! Great acting! Between you and your Mom, Dr. Pearson should be pretty convinced your brother went down with the barn."

The boy responded woefully, "I assure you, my tears are no pre-varication! I merely need to reflect that you're absconding with Jim-mie, and I am most lachrymose. If only Jackie and I hadn't recounted our tale to Coach, our family wouldn't be torn asunder!"

Moved with compassion, Hugh hunched down so he could look Mikey right in the eye. "Good thing you expressed this now so I can set you straight. The Canadian government won't be satisfied with mere hearsay that Jimmie burned in the fire. No doubt, they'll order a thorough probe of the remains and request us to return the ashes of the two bodies to them. If I didn't know about Jimmie, I would have cooperated fully as we have been until now. But it's not in the interests of our government to let them know Jimmie's alive, so when the request arrives, I know how to slow down the procedure long enough for your mother to erect a new building, or better yet, install a huge swimming pool over the site. That'll mess up the ash count!"

The boy's grin communicated that he understood. "But why do you have to take him away?"

"More than that, I'm helping him to get a new name, so he can live in peace." Hugh added gently: "It's safer for him right now to go into hiding away from your family. You understand how important it is for him for everyone to think him dead. And don't think you'll wring any more concessions from me. I've given you a big one, which I'm already regretting."

Mikey perked up. He didn't want Mr. McClury to rethink his promise. "Can we let him out now?"

As the threesome headed towards the secret hideaway, Mikey directed his attention to Coach David.

"Why did you interrupt my discussion with Dr. Pearson?"

In a fatherly way, David put his arm around Mikey's shoulders. "When you disagree with a man's way of acting, it's not always the best thing to take him head-on as you were doing. In the end, you'll get much better results by tossing some seeds in his direction and letting them germinate."

Mike looked thoughtful. "Mom chose another method, didn't she?"

Hugh observed wryly: "Your Mom did some 'power planting.' That can work too, sometimes. And she didn't know Jimmie's still alive."

Mikey switched his attention back to Hugh. "Mr. McClury, would your professional secrecy permit you to divulge why you elected to listen in on Jackie and I informing Coach about Jimmie?" The man chuckled, evidently pleased to share his wisdom with the bright young fellow.

"Elementary, my dear Watson! We FBI folk spend a lot of time observing characters and second-guessing their actions. Now tell me, would your sister really have run into the woods and hidden if she had seen Alf light your barn on fire and wasn't completely occupied in that moment with saving her elder brother?"

He gazed at the boy quizzically. It wasn't necessary for Hugh to explain any further. He witnessed the light go on in Mikey's eyes.

But the older man couldn't help adding, "Cowering in the dark didn't fit the profile of either of you. We don't just keep our eyes on the bad guys, you know. It can help a lot to outsmart the good guys too."

Hugh reached the chassis before the other two. Pushing away the board, he called out, "Lazarus, come out!"

FORTY-NINE

The scene of the burning barn assailed Liz's imagination as she lay in her bed. The flames, her son, and the clones jumbled together, swinging in and out before her mind's eye. She deliberately kept her eyes shut when she heard the bedroom door creak open, Jackie's quiet movement from the chair at her side, and hushed whispers. The door shut, and Liz assumed it was Jackie who sat down on the edge of her bed. Moments ticked by before Jimmie ventured to say one word very softly, "Mom."

Liz shot up into a sitting position. When she beheld Jimmie there, she immediately cringed away from him.

Tremulously she asked, "Who are you?"

Jimmie smilingly pulled back the hair on his left side to expose his tattoo as he leaned towards her. Coach David had told him about it. She reached out her hand to stroke his forehead, still hesitating to believe it was truly her son.

"It's me, Mom. Don't worry."

At that she threw her arms around him and wept heartily.

"Everything's okay. Mikey, Jackie, Coach, and Mr. McClury are downstairs. They're all fine, except that Coach is mad at Mr. McClury for sending all his men away." He added cheerfully, "You'll have to wait until we join everyone else for more of an explanation. Mikey's gotta tell you his fantastic part in the story. You're not going to know whether you should shake him to death or reward him." As her tears subsided he prompted, "We can't keep them long, though, because Hugh needs to be on his way."

Ever the polite hostess, Liz let go of her son and swung her feet around to the floor. "We'll see him off, and then we can celebrate!"

Jimmie replied firmly but gently, "Mr. McClury says I need to go with him. He's going to help me obtain a new identity, and he says it's imperative that nobody discovers I'm still alive. Everyone but the people in this house think I died in the fire."

Liz nodded her head emphatically. "Of course! Jackie, Mikey, and I can be ready in fifteen minutes."

It didn't even occur to her that he intended to leave on his own. She moved to stand up, but Jimmie stayed her with his hand.

"Mom. Mr. McClury's only planning to take me with him."

She didn't get it. "Don't worry. I'll speak to him. Of course we're coming with you."

Jimmie forced himself to speak more assertively. "This time I need to do it alone, Mom. I want it that way, too. Not just Mr. McClury, though he agrees."

She stared back in wonder, hurt at the thought that he would wish to separate from her. "But our family! You would break us up? Where would you go?" She couldn't bring herself to say the words out loud: *Don't you need me?*

Jimmie calmly responded, "This is something I've been thinking about for a long time. I was only waiting to find out who my father was before leaving. Mr. McClury's even going to let me follow my original plan. I'm going to Brazil to do missionary work. Father Matt helped me set this up a while ago."

Still she protested, "But I was happy doing missionary work with Henry when you were young. We could do that with you."

Jimmie shook his head. "I asked for the deep, dark jungle. It's going to be rough going. I couldn't stand the thought of you and Jackie having to tough it out, let alone Mikey. He would be lost, literally speaking."

"Then go somewhere not quite so remote. Roughing it will be good for their character formation."

Jimmie imitated the same reasoning tone he had heard his dad use with his mother at tough moments. "Put yourself in my shoes for a minute. Would you accept having your mother and your siblings endlessly traveling about like vagabonds for your sake? I'm certain you wouldn't! Besides, Mr. McClury says it'll be much easier to hide a single young man than a whole family."

Liz didn't respond right away. Jimmie figured it was time to use his wild card. "Besides, Mom, aren't you forgetting someone?" She looked back blankly at him, overwhelmed at the thought of him being both alive and leaving.

So Jimmie added with a teasing smile, "Mr. McClury is threatening to extradite you to Canada for revealing state secrets unless you're willing to redeem yourself by having enough good sense to marry a certain fine, upstanding citizen of the United States." Liz opened her mouth and closed it again, at a loss for words. "Mom, do you expect Coach David to chase you around the world? Or are you considering dragging him along with you? Imagine: he asked me just now, as the male head of the family, for permission to request your hand in marriage. But I wasn't supposed to tell you, so don't let on I did. Do you really intend just to run off on him like that?"

She hadn't considered David, or where he would fit into the new situation. She attempted a feeble response.

"He can tell you that I've never encouraged him."

Jimmie was adamant: "Maybe you didn't, but do you deny there's something between you?"

He knew she had given in when her tears flowed anew. When she could speak, she protested sadly, "But I haven't had the chance to talk to you about your origins."

He managed a wan smile. "My fellow clones gave me the low-down and Coach explained my false identity. Even more important, you and Father Matt prepared me to accept who I am by making sure I know my heavenly Father. I wish I had normal parents, but your love and God's love will keep me from breaking."

Liz gazed intently at him to discern if he meant what he said. He looked back steadily and peacefully. Slowly, she let out a long breath in relief.

"I've never forgiven myself for the part I had in the experiment. That is, until two days ago. All my life has been directed towards sparing you pain. I would gladly have died for you if that would have helped."

He chuckled. "You almost did die! Dr. Pearson said he had to give you enough sedative to knock out a horse!"

They heard Mikey's voice coming from down the hall, shouting from the top of the stairs to those waiting below.

"Mom's awake. I can hear her and Jimmie talking together."

Jimmie shook his head in amusement.

"It's a good thing you're going to have Coach's help with Mikey! He's going to be a handful in these next couple of years! I'm going to have a man-to-man talk with him about how a gentleman needs to conduct himself."

FIFTY

Liz was stirring the hot chocolate at the stove when David entered the kitchen. He tried to sound nonchalant.

"Jackie and Mikey asked me to let you know that they feel too sleepy after all, even for a drink, so they're heading off to bed."

She was amused. "You still don't know my children very well if you believe them."

"What do you mean? It's after 3:00 in the morning. They sure looked tired to me." She scoffed at him while he poked his head back through the door. "You see. They're gone."

Liz kept her post at the stove. David had been looking forward to a moment when he would at last be alone with her. He knew better than to be put off by her apparent aloofness.

While keeping her back to him, Liz remarked, "I don't approve at all of your staying here overnight. I certainly didn't invite you and I don't think it's wise."

He pulled a chair out from the kitchen table and sat facing her. "Why do you consider it unwise when there's a mad clone running loose out there who's already made one attempt on your life?"

She sniffed. "I'm in full agreement with Hugh and Dr. Pearson that Alpha is long gone. Coming after me now doesn't match his psychological profile."

"Well, I have to admit, there's also the concern that the lady of the house will skip town on me."

She was incredulous. "Now? After the danger's finally over?"

"How do I know you don't have any more secrets? But what's your problem with my sleeping here, anyway? Are you afraid I'll ruin the cushions on your couch?"

Her tone was grave. "It's not proper! You know what people will be thinking!"

"Since when have you worried about what people think and say about you? I distinctly remember you telling me you got over that long ago."

She laughed. "You have a good memory. But you get my point." Her voice softened as she added coaxingly: "If you're really serious about me, then let's do this the right way."

He cocked his head to the side and repeated her word innocently: "Serious?"

Lightly, warmly, she responded, "Yes. Don't you remember proposing something serious to me the last time you were here?"

He acted like he only just grasped what she was hinting at. "Whoa, marriage! Really Liz, you're moving too fast! After all, I'm still undecided about you."

Liz spun around in surprise, hot chocolate momentarily forgotten. "You seemed decided enough then!"

"Sure! That was before I met your cookie cutter cutthroat offspring. To be frank, there are a few things that make me queasy about you." She frowned, trying to read his expression. "For starters…" he enumerated on his fingers as he continued, "if you experience the need to run and hide, will you take me with you? Do you think the odds are very high that you'll get that feeling often? Are you going to want me to help you raise your crazy kids?"

In answer, Liz assumed a meditative expression. Imitating David, she held up her fingers in time to her staccato answers:

"Yes. No. Maybe so."

He stood up, an amorous look in his eyes. Guessing his intentions, Liz snatched a large cup from the cupboard and moved quickly to the freezer for crushed ice. David stepped over to the sink to block her way to the tap. His eyes gleamed triumphantly.

"You're not thinking of pulling the same old ice-water-in-the-face trick on me are you?" Chuckling, she set down the cup of ice and leaned against the fridge. His voice grew tender. "You don't have to run from me anymore, remember?"

He took a determined step in her direction. She feebly held up her hands. "Wait." With a coy smile, she asked: "What are your other concerns about me?"

Very much at ease, he crossed his arms and grinned devilishly at her. "How can you assure me that your father wasn't Frankenstein, that your mother isn't a vampire, that you're not a sorceress who's bewitching me..."

She chimed in, "Or that Mikey isn't a werewolf?"

He nodded. Before he could close the gap between them, Liz suddenly leapt towards him with a shriek of fright. She clung to him, looking about in fear. "Did you hear that noise?"

He could tell she wasn't faking, though he hadn't heard anything worrisome. Taking advantage of holding her protectively, he looked around the room intently, then whispered: "Did it come from your children upstairs? What did it sound like?"

This time they both heard it: an indistinct thumping and scratching from beneath them. Liz whispered back nervously: "We don't have a basement!"

Before they could do anything, a bedraggled Mikey popped out of a trapdoor by their feet and hurriedly scrambled onto the kitchen floor.

"Desist from your intolerably despicable conduct!" Mikey exclaimed. David thought Mikey was addressing him until Jackie stuck her head through the same hole, giggling hysterically.

With a look of deep chagrin, Mikey began, "Mom, Coach, I wish to offer my profuse apologies for interrupting your tryst. I assure you that I had every intention of honoring my word as a gentleman, extracted by Jimmie, to no longer eavesdrop on conversations. However, I made the ludicrous mistake of making my incorrigible sibling privy to my most secret hideaway. It was she who effectively blocked my way from making a discreet retreat."

With one hand, Jackie held her sides in a fit of laughter, and with the other hand she pointed at her brother.

"Mikey's a werewolf! Mikey's a werewolf!"

Mikey tried to look indifferent but didn't succeed. His face was contorted in a grimace. "I'm condemned to suffer these infernal jibes until she alights upon some other sobriquet that touches her capricious fancy. Mother, couldn't you have hit upon something less trite? And in all fairness, shouldn't you have implicated Jackie as well in the whole maudlin affair? You might have suggested that she could be a Harpy, or Medusa, or one of the Furies! I assure you, there's an uncanny similitude between her and each one of them!"

Liz seized the moment to step gingerly away from David, who had joined in the laughter. "The hot chocolate! I hope it's not burned!" As she poured the drinks into cups, she said, looking at each of the three, "I've got a crazy idea. Let's all stay up together the rest of the night!"

EPILOGUE

Hugh McClury didn't like it at all, but he had given his word to the kid. He wondered again how he had given in. For the third time in ten minutes, he swept the crowd with his binoculars. He fixed them first on Jackie, then on Coach David.

Both of them were calling out numbers to the soccer players. With her brilliant mind, Jackie could calculate the steps on her own. David, on the other hand, was merely parroting the numbers he heard through the microphone attached to his ear. That was the part that made Hugh nervous. But none of the commentators seemed to even realize that David was listening to someone.

Mrs. Johnston was filming this national high-school championship playoff soccer game for Jimmie, who was watching from an orphanage by the Amazon River and dictating the tough plays to Coach.

The crowds were enthralled by the mysterious underdog team that had come out of nowhere and played with such amazing finesse. The other team was shaken.

The young water boy was the most enraptured of all. No worries in his stout heart. He was sure of the outcome from the very beginning, and he would not be disappointed.

ACKNOWLEDGMENTS

Special thanks to Lisa Small for editing this book for me long before I submitted it for publication and to Jim Fair for his feedback and encouragement. Thanks as well to all my tutors at Thomas Aquinas College and my professors at the John Paul II Institute in Rome, particularly Monsignor Livio Melina, Bishop Jean Laffitte, Cardinal Marc Ouellet, Dr. Stanislaw Grygiel, and Dr. Gianfrancesco Zuanazzi. Thanks also go to my directors for encouraging me to write, particularly Michelle Reiff, Malén Oriol, Mónica Treviño, Luly Fernandez, and Patricia Camarero. I'm also grateful to the generous benefactors who made this publication possible, particularly Jim and Helen McCleneghen, without whose support this project wouldn't have happened. Finally, thanks to my consecrated companions who listened attentively to many versions of this story, offering so much helpful input and encouragement.